FOR MARLISS,
the queen of the good deeds.

AND THERESIA,
who takes generosity to a
whole new level

ANGEL LANE

Sheila Roberts

St. Martin's Paperbacks

ANGEL LANE

Copyright © 2009 by Sheila Rabe.

All rights reserved.

For information address St. Martin's Press, 175 Fifth Avenue, New York, NY 10010.

Library of Congress Catalog Card Number: 2009012524

ISBN: 978-1-250-05665-8

Printed in the United States of America

St. Martin's Griffin trade paperback edition / September 2009
St. Martin's Paperbacks edition / November 2015

St. Martin's Paperbacks are published by St. Martin's Press, 175 Fifth Avenue, New York, NY 10010.

10 9 8 7 6 5 4 3 2 1

ACKNOWLEDGMENTS

I have made some great new friends in the process of writing this book, and I'm indebted to the following people for giving me a glimpse into their lives as shop owners and busy women. Thanks to Mona Newbauer, the owner of 1 Angel Place Chocolate Bar in Langley, Washington, for sharing with me a day in the life of a chocolatier. Mona, your truffles are to die for, and if I had to get up at the crack of dawn like you do, I would die. Huge thanks also to Valerie Wood at Material Girls Quilt Shop in Silverdale, Washington, for showing me how much is involved in running a quilt shop. What a labor of love! And speaking of labors of love, huge thanks to Helen Ross, über-quilter, for her patient explanations of the complexities of quilting. Thanks, too, to Kathy Nordlie and Maria Parra-Boxley for the wonderful candy recipes you contributed. Thanks to the Bainbridge Island Brain Trust (Susan Wiggs, Suzanne Selfors, Elsa Watson, Carol Cassella, and Anjali Banerjee) for their invaluable input. And, finally, thanks to Paige Wheeler, my agent, and Rose Hilliard, my editor, and all the wonderful people at St. Martin's Press who continue to make writing such an enjoyable adventure.

ONE

$\mathcal{A}$nother day in Mayberry, Jamie Moore thought as she waved the last two customers of the day out the door of the Chocolate Bar. A gust of autumn wind slipped in as the old women left, tickling the chimes hanging in the window: little chocolates nesting in pretend paper cups dangling from a pink, heart-shaped chocolate box. They looked good enough to eat, just like the vast array of temptation Jamie kept on trays behind the glass counters. Except Jamie's truffles and fudge and other chocolate concoctions weren't simply good enough, they were great, to die for. That was what all her customers said anyway.

Jamie watched through the window as the two women started their snail-paced progress down the sidewalk, the late October wind whistling under their skirts. On the other side of the street another gust playfully stripped blushing leaves from the big maple on the corner. They danced off, swirling onto the sidewalk. The swirling leaves made Jamie think of fairies, and that made her smile, something she'd done a lot lately. Maybe it was Heart Lake, maybe it was the magic of chocolate—whatever it was that she'd found here, it had given Jamie back her smile. Her struggles in L.A. were behind her now and she had a new business and a new life. She had come home, stepped back in time, and found herself again.

Jamie hadn't found a fortune, though, at least not yet, so that meant only part-time help, low-rent living, and a beater car. But the low rent was on a lakefront cabin that her aunt, Sarah Goodwin, had found for her. And the beater was a Toyota that gave her pretty good gas mileage. So it was all good.

She turned the sign on the door to CLOSED, then hurried through her closing chores, cleaning the espresso machine, wiping down counters, and washing dishes. Her final chore was to jot down her grocery list. She bought her chocolate from a supplier in Seattle who had it shipped from France, but for her other supplies she shopped locally. Tonight she needed to get cream, a necessary staple for really good truffles. She also needed some more strawberry liqueur, which Tony DeSoto at Bere Vino was holding for her.

Tomorrow she'd be in the shop by five, making truffles. Her part-time help would join her at ten and man the counter. Wednesdays were always busy thanks to a walking group, the local MOPS moms who came in after their weekly meeting, and Lakeside Realty, who always bought truffles to serve at their realtors' open houses every Wednesday. And that was only the morning customers. Just thinking about tomorrow made her tired, but that was nothing compared to how tired she felt when she thought of Fridays, when half of Heart Lake came in searching for hostess gifts, shower presents, and a little something to help them celebrate TGIF. Tired is good, she reminded herself, it means your business is growing and you can pay the rent.

By the time Jamie stepped outside and locked the chocolateria door behind her those gusts of wind were spitting rain everywhere. Look at all the cars parked out here, she thought, surveying Valentine Square as she prepared to make a dash to her Toyota. Who'da thunk it?

When she was a kid, downtown Heart Lake had been a slow, lazy place, with an occasional old lady browsing a few shops on a long stretch of cement. Vern's Drugs, with its narrow aisles and slightly off-kilter hardwood plank floors, had been the popular destination spot for friends in search of some gossip as well as kids on the hunt for penny candy. The town had grown up all those years she'd been away. Vern's still occupied the same spot on downtown Lake Way, the main drag, but now it was crowded on all sides by new shops. And the downtown district had spilled over into nearby streets like this little U-shaped one, where her shop sat along with a card shop, a jewelry store, a lingerie shop (of course, they'd all chosen Valentine Square on purpose), and an old brick two-story Tudor that housed a divorce lawyer on the ground floor and a romance writer on the top. This street wasn't too crowded, but Lake Way was getting ridiculous. When Jamie had gone to Vern's the week before looking for aspirin she'd had to park clear at the end of the street.

Just two quick stops, she promised her tired self as she drove up Alder, headed for Lake Way. Then she could go home and snarf down the leftover lasagna Sarah had sent her away with after their dinner together the night before.

Poor Sarah. Tomorrow her daughter left for the East Coast. She'd be ready for a chocolate bender when they got together after work for their weekly confab with Emma Swanson.

At the four-way stop where Alder intersected with downtown Lake Way she found herself in a mini rush hour. "What's this?" she muttered. Cars never used to line up for this stop sign coming even one direction, let alone all four.

The car conga line inched toward the stop, each driver reaching the intersection and barely waiting for the next in line to zip across before jumping his or her vehicle forward like a racehorse out of the gate. And there stood her two little old ladies, clutching their Chocolate Bar goody bags and hovering over the crosswalk, afraid to put out so much as a toe. The short, plump one clutched her wool coat tight to her chest and huddled next to her friend as if for protection. Some protection. That woman was taller, but her legs looked like matchsticks. Her thin lips puckered in a frown and she was holding her felt hat down as if she were afraid the back draft from some rushing car would whoosh it right off her head.

Jamie understood that everyone was anxious to get home for the night, but couldn't somebody spare even a minute to let the old ladies cross the street and get out of the rain and back inside their senior housing? If they were still stuck on the curb when she reached the stop sign, she would.

Four more cars bolted across the street and the women remained rooted to the corner, looking uncertainly at the passing vehicles, probably thinking they'd never see Senior Gardens again. Jamie pulled up to the stop and waved them across. They stepped out nervously, linking arms and looking right and left at the other cars, probably mentally begging the drivers not to squash them. Once in the crosswalk they hobbled for the other side like contestants in a slow-motion three-legged race. After a millennium they safely reached the corner. The plump little one smiled at Jamie and blew her a kiss.

She smiled back and waved. That had felt good. And it only took a minute to be nice. People should always be nice. She started to take her turn only to have a red

Mustang holding two high school Britney Spears wannabes bolt across the street right in front of her, gobbling up her warm, Good Samaritan moment with a squeal of their wheels.

"Excuse me?" Jamie laid on the horn and one of them flipped her off. *Well, of all the . . .* She caught sight of their bumper sticker. ALL YOU NEED IS LOVE. "And driving lessons," she muttered. What a couple of little beatches.

Oh, well. Every town had 'em, probably even Mayberry had one or two. Somewhere. Hiding off camera.

Even though the angle parking downtown was clearing out she failed to find a spot close to Bere Vino. By the time she walked through Tony's door she was a cloud with legs, dropping water everywhere.

Tony DeSoto wasn't old enough to be her father, but almost. He was divorced and hungry for sex, and before Sarah took Jamie into the shop to introduce her to him, she had warned Jamie that Tony imagined himself a cross between Sylvester Stallone and Leonardo DiCaprio. He was very fond of blondes, and he'd been known to sing under windows when there was a full moon. The last thing Jamie needed was an Italian-lover wannabe serenading her at the lake, so after Sarah had introduced them Jamie told him how much she and her partner were enjoying their new home. And did Heart Lake have a Gay Pride week? The drool on his chin had dried instantly. Now Jamie and Tony were just business pals, and every once in a while when she came in she'd catch him looking at her sadly and shaking his head.

"That will get around faster than free caviar. Now every man in town is going to think you're a lesbian," Sarah had chided her when they left the shop.

"And the problem with that is?" Jamie had retorted. Like she wanted a man in her life again? Ever? The day her ex broke her jaw was the day she swore off men.

"My God, you look like a drowned cat," Tony greeted her, eyeing the puddles forming at her feet. The first time she'd come into his shop he'd slicked back his salt-and-pepper hair and sucked in his gut. Now the hair stayed untended and the gut hung over his belt, a hedge of untrimmed fat.

"I feel like one," Jamie said.

"Well, I got just what you need to take the chill off: a new liqueur. You're gonna love it."

Tony always had a new something she was going to love. She'd spent a fortune on wine and cheese since she moved back. "Yeah?"

"Blackberry," he said, holding up a little bottle with a gold-foil label.

She walked over to the counter like a fish swimming to the lure.

"Take it home, try some in your truffles, see what Ginger thinks."

Ginger, her imaginary girlfriend. "Thanks," she said, taking the bottle and examining it. Blackberry with white chocolate—that could prove to be a deadly combination.

Tony had set aside her other liqueurs and was now ringing them up. "You should go home and get a hot bath," he advised. "You're going to catch your death. And you'd better buy an umbrella and a warm parka. We're gonna have a nasty winter. My bad knee is already acting up. Football injury," he added, in a moment of macho. "If it does what it did last year, we're gonna have some pretty bad snows."

"I hope not," Jamie said. "My candy is good, but I can't see people coming out in the snow for it."

"Around here people don't come out in the snow for nothin'," said Tony. "But rain? That's another story. I was swamped all day. Everybody getting ready to go home and tuck in with a nice bottle of wine and some cheese."

Actually, that sounded like a good idea. In addition to what she came in for, she left the store with a bottle of white wine, some brie, and a little box of sesame crackers.

At the Safeway store, she dashed from the parking lot, but hordes of icy little drops still sneaked under her jacket collar to torture her with every step. Ugh. That was the one good thing about L.A. Less rain.

But more cement and less green. She'd take Heart Lake and its lush woods any day.

She was chilled and miserably aware of her wet jeans rubbing against her skin by the time she got to the express lane. Where a middle-aged woman cut in front of her. Okay, Jamie obviously hadn't gotten the memo. Today was National Rudeness Day.

Never mind, she told herself. *It's the rain. Everyone's in a hurry to get out of it and get home.*

Including her. All she could think about as she left the downtown area was getting inside her cozy little cabin and sinking into a hot bath. She had some vanilla spice bath melt that made the yummiest bubbles, and she'd light some candles. The way the hanging flower baskets lining Lake Way had been swinging, she might find herself out of power, but if she lost power, no big deal. She'd still have enough hot water for her bath. Bubbles, glowing candles, a glass of wine . . .

A flash of red lights behind her jerked her out of her mental bathtub with a jolt and sent adrenaline racing through her veins. She pulled her car over with hands suddenly damp. She hadn't been speeding. Why was this cop stopping her? She choked the steering wheel and chewed her lip. *It's just a routine stop. Get a grip. AND DON'T DO IT.*

She looked in the rearview mirror and saw the door of the police car behind her open. Out climbed a big man with a chest the size of a whiskey barrel and hands as big as hams. She tried to ignore the irrational banging in her chest and let down her window.

A face appeared. It was a good-looking face with deep-set eyes, full lips, and a strong, angular chin, the kind of face her friend Emma Swanson would have swooned over. It just made Jamie want to run.

Part of her itched to inform him that she wasn't speeding, that he had no right to stop her. It was silenced by a wiser voice, cautioning, "Appeasement works best. Keep your big mouth shut."

"Did you know you have a taillight out?" he asked.

"That's why you stopped me?" Any flimsy excuse to intimidate a woman. Okay, so no reason to embarrass me, she warned her body. *DON'T DO IT*. She took a deep breath and held it, just to be safe.

His eyebrows took a dip. "Did you *know* you had a taillight out?" he repeated.

"Of course not," she snapped. Okay, snapping was dumb on so many levels. She tried again, her voice smoother. "I thought you thought I was speeding," she said, then went back to holding her breath.

"Actually, you were going two miles under the limit," he said, and smiled. The man had a great smile. He could do toothpaste commercials. Hell, he could probably sell anything. He gave the car a friendly tap. "Be sure and get that fixed," he added. "Contrary to popular opinion, cops don't like giving out tickets."

She nodded and he turned and walked back to his patrol car.

She put up her window. *Hic*. Oh, stop, she told herself irritably. Another hiccup rose to mock her. At least they'd held off until the cop walked away. Her little problem would have been too totally embarrassing to explain. She watched him in her rearview mirror, waiting for him to pull out and drive on past her. Of course he didn't. They never did. They deliberately sat there in back of you to make you nervous. Well, she wasn't nervous. So there. *Hic*. She took in a deep breath and then moved out onto the street. He only followed her for a block, and then turned off in search of some new schlub to torture.

A huge hiccup carved a painful trail up her chest. You can stop now, she told her body. It's all over. *Hic*. She took a deep breath and told herself he'd been a nice cop. The policeman is your friend, her mother had always said.

Right. Jamie had thought that until she married one. He had burst her bubble for good. Not every cop was your friend. And the saddest thing was when you married one and expected him to be your best friend and he became your worst enemy.

Rude drivers, rain, cops—it was no wonder she felt grumpy by the time she dripped her way into her cabin. The poor spider lurking on the wall didn't have a chance.

She felt bad after she murdered it. You could have trapped it in a glass and put it outside, she scolded herself. *Not very Mayberry of you.*

Where was everyone? Emma Swanson paced to her shop window and looked out. Not one single person was hurrying up the sidewalk, worried about being late to her big event.

She frowned at the table she'd set up in one corner of her quilt shop, piled with squares of fabric in varying shades of pink, waiting for volunteers to embroider or decorate with fabric paint. She'd advertised in the paper and everything. Didn't anyone want to quilt for the cause? Was she going to be the only quilt shop owner in the whole Northwest who wouldn't be contributing squares?

It was looking very much that way. She should have known. The signs of failure were there in the attitudes of the few customers who had come into the shop in the last couple of days.

Emma had heard all kinds of excuses and evasions. "I'll try." (This was said in a tone of voice, that added, "But not very hard.") "I think I've got something going that night." (Which translated into, "Don't hold your breath.") The most creative excuse had come from one of her older customers. "I don't go out at night, dear. Carjackers."

As if any self-respecting carjacker would go near Heart Lake. It was like Bedford Falls in *It's a Wonderful Life,* only without mean old Mr. Potter. "I could come pick you up," she'd offered.

"Oh, no. You'll have too much to do getting ready for the big event. I'm sure it will be wonderful, though."

Emma sighed. This nonturnout was not wonderful. What had she expected, really? She was having a hard enough time getting people to come into her shop during the day. Why would anyone want to brave a dark, rainy night to do it?

She leaned her head against the storefront window. During the day the downtown shop area was so pretty with its hanging flower baskets and cute shops. But at night, darkness sucked the life out of it, making it look deserted and unloved. Kind of the way she felt right now.

Wait. What was this? Two figures approaching. Yay! Bodies.

Her wave of excitement crashed when she realized it was her mother and grandmother. It wasn't that she didn't appreciate their loyalty. Mom and Grandma Nordby were her two best customers. But having your mother and grandmother as the only attendees at your big event wasn't exactly a hallmark of success.

"Sorry we're late," said her mom, giving her a hug and a kiss.

Grandma Nordby was right behind her. She seemed to

get shorter and rounder every day. "Where is everyone?" she asked as Emma leaned over and kissed her.

"I don't know," Emma said. "This is for a good cause, for crying out loud." Which was exactly what she wanted to do. The decorated squares from all the shops in the greater Seattle area and its outlying districts would be turned into quilts and then auctioned online, with the proceeds going to breast cancer research. She'd said that in her ad. Surely someone cared.

"Well, let's get to work," said Emma's mom briskly. She walked to the table, took a seat, and grabbed a square. "If it's going to be just the three of us, we have a lot to do."

Grandma Nordby shook her head. "I don't understand where Doris is. She promised she'd come. Let me use your phone, dear," she said to Emma. "I'll just call her."

Now they were going to call and plead with people to come make her a success? "That's okay, Grandma," she said. "It doesn't matter."

But of course it did. She so wanted Emma's Quilt Corner to be a thriving business, and she'd envisioned this night as a smashing success, with lots of women from the community working together, enjoying each other's company.

"Come to think of it, Doris was worried she might be coming down with something when I talked to her yesterday," said Grandma.

Maybe the whole town had come down with something. Emma fetched them all mugs of hot cider from one of the enormous Thermoses she'd filled and sat down at the table.

"I know what you're thinking," her mother said in a tone of voice that heralded a motherly lecture.

"No you don't," said Emma, reaching for a fabric square.

"Yes I do, and you're not."

"Not what?" asked Grandma.

"A failure," said Mom, looking sternly at Emma.

"I wasn't thinking that." Well, okay. Maybe she was a little, but she was not telling her mom. She frowned at the fabric in her hand. "Where is our town spirit? Why aren't there any people here?"

"The people who count are here," said Mom with a decisive nod.

It was a valiant attempt to cheer her up, but . . . "You had to come. You're related." Emma sighed.

"Well," said her mother, "if it's any consolation, I think the high school's fall concert is tonight."

"And *Dancing with the Stars* is on," added Grandma Nordby.

"Great. I got beat out by a TV show," muttered Emma.

"And a school event," added her mother.

"This is an event, too," said Emma, "and an important one." Or at least she had thought it was.

Two more women straggled in later, but it wasn't enough to hide the grim reality. She was a failure.

TWO

$\mathcal{B}$lack Wednesday, that was how Sarah Goodwin would always remember this day. She gripped her cell phone like a lifeline. "I miss you," she lamented to her daughter, Stephanie.

"We've only been gone six hours," Steph reminded her.

Only six hours ago her daughter and son-in-law had stopped by Sweet Somethings Bakery to tell Sarah one last good-bye. Her granddaughters, seven-year-old Katie and five-year-old Adeline, had been in tears. Even Sarah's husband, Sam, Mr. Tough Guy Fire Chief, who had run over from the station to help see them off, had been looking a little misty eyed. A box of oatmeal cookies from Nana's bakery had cheered the girls considerably. And Sam went back to the fire station with an apple pie and a smile.

But nothing was going to make Sarah feel better. There was nothing in the bakery, nothing in her life, that could fill the big, empty spot her daughter's family had left behind. It had been a horrible day, bitter as vanilla. She knew this was a big deal for her son-in-law, but his gain had been her loss. Why did companies have to move people around so much, anyway? Children needed to be near their grand-mother.

She sighed. "It's been the six longest hours of my life. Well, except for when I was in labor with you. Ten hours of labor—"

"And this is the thanks I get," her daughter finished Sarah's favorite tease with her. "I know, but think of the fabulous daughter you got out of the deal."

That made Sarah tear up. Fabulous was on her way to upstate New York.

"Remember, we'll be back for Christmas," Steph reminded her.

And then a certain son-in-law was going to get a lump of coal in his stocking. It had been all Sarah could do not to give him a lump on the head when he made his big announcement at her birthday dinner two months earlier. Talk about a crummy birthday present. It had been hard enough letting her son go off to Hollywood, where he was bound to wind up running bare naked all over the big screen to embarrass her in front of her girlfriends, but parting with Steph was ten times worse. Jonathan's departure had been no surprise. Boys grew up and moved away. Daughters, on the other hand, were supposed to stick around, making themselves available whenever their mother felt the need to interfere in their life.

"Here," Steph said. "The girls want to talk to you."

A moment later a little voice piped, "Hi, Nana."

"Katie, my little cupcake with the cherry on top," Sarah said, forcing good cheer into her voice. "Are you having a fun trip?"

"Yes, but I miss you so much."

"And I miss you, too," said Sarah. She began to wipe down the counters in the bakery kitchen with bleach water. Keeping busy was always a good idea when you were feeling down. So was consuming vast amounts of baked goods, but she was too far down for even that to help.

"We went over the mountains," Katie announced, happily switching gears, "and we had a picnic."

"Well, that sounds fun," said Sarah. It was no picnic here in Heart Lake.

"And we got ice cream. Addie got sick in the car."

Poor Steph.

In the background Sarah could hear another little voice, whining, "I want to talk to Nana."

"We're going to stay in a motel tonight," Katie went on. "And when we get to our new house we're going to get a puppy. Mommy promised. And we're going to go to Yellow Park and see bears."

Yellowstone Park. They'd taken the kids camping there years ago. Sarah could still remember the rotten-egg smell of the hot springs and how uncomfortable the bed in that old camper had been. The kids had nearly driven her insane that trip. If only she'd known then how fast they'd grow up. She'd have stayed a lot saner.

The other little voice was getting louder. Sarah heard her daughter now, too, saying, "Give the phone to Addie."

"Hi, Nana!"

"Addie, my little sugar dumpling, how are you doing? Is your tummy all better?"

"Uh-huh. But Katie ate my cookie."

"Did not!" Katie cried in the background.

"Nana will mail you some more. Okay?"

"Okay," said Addie, her voice subdued. Poor little thing, she missed her nana. Or at least her nana's cookies.

There was a moment's silence and then Steph was back on the phone. "That gives you the highlights so far. Ice cream and barf."

"Sign me up," said Sarah.

"I wish I could. We stopped at a gas station and scrubbed

down the car, but it didn't help much. We've had the windows down for the last hour. My buns are asleep and the girls are getting cranky. Are we having fun yet?"

No. "It will get better once you stop for the night."

"If Darrell ever stops." Steph's tone of voice said the boy had better do so soon. "Addie, what's wrong? Oh, Darrell pull off. I think Addie's going to throw up again. Gotta go. Love you!"

Sarah echoed the sentiment although there was no one left on the other end to hear it. With a sigh, she shut her cell phone. She looked around the bakery kitchen. It was so clean the health inspector could eat off the floor.

Chrissy Carroll, who worked the counter, poked her head in. "The last ST has gone."

"Well, then, let's close up and get out of here," said Sarah.

"Ten minutes early. Awesome!" said Chrissy, and disappeared to go home to her family. Lucky Chrissy. Her kids were little.

Sarah looked at the clock on the wall. Ten till five. Well, it was five o'clock somewhere and she was going on a bender.

She locked up the bakery, dropped the day's profits off at the bank, and then squeezed her Cadillac-sized hips into her gas-economical tin can and steered herself toward the Chocolate Bar, Heart Lake's chocolateria.

Change. Sarah hated it, unless it was good and was happening to her. What she hated most was when people moved away. First her sister and brother-in-law had drifted off to California in search of sun—which was highly overrated, if you asked Sarah—and took her nieces. (At least one of them had had the good sense to come back.) Then Jonathan had left. And now Steph was moving.

And speaking of moving, Sarah thought, checking out the strangers driving past her, was Heart Lake some new destination spot? It seemed like lately she was seeing as many new faces as old, familiar ones. Why couldn't life stay the same?

By the time she came through the door of the chocolateria even the sensual aroma that danced around her nose couldn't tease her into a happy mood.

She took in the array of truffles behind the glass counter with a scowl and marched to where her niece, Jamie Moore, stood, smiling and holding out a steaming cup of Sarah's usual weekly treat, a coconut mocha. (Hold the whipped cream—a woman had to draw the line somewhere.)

"I hope that's a double," said Sarah. "I need it."

"A double with decaf so you won't be awake all night," said Jamie. She arched a delicately penciled blond eyebrow. "Is this a two-truffle day?"

"More like a ten, but I'll stop at one. How could you tell?"

"Other than the fact that I knew Steph was leaving today? Just a lucky guess."

Sarah took the mocha with a sigh and moved over to the glass case. A summer of weekly truffle treats at her niece's new shop had already added three pounds to her hips. Even when Sarah was young she'd had a bit of a bubble butt. After she'd opened the bakery it had grown from a bubble to a balloon, and now that she was fifty-six, it was nearing the size of a hot-air balloon. Every once in a while she suggested to herself that changing this weekly coffee klatch to the back room of Emma's quilt shop wouldn't be a bad idea. A girl couldn't get fat on fabric.

Her friend Kizzy, who owned a kitchen shop in town, kept urging her to join her teeny-bikini diet club, but Sarah wasn't ready for that. So Kizzy settled for getting Sarah out for Sunday afternoon walks around the lake. Sarah wasn't sure it did much good. At the rate she was going, to see any improvement she'd probably have to walk all the way to Florida. And back.

Okay, one truffle. She bent over to examine the rows and rows of treats calling to her from behind glass. Flavors ranged from dark chocolate with Grand Marnier filling to white chocolate with lavender. Then there was the fudge: traditional chocolate, rocky road, penuche, and the new caliente flavor with its south-of-the-border bite. And now, with summer giving way to fall, white- and milk-chocolate-dipped apples had replaced double-chocolate ice-cream bars.

"Decisions, decisions," teased Jamie. How she managed to stay a size eight was a mystery. Maybe it had something to do with the fact that the girl didn't eat.

"Don't laugh. It's hard when you're only choosing one," said Sarah. "You could do my hips a good deed and come up with a no-fat, no-calorie truffle."

"I could," Jamie agreed, "if I made it out of cardboard."

"How about the white-chocolate-raspberry?"

"Good choice," Jamie approved, and pulled one out for her.

The shop door opened and in stepped a woman in her early thirties with a round, freckled face, a curvy figure, and strawberry-blond hair pulled back in a ponytail. She had a coat thrown on over jeans and a pink flower-print flowing top. Emma Swanson, proud owner of Emma's Quilt Corner. One Wednesday in September, she'd wandered into the shop just as Jamie and Sarah were getting ready to end their day with a dose of chocolate. The impromptu get-together had quickly become a weekly tradition, and casual friendship had made a fast evolution into sisterhood.

Emma flipped the sign hanging on the door to CLOSED and locked it, announcing, "It's officially five."

"Good," Jamie said with a sigh. "I'm ready to sit down. I'm pooped."

"Too much business," said Emma. "I wish I had that problem," she added with a sigh.

"Be patient," Sarah told her. "You haven't even been open a year yet. Quilting is catching on."

"I hope so," said Emma. "So far my best customers are still my grandma and my mom. And Mom doesn't quilt. Oh, and you, of course," she added, smiling at Sarah.

Sarah had spent a small fortune on fabric a week earlier so she could make quilts for both the girls for Christmas. She'd been so busy with the bakery that she hadn't quilted in years. But she was sure it would all come back to her, like riding a bicycle. She hadn't ridden a bicycle in years, either. She'd rather quilt.

They settled at one of the white bistro tables on the other side of the shop, Emma and Sarah armed with their mochas and truffles and Jamie only with a cup of chocolate mint tea.

"No wonder you're so skinny," Emma said, pointing to it. "I don't know how you keep from eating all your inventory."

"I have Clarice for that. Anyway, I sampled so many truffles when I was first learning how to make these things that I don't care if I ever taste another one again as long as I live. Well, unless it's a new recipe," she amended.

"I sampled a lot of my recipes when I started the bakery, too," said Sarah. "All it did was turn me into an ST."

"Yeah, that was what did it, all right," mocked Jamie.

"What's an ST?" asked Emma.

"Sweet Tooth," Jamie answered for Sarah. "And you were an ST before you even opened the bakery. I was around, remember?"

Sarah shook her head. "This is the problem with

having an older sister who makes you an aunt before your time. You end up with lippy nieces who know too much."

"You imported me," Jamie reminded her with a smile.

"And I'm glad I did. Someone in your family needed to come back home. You make a great addition to Heart Lake." She took a sip of her mocha, then sighed.

"They'll be back by Christmas," Jamie reminded her, accurately interpreting the sigh.

"Seeing them go had to be pretty hard," said Emma. "I know how much you love your granddaughters."

"My mom wore sunglasses when I went to say good-bye," said Jamie.

"Doesn't everybody in L.A. wear sunglasses?" asked Emma.

"In the house?"

"Um, that's weird."

"She didn't want me to see she'd been crying."

"I was brave and didn't cry," bragged Sarah. "Not until they left, anyway."

"Well, we sure could use a few more Stephs here," said Jamie. "You're not going to believe this, but two little twits ran the four-way stop on Lake Way and Alder yesterday."

Emma looked at her questioningly. "Somebody ran a stop sign and you're surprised?"

"Somebody ran a stop sign in *Heart Lake* and I'm surprised," Jamie corrected her. "There were two old ladies at the crosswalk. If I hadn't let them go they'd still be standing there."

"You know, people used to just about kill each other with kindness at that four-way stop," Sarah reminisced.

"Well, they've kept the 'kill each other' part," said Jamie.

Emma sighed. "I wish Heart Lake could stay just like it was when I was in school."

"Nice places like this can't help but grow," Sarah said.

"Everyone wants to be the last person in Paradise. Of course, as more people move into Paradise it gets harder to stay connected. Then people stop caring and it's not paradise anymore." She frowned and took another sip of her mocha.

"That's already happening," Emma said with a frown. "You know, only four people came to my event last night. And two of them were related."

Guilt washed over Sarah. "Oh, no. I completely forgot."

"Me, too," said Jamie. "I'm really sorry, Em."

Emma shrugged. "Oh, well. I tried."

"People are selfish," Jamie said in disgust. "But what are you going to do?"

Emma put her elbows on the table and rested her chin in her hands. "I wish I could do something. It makes me sad to think of Heart Lake changing. It used to be a sweet, friendly town."

"It's still friendly," Jamie assured her. "You were like a one-woman welcoming committee when I first moved here." She beamed at Sarah. "And you were awesome."

"I had to be. We're related," Sarah teased. "Seriously," she added, "Heart Lake is a perfect fit for you."

Jamie had come a long way from the beaten-down woman Sarah had taken under her wing a year ago. Now she was happy, with her own place and a thriving business. No man in her life, though, but Sarah could hardly blame Jamie for putting a NO VACANCY sign over her heart, not after what she'd left behind.

"Maybe that's what we need, some kind of welcoming committee," Emma mused. "That way people would feel connected."

"There was such a thing once," said Sarah. "It was called Welcome Wagon."

"Welcome Wagon? What happened to it?" asked Emma. Sarah shrugged. "It just . . . died. No volunteers to keep

it going, everyone working and no one home to welcome.
I guess people are too busy to be nice."

"It only takes a minute to let two old ladies cross the
street," Jamie said in disgust.

"Well, there's your random act of kindness for the day,"
Sarah told her. "You know," she added thoughtfully, "if
everybody just did one nice thing a day . . ."

"We'd be living in Mayberry," Jamie finished.

"I used to love those old reruns when I was a kid," said
Emma.

Jamie rolled her eyes. "Why am I not surprised?"

Sarah was still thinking. "Why couldn't we do one good
deed a day?" she asked suddenly. "It might be fun to try.
You know, paying it forward."

"Like in the movie," Emma said with a smile.

"That worked real well at the stop sign," said Jamie. She
downed the last of her chocolate mint tea. "Well, here's my
something. Your chocolate therapy is on the house," she
said to Sarah and Emma. It always was, but she cocked
an eyebrow and grinned at Emma. "So, top that."

"Maybe I will," Emma said. "If I see a hot-looking
homeless guy, I'll take him in for the night."

Okay, they weren't taking her seriously. Sarah could see
that. But somewhere in there was a good idea, if she could
just find it.

THREE

At five-thirty Sarah looked at the clock and announced, "I'd better get home and start dinner."

She only had Sam and herself to feed now, and half the time Sam was at the station. But that didn't matter. Sarah cooked dinner for him no matter where he was. In fact, she usually wound up cooking for all the guys at Firehouse Number Nine. If you asked Jamie, her aunt was already the queen of good deeds.

"You know, she might have a point," Emma said after Jamie had given Sarah a kiss and sent her on her way with a truffle for her uncle (which would, of course, never make it home).

"About the 'pay it forward' thing?"

"I mean, why not? People are basically good."

Jamie made a snort of disgust. "I don't know who told you that, but he lied."

"Most people are basically good," Emma amended. "And my grandma told me. I think, deep down, people want to be good."

"Not all people," Jamie said under her breath. Emma's pitying look made her suddenly antsy. She got up and went to the kitchen at the back of the shop to put their mugs in the dishwasher.

Emma followed her. Jamie could feel her friend watching her with those big, blue naïve eyes. "Hey, it's not like I don't love this town," Jamie said, "and I'd hate to see it grow into an anthill of strangers. But I don't know how you stop a place from changing."

"Too bad we can't take a picture of Heart Lake, stick it in a frame, and then just jump in," said Emma with a sigh.

Jamie picked up her keys to lock up. "With all the new people the picture would probably fall right off the wall anyway."

"Want to come over for dinner?" Emma asked as they walked out the door. "I made chicken curry soup last night and I recorded *Bell, Book, and Candle* with Jimmy Stewart and Kim Novak."

Emma and her old movies. "What's it about?" Jamie asked suspiciously.

"Witches. Perfect for Halloween."

"Just witches?" *No sappy love story?*

"It's really cute," said Emma. "And don't forget, you get a free meal, too," she added.

What the heck? Jamie wasn't exactly booked solid. Since coming to Heart Lake her social life had consisted of weekend bike rides around the lake, trips to the gym, and visits to Sarah for cake-decorating lessons, followed by more trips to the gym to counteract the damage done by the visits to Sarah.

Other than that, all she had was movie nights at Emma's little duplex. When they first started hanging out, Emma and Jamie had done crafty things like making candles and dried-flower arrangements. That had evolved into crafts followed by a flick. It hadn't taken more than a couple of times for Jamie to realize that Emma was an old-movie addict. She especially loved tearjerkers such as *The Ghost and Mrs. Muir* and *An Affair to Remember.* Movies like *Kill Bill* were more to Jamie's taste, so they had negotiated a compromise. Jamie would wander around in old-movieland with Emma as long as no woman was verbally abused or got a grapefruit pushed in her face by James Cagney. And no cop movies. No sappy romances, either. That last one was hard for Emma. Still, witches sounded safe enough. Bubble, bubble, and all that.

But they weren't. Jamie knew it right from the scene where Jimmy Stewart stumbled into Kim Novak's creepy little shop. She sat on Emma's old sofa, curled under a fan quilt, grinding popcorn between her teeth while Emma tried to look clueless as she finished the binding on a quilted wall hanging destined for her display window.

When Jimmy and Kim finally got together and Kim declared with tears in her eyes that she was only human, Jamie frowned at Emma, sitting red-faced in her overstuffed chair, then grabbed the remote and put an end to the ending credits. "Just witches, huh?"

Emma's face turned redder—a bad color combination with her pink top. "I forgot about the romance part. I really did. I just remembered the funny scene with Jack Lemmon turning off all the streetlights."

"It wasn't that funny," Jamie informed her.

Emma hung her head. "Sorry."

"Never mind. It's all good," Jamie said with a shrug, trying to be a sport. Anyway, it served her right. She should have bailed and gone to the gym when Jimmy and Kim started getting sloppy. She threw off the quilt, saying, "I'd better go. I have to get up early tomorrow and replenish my caramel truffles and do some more apples."

Emma nodded, obviously relieved to be off the hook. "What are you going to give out for the Goblin Walk? Have you decided?"

"Suckers for the kids. And I'm going to sample out fudge for the grown-ups."

"Good advertising," Emma approved. "You'll probably even get some new customers out of it. Everyone likes chocolate."

"You know, I'm kind of looking forward to it," Jamie said. "I remember doing the Goblin Walk when I was a little kid. I never thought I'd be doing it now as a shop owner."

"All those little witches and princesses and fairies— they're so cute," said Emma. "Kind of makes you want to have some of your own, doesn't it?" she added in an attempt to be sly. And of course, to go along with those children, Jamie should have a man. When she wasn't busy at her shop, Emma Swanson moonlighted as Cupid.

"Uh. No."

"You are so lying."

Jamie shrugged. "Okay, so I'm lying. Maybe I'll adopt someday."

"Someday? You're not getting any younger, you know," Emma reminded her.

"Thanks."

"Neither of us are," Emma said with a sigh. She pointed a finger at Jamie. "What you need is a Jack Colton."

"A who?"

"You know, from *Romancing the Stone.*"

"Oh, yeah. That's what I need." Emma lived in la-la land. Jamie put on her denim jacket and scooped up her purse. "The soup was great. Next time's at my place. We can start making those pinecone candle wreaths I told you about."

Emma reluctantly set aside her Cupid wings and nodded.

Emma watched her friend climb into her old Toyota and drive off into the night. Alone. What a waste of blonde. With her thick, long hair and hazel eyes Jamie always made Emma think of Viking princesses. She had the perfect face—not too long, not too fat (like Emma's), and no freckles—just perfect, creamy princess skin. She also had a little dab of a nose and a little dab of a chin that made her look helpless and delicate. Oh, and a perfect little body that also helped with the delicate look. Jamie was a princess in need of a prince.

Aren't we all? Emma thought. But she was more like Drew Barrymore's pudgy stepsister in *Ever After*—not exactly the kind of girl a guy went looking for, glass slipper in hand.

Even if one went looking, he'd have a hard time finding her. Princes tended not to wander into quilt shops. "You've got to get out there where the men are," her mom had urged her. So she'd tried Internet dating. That netted her a nineteen-year-old nerd, a fat Trekkie, and a middle-aged bald guy. Baldie was strike three and she was out of there.

Single wasn't so bad. She didn't have to fight anyone for the remote and she could watch her fill of real men on her classic movie channels.

Jamie was different, though. She was simply too pretty to be alone. Anyway, Emma was thirty-three. She still had time. Sort of. Okay, not really. But Jamie was older. In five more years her thirties would be history. Couldn't she hear her biological clock ticking?

Of course she heard it. She was probably trying her best to drown it out. A waste, a total waste. Emma would have to find a way to help her friend; that was all there was to it. She'd think of something.

Meanwhile, she had things to do. She got into her pajamas, and then plunked in front of her computer to take care of the business of life. Online life.

She clicked in her password and entered My World, a Web site rather like a giant Internet model of the old Milton Bradley game of Life. Only more expensive. People who lived online paid for the privilege, buying land and businesses, doing social networking. Emma's avatar owned a fancy restaurant, and her name was Tess L'amour. Tess didn't run the restaurant, though. She was a movie star, the size eight variety, and she had flowing black hair. She juggled six boyfriends, each of whom thought she was dazzlingly funny and brilliant. She drove a black Mercedes convertible and she was hot. Today she had to organize for a big soiree with a guest list of fifty movers and shakers. Three of the guests were her boyfriends. That could prove interesting, a lot more interesting than Emma's offline life.

It was easy to believe in happy endings when you'd never experienced a sad one, Jamie thought as she tooled home on balding tires. But once you'd seen the ugly underside of the storybook love story you couldn't be a believer.

Grant had seemed like the perfect man, but he'd been acting, just like the men in those movies Emma loved so much.

A flash of red lights behind her brought Jamie out of her painful musings. Oh, not again. She pulled over and watched in her rearview mirror. Out came the giant.

Hic.

This was just sick and wrong. She suddenly thought of the movie *Groundhog Day,* probably another favorite of Emma's. Just what she wanted to relive, getting stopped by a cop.

She took a deep breath to quell the stupid nervous hiccups

and held it while he approached the car. Then she let down her window and started talking the second his face came into view. "I haven't had a chance to get the taillight fixed, but I've got an appointment." Total lie. She was lying to a cop. This was no way to make a deposit in the old karmic bank.

"Do you know how fast you were going?"

Speeding? *Hic.* She never sped. *Hic, hic.* Well, when she was paying attention to what she was doing, she never sped. She crossed her arms over the steering wheel and laid her head down. "I'm in hell."

"You were going thirty-five in a twenty-five-mile-an-hour zone," he informed her.

She stared at him. "I was?"

He was looking at her suspiciously. If only she'd gotten something useful out of that dumb movie, like a spell for making a cop disappear. If only she was Samantha the Witch. She'd wiggle her nose and have this guy gone in an instant. On impulse, like in some crazy dream, she wiggled.

He raised his eyebrows. "Are you all right, ma'am?"

"As all right as I can be under the circumstances," she replied. "I have allergies." *To cops.*

He frowned like he could read her thoughts.

Another hiccup escaped her. Great. Just great. Stopped by a cop and hiccupping.

He checked out the back of the car, looking for a half-consumed bottle of booze, probably. Whatever happened to innocent until proven guilty? "May I see your license and registration?" he asked, politely neutral.

She frowned and took her license from her wallet. "I haven't been drinking if that's what you're thinking. I just get the hiccups sometimes." *Like when I'm nervous.* She got her registration from the glove compartment and handed it over. "Go ahead, make my day," she said grumpily.

"Like I haven't heard that one before," he said, and went back to his squad car.

She watched his retreating backside. It was a thick, well-muscled backside that made her think of football players—a great backside. For Emma or someone else. Not for her.

"So, did you find anything on my record?" she greeted him when he returned. "Drugs? Grand theft auto?"

Dumb. That smart mouth of hers was what got her in trouble so much when she was married. Big, testosterone-laden men were like bumblebees. They were slow mental movers. But they packed a wallop when they hit.

A corner of his mouth slipped up. "Nope. Maybe I should look again."

Cute. A cop who moonlighted as a comic.

"I'm letting you go with a warning."

She stared at him. "That's unheard of."

"What's unheard of?"

"Stopping someone twice and not giving her a ticket. In most places you don't even do that once."

He shrugged. "This isn't most places. It's Heart Lake."

"Mayberry," she murmured.

"Just call me Barney Fife," he said. "And get that tail-light fixed. Third time you get a ticket, even in Mayberry."

"Yes, Officer," she managed. And swallowed a hiccup. *Ouch.*

"Hold your breath," he advised. "Best cure for hiccups."

"We both know scaring me doesn't work," she muttered as he returned to his car.

He may have scared her, but not on purpose, or so he would have said. He was just doing his job. She still couldn't believe the man hadn't given her a ticket. Her conversation with Sarah and Emma about good deeds came to mind. Maybe she was this cop's for the day.

Or maybe the nose-wiggling had really helped. Who knew?

Who cared? He was gone and that was all that mattered.

FOUR

Emma's Quilt Corner was *the* place to be if you were a quilter. Sadly, there didn't seem to be many quilters in Heart Lake, and that was a mystery to Emma since quilting was getting more and more popular. All a woman had to do was look on the Web.

Maybe all a woman had to do was shop on the Web, too, she thought glumly as she worked on her new window display. Everybody lived on the Internet these days, she understood that. But the Internet couldn't look at a quilter's project and show her how to fix her wavy borders. The Internet couldn't demonstrate how to put on binding. Never mind, she told herself. You can beat the odds.

The quilt-draped rocking chair she had placed in the display window two weeks ago was too old-fashioned, she'd decided, so she'd replaced it with several wall hangings, all dangling at different levels—gigantic lures to catch passersby. The first week of November she'd be adding a machine-quilted rectangle that reminded Heart Lake residents "Christmas Is Coming." She'd scripted a sign announcing her next quilting class (free when you buy your materials at Emma's), which was now propped on an easel. She moved the easel six inches and stepped back to check out the overall effect. Perfect. People would see it and the lovely hangings on display and rush through the door to sign up.

Hopefully.

Emma looked out the window and surveyed the street. It was a rainy (big surprise) Monday and the only ray of sunshine came from the gold mums showering in their heart-shaped hanging baskets along the street. Soon those mums would be replaced by swags and candy canes. Then, after a short break, the hearts would be back, filled with plastic red roses for Valentine's Day. The roses would stay until spring, when real flowers could make their appearance.

It was little touches like this that made people want to live here. Emma sure didn't want to live anywhere else. Not that she'd been many places. She'd gone to Mexico once when the church youth group went to some remote part of the country to build houses for the poor, and she had made several trips to eastern Washington to visit her cousins. She'd been to Victoria once, too. It had been fun to ride the Clipper.

It wasn't much compared to Heart Lake kids like Kelsey Bleecker, who had moved to New York to become a star on Broadway, or Jamal King, who Emma heard was now in L.A., working on films. So many kids had fled after graduation, vowing never to come back. But what had leaving town really gotten them? So far she hadn't seen Kelsey on TV, accepting a Tony, and from what Jamie had told Emma about L.A., Jamal could have it.

The shop door opened and in came Kerrie Neil, with her two-year-old, Nesta, crying in her arms. "Just one more stop," she told the toddler, then greeted Emma with, "Hi. I need some white thread."

Good old Kerrie. She wasn't into quilting, but she and Emma had been in student council together. They had fought to keep the Heart Lake High Good Citizen Award going, even though most of the student body preferred to play mailbox baseball, climb the water tower, and sneak pot rather than look for ways to be good citizens. Now, even though Kerrie didn't quilt, she was still earning her good citizen award by helping to support Emma's business.

She grabbed the spool of thread and looked around the shop as if searching for something more to buy. So far she'd purchased embroidery thread and dish towels for her great-aunt's birthday, a book on quilting—which she claimed she would be using as soon as Nesta was in school and she had more time—and Emma's quilted Noah's Ark wall hanging for Nesta's bedroom. "I guess that's it for to-day," she said at last, setting her purchase on the counter.

The little spool of white thread looked pitifully small squatting on that big, long counter, but a sale was a sale, and Emma appreciated the business. "How's Miss Nesta doing?" she asked, smiling at the toddler as she rang up the purchase.

Kerrie frowned. "We're going home after this. She needs a nap. I need a nap." She heaved a sigh. "You know, when you get pregnant everyone says, 'Oh, awesome, you're going to have a baby.' But nobody tells you what that really means. It means you're going to end up with a figure like a kangaroo, get no sleep, and be too tired for sex."

"Which is what got you in this mess in the first place," teased Emma. "You've done such a great sales job I think I'll have to grab a man on my way home tonight and have wild, crazy sex so I can get knocked up."

Kerrie smiled down at Nesta, who was pretending not to listen to the grown-ups by offering intermittent whimpers. She ran a hand over her daughter's dark curls. "Then Nesta can have a best friend in the student council when she's in high school. Good idea." She smiled at Emma and heaved a rueful shrug. "I wish I knew someone I could gift wrap for you. It seems like most of the single guys have left town."

It seemed so to Emma, too. She'd done her share of checking out guys in Safeway's produce department. They all had gold rings on their left hand. "Oh, well," she said with a shrug. "I'm waiting for Jimmy Stewart's great-great-great-grandson to come to town anyway."

"Does he have one?" asked Kerrie, wide-eyed.

"I don't know. He should."

Kerrie shook her head at Emma. "You and your movies. You are such a hopeless romantic."

"No, hopeful," Emma corrected her.

"Whatever," said Kerrie. "Listen, I had another reason for coming in. I was just wondering . . ."

Emma knew by the sudden awkwardness, the hesitation, exactly what her old friend was going to ask. It happened a lot, and she didn't mind, really. "Yes."

"You don't know what I'm going to say," Kerrie protested.

"Yes I do. I'll make a quilt for you. What's the cause?"

"The wildlife shelter's annual New Year's auction. I don't need it till after Christmas."

It wasn't much time, but she could do it. She sure had enough inventory on hand. Sadly. "No problem."

"Thanks. You rock."

Either she rocked or she was the world's biggest soft touch.

It was an hour before another customer came in. Actually, two women entered the shop within a few minutes of each other, but Emma knew right off only one would be a paying customer. Ruth Weisman, who not only quilted but also sewed clothes for her granddaughters, was always good for a few yards of fabric. Shirley Schultz, however, was another story. She was somewhere in her seventies and she loved to quilt. She always had a project going, which should have been a good thing for the shop. Except Shirley didn't believe in credit cards and she had a habit of forgetting her checkbook. Of course, she never had any cash with her, either. Emma now kept a running tab for Shirley. And it was definitely running—away from Emma.

She knew she should be firm with Shirley and insist she bring in her trusty checkbook and catch up on what she owed, but Emma couldn't bring herself to do it. Shirley was old enough to be her grandma. How could a girl be mean to her grandma? On top of that, Shirley was a widow, and judging from the frayed condition of her black wool coat and the shabby tennis shoes she always wore, she was probably squeaking by on Social Security.

"This flannel will be perfect for matching pajamas," said Ruth, fingering the bolt of soft pink fabric with its pattern of stars and rainbows that Emma had suggested. "It will look adorable on the girls."

"It's a great idea to be thinking ahead," said Emma. "Christmas will be here before we know it."

"I just give the children a check," said Shirley, who was moving toward the bookshelf. "It's too hard to shop anymore. They never like what I give them anyway."

Emma had a sudden image of the old lady in the *National Lampoon* Christmas movie who wrapped up her cat and gave it away as a Christmas present. She could just see Shirley showing up for Christmas dinner with a jumping, yowling, beribboned box. Probably Shirley's pittance five- or ten-dollar check would be a welcome relief from whatever she chose to give.

Ruth raised an eyebrow and turned in Shirley's direction. "You can always give gift cards." With her freshly dyed and styled hair, her acrylic nails, and her Lands' End clothing, Ruth obviously didn't have to worry about making do on a fixed income.

Shirley frowned. "Someone could steal a gift card. I read somewhere that thieves take the numbers right off them in the store and then cash in." She shook her head. "People have no scruples. Oh, you have a book of Christmas crafts. How lovely!"

Ruth's eyes lit up at that. "Really." She moved to where Shirley stood.

Shirley clutched the book to her scrawny chest. "It's the last one."

Ruth looked down her nose at Shirley. "What do you want it for? You just said all you give is checks."

"I might do something different this year," Shirley argued.

Maybe she'd do something different right now, and actually pay for the book. "Not to worry," Emma said to Ruth. "I've ordered more and they'll be in next week. I'll put one aside for you."

Ruth shot Shirley a look of disgust, but said, "That will be fine," and Shirley moved to the counter with her treasure.

"So, the book will do it for you today?" Emma asked pleasantly, all the while willing Shirley to pull a checkbook out of her purse.

Shirley nodded and patted her wiry, gray hair while Emma rang up her purchase.

"That will be sixteen forty-nine," Emma said brightly. "A bargain at any price." *So please pay me.*

Shirley smiled and opened her capacious, old handbag. And then it began. First she scrabbled around in its depths. "Hmm. That's odd." Next she began to remove the contents. Out came her hankie, a bottle of antacid, breath mints, a coin purse, three pens, a comb, various slips of paper with shopping lists, a folded envelope. "Oh, dear. I seem to have forgotten my checkbook."

You have to stop this. Be strong. "I can hold the book for you and you can get it the next time you come in," Emma offered.

"Or I'll take it," said Ruth sweetly.

Shirley ignored her, concentrating all her energy on looking pitifully at Emma. Her lips (bright red—Shirley liked to make a statement) dipped down at the corners. "Oh." And, just in case Emma had missed the pathos in her voice, she said it again. "Oh." And added, "I was so hoping to start some of those crafts this week."

It would probably be her only pleasure. Emma suddenly felt like mean old Mr. Potter from *It's a Wonderful Life,* about to foreclose on some poor old lady. All her resolve crumbled. "Okay. Tell you what. Let's put it on your tab."

Shirley beamed at Emma like she'd just offered her a lifetime supply of free Metamucil. "That's a great idea." She reached out and patted Emma's arm. "You're an angel."

A stupid angel.

"You'll make some man a wonderful wife someday."

I hope I make a better wife than a businesswoman, Emma thought.

"Are you dating someone?" asked Shirley.

"As if that's any of our business," said Ruth.

"I'm way too busy with the shop," lied Emma.

Shirley shook a cautionary finger at her. "Just remember, a loaf of bread sits on the shelf too long and it goes stale."

"I'll remember," Emma promised. How could she forget an image like that? She pictured a loaf of bread on the top shelf at the Safeway with her head sticking out one end of it and every man in Heart Lake walking right by. Most of them were wearing wedding rings. She sighed and watched out the window as Shirley sailed out the door with her treasure.

"You're too soft," scolded Ruth.

"It's what George Bailey would have done," said Emma.

Ruth shook her head and frowned. "This isn't Bedford Falls."

"No, but it's as close as a place can get," Emma countered.

"Not for long, probably," said Ruth, pulling out her charge card.

That was a sad thought. Emma remembered Sarah's suggestion that they try to do one good deed a day. Shirley had just been hers. What if everyone did that? she mused as Ruth left the shop.

A town was like a quilt—one work made of many small pieces. When you fit all the pieces together just right you got a thing of beauty. Why couldn't they try and fit the pieces together just right? If each person did his or her part . . .

The sky turned late-afternoon dark and the rain began to sheet. Emma decided to close early. What was the point of staying open? All her clientele were tucked in their houses now, happily quilting or taking an afternoon nap.

She went home and took a long, hot shower. Then she heated up some of the soup she'd made the night before and took it into her office to eat while she walked Tess through a land auction on a prime corner lot where Tess planned to build a spa. It was exhausting and stressful, so afterward Tess went to her favorite dance club and dazzled everyone with her beauty and grace. After Emma finally got Tess tucked in for the night, she settled in front of the TV to do some hand stitching on a wall hanging for the church nursery and watch Jerry Maguire. She knew most of the lines by heart, and beat him to the punch when it came time for him to deliver the most romantic words of all time: "You complete me."

People needed each other. A person alone was like a scrap of fabric looking for a square. She sighed. She'd find her square someday. On that encouraging note, she turned off the lights, brushed her teeth, and ambled off to bed.

And had the most amazing dream. Jerry Maguire didn't show up (darn!), but a lot of familiar faces from town did. There was Kizzy from the kitchen shop and Dan the checkout guy from Safeway, Hope Wells, who owned Changing Seasons Floral, and Sarah and Jamie, and some of Emma's customers, and they were all giant squares of fabric, floating around downtown Lake Way, right in the middle of the street. More and more fabric-square people joined them, coming out of various shops, and they all started folding into one another and forming the most beautiful quilt Emma had ever seen.

Her eyes popped open. "Wow," she breathed. She checked the clock. Five A.M. Sarah would already be at work. Emma scrambled out of bed, ran to the phone, and called Sarah's private kitchen line at the bakery. She barely gave Sarah a chance to answer. "I know it's not our usual day, but can you meet at Jamie's after work? It's important."

"Well, sure. What's up?"

"You were right and I've got an idea."

FIVE

So, what's the big news?" asked Jamie once all three women were settled at one of her bistro tables with their various chocolate fixes.

"I had the most amazing dream last night," said Emma. Just remembering it made her want to jump up and do the Snoopy dance. She could barely stay still in her seat.

"Did one of us inherit a million bucks?" Jamie teased.

"Even better," Emma said, and then proceeded to tell them what she'd seen in her dream.

Jamie cocked an eyebrow. "So you dreamed we were all giant pieces of fabric."

"It was symbolic, like . . . a vision."

"Oh." Jamie nodded as if Emma had gone around the bend.

"Think of what was at the center of the quilt," Emma urged.

"A heart. It probably meant you had heartburn," said Jamie, determined to be dense.

Emma heaved an exasperated sigh. "Don't you see? It proves Sarah was right."

"About what?" asked Sarah.

How could she have forgotten? "About the 'random acts of kindness' thing. Guys, we could start a movement and save Heart Lake."

"I hate to say it, Em, but it wouldn't last," Jamie predicted.

"Yeah? Good thing nobody told that to the twelve disciples or the abolitionists," Emma countered.

Jamie's eyebrow went up again. "And which of them are you comparing us to?"

"You know what I mean," said Emma, but suddenly she didn't feel as confident. Maybe it was only a silly dream. She could feel her enthusiasm draining away like a slow leak.

"I know what you mean, and I'm all for exploring this more," Sarah said firmly.

Emma shot her a grateful look.

"Did you have something specific in mind?" asked Sarah.

"Actually, yes."

Jamie waved a hand in surrender. "So, let's hear it."

"Well," Emma began, warming to her subject, "the 'acts of kindness' thing is great, but we need a plan to make it all come together, just like if you're making a quilt. You have to have a pattern, some way to make the pieces fit."

"And so?" prompted Jamie.

"I'm getting to that." *Sheesh.* "First we need a name. That will be our pattern. We could call it the 'Have a Heart' campaign, and our slogan could be 'Keep the Heart in Heart Lake.' "

Jamie nodded, looking reluctantly impressed. "Not bad. But how do you make it all happen?"

"Call a community meeting," said Emma. "Maybe we could get the Grange Hall for a night, put an ad in the paper."

Now Sarah was nodding and smiling. "Great idea."

"Okay, so now we've got a bunch of people at the Grange," said Jamie. "Then what?"

"Then we get everyone to pledge to do one good deed a day," said Emma.

"Maybe we could even make up T-shirts that say HAVE A HEART," Sarah suggested. "That way we have something tangible. On the back we could print KEEP THE HEART IN HEART LAKE. We could sell them and give the proceeds to Helpline."

"Money for the food bank—I love that," said Jamie, pointing at Sarah as if she were brilliant.

Emma wouldn't have minded getting a little credit, but oh, well. At least Jamie was on board. "And if we invite a reporter from the *Heart Lake Herald,* we could get an article out of the deal. Free publicity."

"I'll call the Park and Rec office tomorrow and see if they'll let us use the hall," Sarah said. "We could shoot for the first week in November. The timing is perfect, just as we're coming into giving season, when people feel most generous."

Emma frowned. "We don't want to limit this to a season, do we? I mean giving season should last all year."

"There's another great slogan," Sarah said, saluting Emma with her mug. "And I agree. I'm just saying this is a great time to kick off a campaign to do good deeds. People are already predisposed to accept it." She turned to Jamie. "What do you think?"

Jamie nodded. "I don't know if it will work, but I'm in."

"Let's all start this week so we have some testimonials for the meeting," said Emma, excited.

"Sure. Why not?" Sarah agreed. She hoisted her mug. "Here's to giving season. May it last all year long."

Emma had tears in her eyes now. This was such a beautiful idea. "This is a true movie moment."

Jamie rolled her eyes. "I'm going to go into insulin shock here." But then she grinned and raised her mug, too. "To giving season."

"This is going to be awesome," Emma predicted.

Jamie wasn't so sure about that, but she decided to try to keep an open mind. No opportunity to do a good deed presented itself between the Chocolate Bar and home. In fact, nothing at all happened between the Chocolate Bar and home. Everyone was behaving at the four-way stop, probably because she'd missed rush hour. No person in need crossed her path. No cop, either, thank God. Naturally, she didn't run into the big, bad cop because she now had her taillight fixed. If she hadn't, of course he'd have been right behind her like a hound on the scent of a terrified fox.

Tomorrow would be soon enough to do something nice, she decided. Tomorrow she would send her mom some chocolates, just because. Mom was as bad a chocoholic as Sarah. She'd love it.

Jamie was in her shop kitchen by five the next day, making ganache. Before opening at ten she had chocolates to dip and decorate and fruit to enrobe, and she had to fill the espresso machine with beans and make her dark and white truffle shots and hot chocolate. By the time Clarice, her counter help, showed up, she was ready for a break, so she decided to go put her mom's surprise in the mail. Just before she left for the post office, it occurred to her that simply sending chocolates to her mom didn't really qualify as a good deed, so she filled a little plate for Carolyn the postmaster and her assistant Walter. If any pair deserved a good deed it was those two. They knew every one of their post office patrons by name as well as their dogs, and Carolyn always kept treats on hand to give to her four-legged visitors.

Carolyn saw the plate of truffles and her eyes lit up behind her glasses. "What have we got here?"

"A little something to thank you guys for working so hard," said Jamie.

"All right," said Walter, leaning over from where he was sorting letters into mailboxes and grabbing one.

Noting the bit of belly beginning to sneak over Walter's belt, Jamie couldn't help but wonder if this really qualified as a good deed. Walter's wife, who tried to watch his weight, would probably come into the shop and club her with a scale.

"That was really sweet of you," said Carolyn as she weighed Jamie's goody package for Mom.

Jamie shrugged. "Just trying to keep that small-town feeling alive. In fact, Emma Swanson, Sarah Goodwin, and I are starting a movement."

"A movement?" Carolyn looked at her like Jamie was about to try to lure her into some strange cult.

"Yeah. We're going to try and encourage everyone to do one nice thing for somebody every day."

"Kind of like paying it forward?" asked Walter, reaching for another chocolate. Carolyn moved it out of range and he pouted.

"Something like that," said Jamie. "You know, help keep the heart in Heart Lake."

"That's a great idea," said Carolyn as Jamie handed over her money.

"So, what do we have to do?" asked Walter.

"Anything," Jamie told him. "Let somebody go ahead of you in the checkout line, change a flat tire for someone—whatever comes to mind."

"That could be kind of fun," he said. "How long are we doing this?"

"We're not exactly thinking of putting an expiration date on it."

Walter shook his head. "People will never keep it up."

Jamie conveniently forgot that she had thought the exact same thing. "You never know. Maybe it will become a habit."

"It sounds like a good habit to me," said Carolyn. And as Jamie left the post office, she heard Carolyn say to the next person in line, "Let's start right now. Would you like one of my truffles, Mrs. Gormsley?"

"Chocolates?"

Jamie looked over her shoulder and saw one of Heart Lake's senior citizens with her fingers poised over the plate, a smile on her face. That felt good. She could get into this. So, what else could she do?

Gift jars. She and Emma could fill quart-sized Mason jars with candies or cocoa mix, decorate them with cute lids, and randomly give them away to anyone who looked tired or down or stressed. That would be fun. Maybe they could make a bunch and take them around to the residents at Senior Gardens.

She called Emma at the quilt shop to share her idea.

"Emma's Quilt Corner," snarled Emma.

"It's me. Are you okay?"

"Yeah," Emma said with a sigh. "I just let Shirley Schultz make off with half a yard of free fabric and two spools of colored thread."

"Oh. The woman who never remembers her checkbook."

"That would be the one. We're like Lucy and Charlie Brown with the football. Wouldn't you think I'd get smart?"

Jamie decided that was probably a rhetorical question. "At least it wasn't much."

"It all adds up," Emma said, sounding grumpy.

"Look at it this way. There's your random act of kindness for the day."

"It wasn't random, it was planned. And a good deed isn't much of a good deed if you feel like you were tricked into it."

"Then tell yourself you're not being tricked," reasoned Jamie. "You know what's coming."

"Yeah, you're right," Emma said. "Maybe I'm just tired of getting suckered by old ladies. It doesn't feel very noble."

"Well, then, have I got a deal for you," Jamie said, and explained her idea.

"Oh, I love it!" gushed Emma. "Let's start tonight."

"Why not? You bring the material; I'll go scrounge jars from Aunt Sarah. I know she's got a ton in her basement."

"And I'll pick up a pizza."

"Great. You can count that as your good deed for the day," said Jamie. "My fridge is empty and I'm broke."

"Me, too," said Emma. "But I'm so far in the hole, what's another inch?"

Emma hung up feeling excited again. Jamie was right, of course. Helping Shirley was a good thing to do, and she shouldn't take the shine off the act of kindness by feeling resentful. The small amount of merchandise Shirley got away with wasn't going to make or break her. Her meager supply of customers was going to do that.

No negative thinking, she told herself sternly, and no more bad attitude. From now on she was going to help anyone and everyone and not worry about feeling tricked or taken advantage of. And she'd keep her eyes open for more ways to help others.

She didn't have to keep them open for long. After an evening of topping jar lids with fabric and ribbon at Jamie's little lake shack, she bolted from her car to her duplex under a deluge of rain. As she unlocked the door, she heard a pitiful yowl. She peered around in an attempt to locate it. There it was again, just off to the right of the porch. Bending over and looking under the juniper bush, she saw two green cat eyes peering back at her. The animal gave a low-throated rumble.

"Oh, kitty. Why aren't you home and out of the rain?" she cooed.

The cat explained with another yowl, this time softer, like it was now too low on energy to cry for help.

Now here, indeed, was an act of kindness waiting to happen. "Oh, poor thing." She bent over and held out a hand. "Come here, sweetie."

The cat backed up with a growl.

"Of course you're afraid," she explained to both of them. She unlocked her door and opened it. "You want in?"

The cat didn't respond. Its mama had probably told it never to talk to strangers.

Emma sighed. It was hard to be kind when the animal you were trying to help wanted no part of you. "Okay, wait there," she said. She went inside, ran to the kitchen, and found a can of tuna in the cupboard. She opened it, then went back to the porch and set it down on the welcome mat. "There you go. Maybe that will help."

Sure the cat wouldn't come out of hiding until she was gone, she stepped back inside and shut the door. She couldn't see from the peephole in the door or her front window. She hoped the cat was enjoying its feast. One thing she knew for sure, she'd enjoyed offering it.

She washed up, threw on her pajamas, and climbed into

bed. She was just drifting off when she remembered that Tess was supposed to pay for the land she won in her latest land auction.

Tess could wait.

SIX

$\mathscr{S}$arah took weekends off. Sweet Somethings Bakery was closed on Sundays, and on Saturdays she left the bakery in the capable hands of Chrissy Carroll and Amber Howell. Amber would come in at five and turn herself into Sarah, baking up a storm. Then Chrissy would arrive at seven and together they'd handle the morning breakfast rush of Heart Lakers looking for quiche´ and Sarah's famous scones—a rush that started the second they opened their doors at eight. And while things were humming at the bakery, Sarah and Sam, who managed to be home at least part of the weekend, would enjoy a quick bout of middle-aged sex, followed by Sam's breakfast specialty: scrambled eggs and toast. It was the only thing he could make, but it was something, and Sarah never discouraged him.

Except this Saturday. This Saturday she was as disgruntled with scrambled eggs as she was with middle-aged Saturday-morning sex. It might have had something to do with the fact that another Saturday tradition was suddenly lacking: no granddaughters coming over in the afternoon to bake cookies.

"It wouldn't hurt you to learn how to make coffee cake," she grumped to Sam. "Or pancakes. Pancakes are easy."

He frowned. "Eggs are good for you. They stick with you all day."

"They especially stick to your arteries," Sarah informed him without so much as a smile. She watched as he randomly shoved the plates into the dishwasher. Without rinsing them, even though she'd told him a million times over the last thirty-five years that, no matter what the manufacturer told you, you really had to rinse the dishes first or the food would bake on. They'd married young. He should have been trainable, for crying out loud.

She got up from the washed-oak kitchen table, scowling, and trudged to the dishwasher. "Here. If you're not going to do it right I may as well load the dishes." Maybe some good, old-fashioned guilt would motivate him to respect the Sarah Goodwin Dish Loading Method.

She supposed she could just load the dishes and shut up and let it be her good deed for the day, but she'd already faked an orgasm. That should count for a whole week's worth of acts of kindness.·

Sam scowled back at her. "What is with you? I haven't seen you this grumpy since Kizzy beat you out in the Fourth of July pie-baking contest."

"I am not grumpy," she snapped, and then burst into tears. "Yes I am. I'm sorry."

Sam pulled her into a big bear hug. "I know you miss the girls, babe, but it'll be Christmas before you know it and they'll be back."

"Only for a visit." Sarah sniffled. "I'm grandchildless."

"No you're not. They're just in a different location."

"The house is so empty," she continued.

"So, let's go to the pound and get a dog," Sam suggested.

"Oh, leave it to a man who is gone half the week to suggest getting something to housebreak," Sarah said in disgust ending their embrace. "And how can you compare a dog to a grandchild?"

"They both make messes?" he guessed.

"That is not funny, and it's not funny that the girls are growing up without their nana."

"The girls have been gone a week, and you've talked to them on the phone every day."

"It's not the same as having them here." Sarah threw up her hands in frustration. "What is the point of surviving parenthood if you don't get to enjoy being a grandparent? And what's the point of having all this baking knowledge if I don't have someone to share it with?" She turned back to the sink and scowled out the kitchen window at the gray sky hanging over the lake.

"You share it with me," Sam said, hugging her from behind. "In fact, it's kind of nice to have the house all to ourselves, dontcha think? Like being newlyweds again," he added, a hand sneaking up toward her breast. "I might get to see more of my wife now that she's not always running off to babysit and bake cookies."

Sarah squirmed away. "You are not listening to a word I'm saying."

"Yeah, I am," he insisted. "But maybe we're headed into a new phase. Let's just relax and see where it leads."

She crossed her arms. "I already don't like where it's leading." She was going to be a stranger to her grandchildren at this rate.

Sam frowned. "So, go find some kid to bake with. Aren't you looking for ways to pay it forward? You shouldn't have trouble finding a kid somewhere in this town who likes oatmeal cookies," he added, pulling the half-read copy of the *Heart Lake Herald* from the kitchen table and making for the living room.

"Where are you going? What happened to doing the dishes?" she called after him.

"I'm saving you the trouble and firing myself," he called back.

"You are not funny. Not even remotely." She abandoned the dishes and left the kitchen. If he thought she was even going near a dish on her day off he was delirious.

But what was she going to do? She decided to work on her quilts. She went to her craft room and pulled out the fabric she'd bought at Emma's shop.

Fabric wasn't the only thing she'd gotten. Quilting was a hungry hobby that ate lots of money. She'd also purchased batting, a cutting mat, fabric-marking pencils, a quilting hoop, a quilting thimble, safety pins, and a rotary cutter. But it had been worth the cost. The girls would have special quilts to curl up under and remember their nana. She sighed and set to work measuring and making her squares. Emma had suggested starting with something simple, so Sarah was putting together two twin-sized quilts made with the traditional four-patch blocks. She should have them done by Christmas.

But Christmas of what year? Two hours later, she straightened up, cracking half a dozen vertebrae in the process, and looked at the pile of squares in front of her. "You're making progress," she told herself. Slow progress, but that was the way of all artistic creations. Whether they were made from flour, sugar, and eggs or out of fabric, works of art took time.

They also gave a girl an appetite. She needed fortification. She went to the kitchen in search of coffee and a cookie. She could hear the sound of hammering coming from the garage, which meant Sam was working in his shop.

She filled a mug and wandered over to the living room window. The early-morning clouds had moved on and now the sun was out and making the lake sparkle like a gigantic sapphire. When she was a child her parents had owned a cabin on the water. They sold it after the first permanent residence made its appearance, trading the place in on some property at the ocean. But Sarah always loved the lake, and when she and Sam married, they moved there. They couldn't afford to be on the water, so they wound up across from it, and because the houses on her side of the street were slightly uphill, they still got a view. The neighborhood was friendly and the street was quiet, except for the occasional noisy barbecue. And she and Sam were usually present for those, contributing to the noise, so who cared?

Today Anna Grueber was out walking her schnauzer, Otto. Across the street the Morioka boy was raking leaves. And a U-Haul moving van was pulling up in front of the corner lakefront rambler that she and Sam had considered buying. They'd been too slow, so she'd heaved a mental shrug and reminded herself that she was perfectly happy with her lovely view.

Still, she'd been curious to see who beat her to the punch. She'd heard the new people were supposed to move in after the first of November. They must have fudged the moving date a little. She craned her neck for a better look.

Another car pulled up behind the U-Haul—an old beater of some kind. American made. Sam would know the make and model in an instant. Out spilled two young men who looked to be somewhere in their thirties. Another young family. Great. But where were the women?

The U-Haul cab door opened now and out stepped a middle-aged man. He was short and square with salt-and-pepper hair and was wearing jeans and a leather bomber jacket. He walked over to one of the young men and clapped him on the back, and for a moment all three stood surveying the house. Where were the women?

The men sprang to life, opening the moving truck, letting down the hydraulic lift. She tried to get a better look at what might be inside and banged her forehead on the window. Maybe the missus was coming in another car. Maybe she'd be showing up any minute and wondering what kind of neighborhood she'd moved into.

This was a perfect opportunity to keep the small-town spirit alive. Sarah hurried to the kitchen and pulled out the recipe for her coveted huckleberry coffee cake from the old, wooden recipe box that had been her mother's. Then she got to work.

She was pouring batter into the pan when Sam ambled into the kitchen. "Looks like we've got new neighbors," he said, peering over her shoulder into the bowl.

"Did you meet them?"

He looked at her like she'd suggested something ridiculous. "No. They're trying to get moved in."

"You could go offer to help."

"Nah. Looks like they're almost done." He dipped a finger in the batter.

"I know you didn't wash your hands," she scolded.

"Germs are good for you," he retorted, and stuck his batter-dipped finger in his mouth. "When will this be done?"

"In about a half hour," she said. "But don't get excited. It's not for us."

"It figures," he said, his voice frosted with disappointment. "Let me guess. It's for the new neighbors."

"I thought it would be a nice way to welcome them to the neighborhood."

"And to get inside the house and see what's going on," Sam teased.

"Ha ha, very funny," she said, pretending to be offended. "And that's not why I'm making this."

"Right," he said with a knowing nod.

Okay, so she did want to get in and see what was going on with the new neighbors. But she also wanted to be nice. Taking a little something to new neighbors was exactly what the Have a Heart campaign was about. It was a sure way to keep that small-town friendliness.

So forty minutes later she was crossing the street, filled with friendliness. It was a perfect fall day. The air smelled like freshly washed earth . . . and coffee cake.

A delivery van from the nearest Macy's was parked at the curb now, and two men were unloading a recliner. She followed them up the walk. The front door stood open. From inside she heard the sound of male laughter. No women yet? Hmmm.

The deliverymen disappeared inside, and as she approached the front porch she heard a velvet voice that sounded like a radio DJ say, "Just put it over there. That's great."

She hesitated on the porch. Maybe this wasn't a good time.

Oh, that was silly. It was always a good time to deliver a gift. She rang the doorbell.

A moment later one of the young men was at the door. He was slim and cute, all-American fresh looking, the kind of boy a woman wanted for a son.

"Hi," said Sarah. "I'm one of your neighbors. I thought you might like something to eat."

"Hell, yeah," he said, eyeing the cake. "Hey, Dad, there's a woman here for you."

The older man came to the door. He had a smelly cigar in his mouth, and that made Sara think of George Burns. Except with his slicked-back hair and fake tan he looked more like George Hamilton.

He took a chew on his cigar and checked her out. "Well now, what have we got here? Is this something for me?"

The way he was looking at her made Sarah wonder if he was referring to her or the baked item in her hands. "Coffee cake," she said, holding it in front of her like a shield. "I figured you and your wife and family might be hungry."

His features took on an attitude of faux regret. "No wife, I'm afraid. It's just little old me."

"Oh." If she'd known that, she wouldn't have come hurrying over here with her coffee cake, looking like a fowl on the prowl. She shoved it at him. "I'm Sarah Goodwin. My *husband* and I live in the green house over there," she said, pointing.

"That green one? Nice house. I'm Leo Steele. Nice to meetcha. I'm glad I moved into a friendly neighborhood. A guy gets lonely." With that voice he should have been on the radio.

"Well, you'll love it here," said Sarah. "All the neighbors are very friendly."

"Yeah?" He smiled around the cigar, and words from an old poem suddenly popped into Sarah's mind. *"Step into my parlor," said the spider to the fly.*

This man probably had a different definition of "friendly" than she did. She took a step back, nearly falling off the porch. "Well, it was nice to meet you. If you need anything my husband will be happy to help you."

He pulled out his cigar and pointed it at her with a George Burns smirk. "Don't be a stranger. You and your husband."

"Thanks," she said for no logical reason. She turned and fled home.

Sam was getting ready to run by the station when she got back. "So, did you get the skinny?"

"He's single," she announced. That didn't quite sound right. "No wife."

"No new neighbor to gossip with," Sam teased. "Bummer."

"Yeah, bummer," she said. She'd probably better direct her random acts of kindness in a different direction.

SEVEN

$\mathcal{I}$t was six P.M. and the night was blacker than a witch's hat. Bare-branched tree skeletons clawed at the sky. Somewhere a dog howled.

Not that anyone noticed. At the annual Heart Lake Goblin Walk, even a banshee would have had a hard time making itself heard above the din of music, laughter, and childish squeals coming from the crowd prowling Lake Way and all its tributaries. Parents and grandparents escorted little princesses, superheroes, and skeletons on their hunt for treats while costumed shop owners stood outside their shops with giant bowls of candy and trinkets. Both the fire and police departments were manning booths, giving away stickers and flyers on fire safety.

"Aren't you so cute," Emma cooed over a little princess who had stopped to dip into her witch's cauldron for a packet of M&M's. "Did your mommy make your costume?" she asked, smiling at the woman holding the princess's hand. A potential fabric customer—she hoped she wasn't salivating too obviously.

"Her grandma in Oregon made it," said the woman. "I don't have time to sew," she added in a tone that implied sewing was only for people who didn't have a life.

Before Emma could think of a reply, the princess and her mother the queen vanished. They were replaced by a group of sugar-buzzed superheroes. One of them vacuumed up Emma's candy supply as though he were collecting food for his last meal. The others quickly followed suit. Neither of the two dads in charge of the group said anything. That was probably because they were too busy checking out a woman on the other side of the street in a Catwoman outfit to pay attention to what the kids were up to.

Oh, well, Emma decided. There was her good deed for the day. She wondered how Jamie was doing.

Valentine Square didn't have the mob that the shop owners one street up were facing, but they were getting a steady trickle. Just enough to make Jamie feel guilty every time she considered taking her Tootsie Rolls and packing it in.

"Are we having fun yet?" called Roxy Reynolds from her post in front of the card shop. She stood chatting with her assistant and Monique, the owner of Whisper, the lingerie shop, who was wrapped up like a mummy. Monique could barely move, but Jamie was willing to bet she was at least warm.

"Oh, yeah," Jamie called back.

"If you think this is fun, you're whacked," said Clarice, Jamie's part-time help, as she refilled the bowl. She had dyed her hair orange in honor of the holiday and was all dolled up with fake blood, her face painted corpse white. "Okay, that's the last of the candy. When it's gone, you're done. And speaking of done . . ."

"I know, I know," said Jamie. "You can take off. Have fun in Seattle."

Clarice grinned. "We will. Borg is sure to win the costume contest tonight. He's going as a chick magnet, with a big, shiny red magnet around his neck. It even glows in the dark. So do other parts of him," she added with a smirk.

"TMI," said Jamie, rolling her eyes. "Get out of here already."

Clarice skipped off like a giant kid. Come to think of it, at barely twenty, that was what she was.

Jamie couldn't help smiling. Next to Christmas, this was the best night of the year for kids, both big and little. She used to love Halloween. She still did. It was the one night of the year when the monsters were pretend.

She greeted a well-rounded woman escorting two girls and a little boy wearing a Frankenstein mask who looked more like a beach ball with legs. All three kids carried king-sized pillowcases, which they had barely filled. She guessed they'd go on to raid Heart Lake Estates after doing downtown. Jamie offered her plate of fudge to the woman and the bowl of cheap candy to the kids. The beach ball dove right into the bowl.

The girls were no fools. They snatched the fudge. "That's good," said one, and helped herself to another piece.

"Don't be a pig," scolded the woman, who also took a second helping.

Hmmm. Oink, oink. But pigs made good customers. "If you think that's good you'll have to come by sometime and try my truffles," Jamie said.

"Do you give samples?" asked Miz Piggy.

Jamie suspected this woman could easily sample her right out of business. "Sometimes," she said evasively.

"I'll have to come check them out," the woman promised, and took a third piece of fudge. "Thanks."

Maybe she should have just given the woman the whole

plate and been done with it. Oh, well. What did she expect? She was offering free chocolate. Who could resist that?

A little ghost of wind swept under her gypsy skirt, raking her legs with icy fingers and making her shiver. If she'd known she was going to be so cold she'd have bought some long underwear. Thank God this ended at seven. She and Emma had a date with a bowl of candy corn, a scary movie (or so Emma claimed), and some drink called a Vampire's Kiss that sounded like it involved enough alcohol to stock a liquor store. Maybe they should have had the alcohol before the Goblin Walk. It would have helped her stay warm. She sneaked a look at her watch. Six o'clock. An hour left to go. Ugh.

Next time she checked her watch she still had forty-five minutes left to stand out in the cold. Time wasn't exactly flying. It wasn't even marching. It was just strolling by, taunting, "Neener, neener," with each icy breeze that tickled her skin. She was so not doing this again. She didn't care if it was good for business. They didn't get as many people down here anyway.

She looked across the way. Roxy and Monique were packing it in, turning tail on the approaching stream of trick-or-treaters and ducking into their shops. Jade Forrester, who owned Jade's Jewels, hadn't even bothered to show. That left only her, and she didn't have the heart to close up. She sucked it up, pasted on a smile, and braced herself for the next wave that came at her in a wall of noise.

It was almost like some giant amoeba, she thought, just one big, noisy cloud of masks, robes, and reaching hands. The blob surrounded her. It took, squealed, and then moved off down the street, making her think of dragons parading through San Francisco's Chinatown on Chinese New Year. Somewhere toward the end of the tail, however, she distinguished a sound that wasn't happy. Crying.

She peered past a noisy clump of teenage boys trying

to hide their age and size under bedsheets to see a wilted little fairy with chestnut curls dragging a plastic pumpkin full of candy and looking like she'd witnessed the end of the world.

Jamie left her candy bowl for the boys to raid and hurried to the little girl. "Sweetie, are you lost?" Of course she was. "Where's your mommy?" Well, duh. Like the kid would know?

"I want my grandpa," the child sobbed.

Lost children weren't exactly Jamie's specialty, but she did know enough to call the cops. "Here," she said, putting a hand to the child's back and propelling her toward the store. "Let's go see if we can find him."

The little girl moved right along with her, which was good in a way, because Jamie could get her to safety and hang on to her. But this kind of cooperation made her wonder if the little girl's parents had ever warned her against talking to strangers. "What's your name, sweetie?"

"M-M-Mandy," the child sobbed. "I want my grandpa."

"I know. We're going to find him. What's your grandpa's name?"

"Grandpa."

That narrows it down. Jamie unlocked the shop and brought Mandy the fairy inside, locking the door after them so no one would think she was open for business and come in. She quickly flipped on the light as Mandy's crying had gotten louder the second they entered the dark shop. She settled the child at one of the bistro tables, saying, "Now, I'll just get my phone and then we'll call and tell the police where you are so your grandpa can find you. Okay?"

The child didn't say anything, just slumped in her seat, clutched her pumpkin full of candy and cried.

This was like getting punked by gremlins. Jamie could barely take care of herself and now she had a lost child on her hands.

It's okay, she assured herself. *You're in Heart Lake now. Call for help.* She hurried to the back room and dug her cell phone out of her purse, calling over her shoulder, "Don't worry, Mandy. It'll be okay." How long would it take for the cops to get here? What could she do in the meantime to keep Mandy the fairy from having a nervous breakdown? To keep herself from having one?

"Nine-one-one," said an operator.

"I have a child," Jamie blurted. "I mean I found a child. She's lost and her name is Mandy. We're at the Goblin Walk. Can you send someone to help?"

"Can you give me an address, ma'am?" asked the operator.

Oh, yeah, that. "I'm in Valentine Square, in Heart Lake. The Chocolate Bar. How soon can someone get here?"

"Someone will be there in just a few minutes," the operator assured her.

Just a few minutes felt like an eternity when you had a crying child on your hands. "I know," Jamie said to Mandy. "Let's have something to eat while we're waiting for your grandpa. You want to come and choose a truffle?"

The crying downgraded to small sobs. Mandy slipped from her seat and walked tentatively over to the glass case where Jamie was standing.

Jamie knelt beside her. "We have a lot to choose from. Do you like chocolate?"

Mandy nodded solemnly, looking at her with big, brown eyes.

"Caramel. Do you like caramel?"

Another nod. The sobs were dying down, thank God.

"How about a chocolate caramel then?" Jamie suggested. She slipped around back of the counter, returning with a chocolate caramel for each of them. Mandy wasn't the only one who needed chocolate. "There you go." She handed it over and the child took it and studied it. Maybe she'd been told not to take candy from strangers. Jamie took a bite of hers to prove it wasn't poisoned. "Mmm, good." Except maybe she shouldn't be giving candy to Mandy the fairy.

Before she could suggest Mandy wait until her grandpa showed up, the child popped the entire goody into her mouth. In less than a second she was drooling chocolate. But she also wasn't crying.

Jamie felt pleased with herself. "Good stuff, huh?"

Mandy nodded and looked at her with a "what's next" expression.

Now what? "Are you thirsty? Would you like a drink of water?"

Mandy nodded.

So they had a drink of water. Now what? Where the hell were the cops?

"I'm a fairy," Mandy announced.

Okay, she was feeling better. "You're a very pretty fairy," said Jamie. *Why on earth wasn't your mom watching you?* "Do you know your address?"

"One-two-three Willow Road," said the child.

"Good for you," Jamie approved. At least they'd have some information to give the police. It would be enough to match Mandy the Fairy with her mother.

A sudden banging on the shop door made Jamie jump. The cops. Thank God.

But it wasn't cops. It was one cop. *The* cop, and he had people with him—a paunchy sixty-something man with shortly cropped gray hair and a princess a little older than the fairy, but with the same big eyes and brown curls.

As soon as Jamie opened the door, the princess pointed at Mandy and cried, "There she is!"

"Mandy. Thank God," breathed the cop. He rushed to her, arms wide open. "Come here, baby!"

"Daddy!" The child jumped into his arms and he swept her up. "I had chocolate," she told him.

"I can see that," he said, taking a wipe at her chin, which looked like she'd painted it with chocolate syrup.

The older man fell onto the nearest chair. "I think I've aged twenty years."

"You were supposed to hold Grandpa's hand," scolded the princess. "Daddy was mad."

"Not at you, baby," said the cop. He walked over to Jamie, the other child tagging along at his side. Jamie was sure the floor was shaking with every heavy footfall. She could feel her heart rate stepping up. He looked like a super-sized Superman in a police uniform. "Thanks for keeping my daughter safe. We owe you."

"For being a good citizen? No you don't."

She only came up to his shoulder. With those big hands of his he could crush her head like a walnut. He smelled like the outdoors and aftershave, but something else, too. Could you smell testosterone? *Hic.* Oh, great. Not again.

"Well, you saved the day big-time," he said.

"That's for sure," said the older man from his chair. "My God, I've never been so scared in my life. One minute I had her and the next I didn't."

"By the way, I'm Josh Armstrong," said the cop, holding out a hand.

She took it and hers was immediately swallowed. But it was a gentle swallowing, and that was a surprise. "I'm . . . I guess you know." She tried to hold in a hiccup and he tried not to smile.

"Can we go get more candy now?" asked the other child.

"No," said her father firmly. "We're done for the night and Dad's got to get back to work."

"And Grandpa's pooped," added the older man, pushing off from his chair.

"But we didn't go to the toy store," the princess protested, her voice full of disappointment.

"We're done," said her father. "Anyway, it's after seven. The Goblin Walk is over."

After seven already? Wow. Time flew when you were . . . stressed.

"Your poor old gramps can't take any more adventure tonight, Lissa girl," said the older man.

"Would you like to take a truffle with you?" Jamie offered.

That pulled the princess immediately out of her pout. "Okay."

"Come on over and look and see what you'd like," Jamie said, and stepped behind the counter.

Lissa the princess stood in front of the case, studying everything.

"Do you like coconut?" asked Jamie.

Lissa nodded, her eyes sparkling. "I love coconut."

"And white chocolate?"

Lissa's brows furrowed as she thought about it. "I don't know. But it sounds good," she added.

"Well," Jamie said, cutting off a piece of white chocolate coconut fudge laced with lemon. "Let's see if it's as good as it sounds." She handed it over to Lissa, who took a delicate bite. She smiled and nodded enthusiastically. "It's good."

Jamie smiled back. "I'm glad."

"What's your name?" asked Lissa.

"Jamie."

"I'm Lissa. I'm nine. My sister's only six. She's a baby."

"Am not," shot Mandy from her father's arms.

"Are, too," said Lissa. "You got lost."

That started Mandy crying again. "I think we'd better go," said Josh. "Thanks again for finding my daughter."

"No problem," said Jamie.

They filed out the door just as Emma arrived. Jamie saw the undisguised lust in her friend's eyes as she and Josh exchanged polite hellos. There had been no mention of a mommy. Josh the cop was single. Talk about perfect for Emma.

A moment later Emma was shutting the shop door behind her. "Who was that? He's gorgeous."

"Josh Armstrong. His kid was lost."

"And you found her?" Emma was lighting up like a theater marquee. "Oh, my gosh, that's such a movie moment."

Jamie made a face. "How did I know you'd say that?"

"And talk about a good deed. Wow! Is he single?"

"I'm not sure, but I think so. I'll introduce you to him."

"Like I could compete with you and all that gorgeous blondness," Emma said. "Anyway, you saw him first."

"That doesn't mean I want him," said Jamie, going to fetch her purse.

"You'd be crazy not to."

"Well, then, call me crazy. I don't need another cop in my life. Been there, done that, bought the T-shirt. Took it back."

Emma shook her head as she followed Jamie out of the Chocolate Bar. She couldn't blame Jamie for being scarred for life. Married to any man who smacked her around would be enough to scar any woman. At least Jamie had had the sense to get out quickly. This policeman sure didn't seem like the smacking type, not from the way those little girls were climbing all over him. He looked like the catch of the day. He also looked like the kind of man who went for women like Jamie. And Tess L'amour.

Emma sighed inwardly. Oh, well. She had Jimmy Stewart waiting at home. *Rear Window,* candy corn, and a Vampire's Kiss—now, that was living.

But back at Emma's place Jamie didn't seem to think so. She only drank half of her Vampire's Kiss, even though she was sleeping in the guest room. (Also the office and fabric room, but Emma had managed to uncover the day bed.) And she thought *Rear Window* was boring.

"How can you say that?" Emma protested. "That movie is a classic."

Jamie pulled a DVD out of her purse. "Now, here's a classic. Let's watch this next."

Emma took it. "*Friday the 13th*. Oh, gross."

"We each got to pick one," Jamie reminded her.

Emma made a face. "Ick."

"My turn, my pick."

"We could make some more gift jars," Emma suggested.

"While we watch the movie," said Jamie with a wicked smile.

"You're sick," Emma muttered, but she put the movie on.

It was totally disgusting and creepy. Emma sat at the card table with her back to the TV while they did their craft projects, but just the screams were enough to make her want to run and hide under her bed. "I'll never be able to sleep tonight," she complained when it was done.

"Good thing it's Saturday. The shop's closed tomorrow and you can sleep in," Jamie said heartlessly.

"You have rotten taste."

"Thank you." Jamie dumped the last of her Vampire's Kiss in the kitchen sink, then started down the hall to the guest room, calling over her shoulder, "Pleasant dreams."

"Oh, fine. Scare the liver out of me and then leave me to turn off the lights by myself."

Emma had lived on her own ever since she graduated from college, and being alone never bothered her. It certainly didn't now, she told herself, especially when she had another person in the house with her. Like Jamie would be any help against a crazed killer. Or Mrs. Nitz, who lived on the other side of the duplex and was eighty and deaf as a stone. Emma thought of that big, gorgeous policeman. Was he still on duty?

The wind had picked up outside. She could hear her wind chime tinkling like crazy. It was a dark and stormy night, just the kind of night that movie murderers picked to wreak mayhem.

Oh, stop.

The sound of a familiar pitiful yowl drifted in from outside: the scared kitty from the other night. She'd once heard black cats were an endangered species on Halloween, that devil worshippers kidnapped them and cut them up. It probably wasn't true, but she hated to take a risk on that poor lost cat. Who knew which of its nine lives it was on?

She went to the door, opened it a crack, and peered into the darkness. She could see shadows of trees swaying in the breeze like giant monsters. "Kitty?"

A forlorn meow answered her.

She turned on the porch light and stepped onto the porch. "Are you there?"

A head peeped out.

"Oh, you poor thing."

The cat took a tentative step out into the open. And then another, sizing her up. Maybe wondering where the tuna was.

"Come here, kitty," she cooed, leaning over.

It took one more step, a poor little animal craving affection, a good deed in need of doing.

She reached out a hand to pet it. And got a nasty Halloween present.

EIGHT

*Y*ow!" Emma howled, grabbing her hand.

The black cat dove back into the bushes, and Emma went inside and slammed her door. "Fine. No tuna fish for you."

"Who are you yelling at?" Jamie was coming down the hallway in an Old Navy black ribbed top and plaid jammie bottoms, her slender feet stuffed into fuzzy pink slippers. She looked like Cameron Diaz. Only better.

If Emma stopped eating things like candy corn and went to the gym three times a week, she, too, would look like . . . Wait a minute. Who was she kidding? No she wouldn't. "Do you ever look bad?" she said in disgust.

Jamie rolled her eyes. "Never. You're bleeding." She pointed to Emma's hand. "Very Halloween of you."

"My good deed scratched me," Emma said, and moved to the kitchen. "I think I've got a homeless cat camping in my flower bed."

"You've got a pissy cat camping in your flower bed," Jamie corrected.

"You'd be pissy, too, if you were scared and cold," Emma said, already forgiving the cat for its bad manners. She turned on the faucet and ran her bleeding hand under the water. "It's hungry. I gave it a can of tuna last night. Maybe that was its last meal. I know I get grumpy when I don't eat."

Jamie walked over and inspected the long scratch. "Grumpy is one thing. That animal needs to be in a horror movie."

"It just needs more food." Emma blotted her hand dry with a paper towel and went to forage in the cupboard where she kept her canned goods. The cat was in luck. She had one can of tuna left. "Well, there goes the tuna casserole I was going to make for dinner tomorrow, but what the heck. It will be my good deed for the day, although feeding a cat's not exactly up there with rescuing a lost child."

"Saving an animal from starvation hits my top ten," said Jamie.

And so another can of tuna fish went out on the porch. And come morning it was empty and there was no sign of the cat.

"It'll be back," Jamie predicted. "It's found a sucker."

"I think I'd better buy some cat food," Emma decided.

"I think you'd better wear work gloves next time you feed the thing," said Jamie. "Scratches won't exactly make a shining testimonial when we're launching our good deed campaign."

"I'll be fine by then," said Emma. "Gosh, I hope we get a good turnout."

The ghost of her last failed event rose from where she'd buried it at the back of her mind and whispered, *Failure.*

What a terrible thought.

Jamie shrugged. "If not, we can at least say we tried."

Obviously, Jamie wasn't holding out much hope for the success of this campaign.

Maybe it had been a stupid idea, like so many of Emma's ideas. Things always played out in her head like a happy ending on the big screen. It was so frustrating that in real life those great endings tended to fizzle.

But not this time, Emma told herself firmly as she began the countdown to the big meeting. They were getting free publicity, thanks to the *Heart Lake Herald,* and she had other people on board, people like Sarah who was a pillar of the community. This was a great idea. Others would catch the vision.

She tried to talk up the meeting to her customers when they came in.

"I'll be with you in spirit," her friend Kerrie promised. "But the in-laws are coming to town and we'll be in Seattle that night. We've got reservations at the Space Needle. Do you know how long it's been since I've been to the city, not to mention a nice restaurant? And I've actually never eaten at the Space Needle."

"Say no more," said Emma.

It seemed everyone had an excuse. Shirley Schultz thought she was coming down with something. Ruth Weisman had her book club meeting at her house that night. The teller at the bank had to take her beagle to dog obedience classes.

No one was coming.

"Well, I am," her mother had promised when they talked on the phone. "And I'll bring Grandma."

At least there'd be three of them. No, five. Sarah and Jamie would be present, too. Five people was better than no people, she told herself. But hardly.

"Don't worry," Sarah said when Emma called her. "We'll have some bodies. Sam's coming, so the fire department will be represented, and I think Pastor Ed will be there. Everyone likes Pastor Ed, so if he gets on board this thing will really get off the ground."

"That would be awesome," said Emma. A vision of the Grange Hall packed with people sprouted in her mind. "If you build it, they will come," she murmured. It would be her new mantra.

"Something like that," said Sarah. "But if you're worried we can always make some flyers and pass them around."

"Oh, great idea," said Emma. Mantras were good. Flyers were better. "I'll print some out when I get home tonight."

She did. With her pretty, red script and the red heart in the corner, the flyers looked like a graphic artist had designed them. "You've got the eye," she told herself with a smile. She'd drop some off to Sarah and Jamie, and the day before the meeting she'd close the shop early and walk around the neighborhood and pass some out.

"These are great," said Jamie. "I'll give out one with every purchase."

"With all the customers you get, that should take care of your pile," Emma said. "Me, I'm going to walk the streets."

"Business is that bad?" Jamie teased.

Actually, it was. "Maybe someone will get inspired and decide to make me their good deed and come in and buy a truckload of fabric."

"Or you could put an ad up on Craigslist: 'Sugar daddy wanted. Must love quilts.' "

"Good idea. I'll post your picture," Emma retorted as she sailed out the door.

Sarah was equally impressed by the flyers and promised to distribute a bunch to her neighbors and put some out on the counter at the bakery. "There's nothing like

a personal invitation for getting people to attend something they'd otherwise be too lazy to come to," she said.

Although the last thing Sarah wanted to do after being on
her feet all day was to wander around her neighborhood
passing out flyers. But she'd promised Emma. It won't take
that long, she told herself.

Of course, she'd forgotten about Betty Bateman. "Oh,
Sarah, I haven't seen you in ages. How have you been?"
Betty was a vision in faded green sweats and pink bedroom
slippers. She put a hand to her rumpled red hair in an un-
conscious attempt to comb it.

Sarah barely had time to answer before Betty started
talking. "What is this, a meeting at the Grange? Oh, good
deeds! I love the idea. But wouldn't you know, I have to
babysit for the kids that night. Oh, speaking of, you've got
to come in and see the latest pictures of the grandchildren."
She threw her front door open wide, urging Sarah into her
overstuffed living room. "We just went to Ocean Shores
last weekend with them. Little Beanie is nine now. Can you
believe that? And such a cutie. Now, what did I do with
those pictures?" She scuffed over to a TV table set up in
front of an easy chair, which was overflowing with enve-
lopes and bills.

It could take Betty hours to search, not only the TV tray
but the various piles of papers and magazines stacked on
the coffee table, end tables, and kitchen counter. And if
she ever found the pictures, it would take her hours to
tell Sarah about each one. "Gosh, Betty, you know I'd
love to see them," Sarah lied, "but I've got a lot of houses
to hit today. How about a rain check?"

Betty frowned. "Of course. I understand."

And she did, which made Sarah feel guilty. "Bring
some in to the bakery. We'll take a coffee break and the

coffee will be on me." And that would be her good deed for the day.

Betty smiled like they were now best friends. "Great idea. I'm sure I'll find them right after you leave."

"Isn't that how it always goes?" Sarah said, edging toward the door.

"I just had them." Betty was scrabbling through another pile of papers now.

"I'm sure you'll find them. See you soon." Sarah opened the door and fled.

The rest of the neighbors didn't take long since most of them weren't home from work yet. (So much for the personal invitation.) Only a couple of houses left. And one of them belonged to their new neighbor, Leo Steele. Maybe she could just overlook him. Or not ring the doorbell and leave a flyer on his front porch. Good idea. That was what she'd do.

But when she got to the porch, the front door opened and there he stood, chewing on his cigar and smiling at her. "I saw you coming."

"Oh. Well."

"You giving away coupons for free coffee cake? If you are, I'll take a handful. That was the best thing I've had in a long time."

If that was a hint for more coffee cake, she wasn't taking it. "Just an announcement for a little movement we're starting to make Heart Lake friendlier."

"It already seems pretty friendly to me," he said. His grin made Sarah think of lounge lizards. He took the flyer and perused it. "I might just have to check it out. Will you be there?"

"I'm one of the organizers."

"Well, then, I'll come. Thanks for thinking of me, Sarah."

"You and the whole block," she said, keeping her voice

light. She motioned to the empty street as if someone were waiting for her. "I'd better be going."

He gave her a friendly salute. "See you at the meeting."

She hoped not. Maybe he'd forget.

Emma closed up shop at four on Tuesday so she could get home before dark to invite her neighbors to the big meeting the next night, but other than Mrs. Nitz, who couldn't hear the doorbell over her blaring TV, no one appeared to be home.

Don't give up, she told herself, and marched up to a two-story yellow Victorian.

There she actually found someone—a woman about her age with a three-year-old girl peeking behind her.

"That sounds great," said the woman, taking the flyer. "My husband works nights, so I don't have anyone to watch our daughter."

"Bring her," Emma urged. "We'll have cookies." She'd pick some up at Safeway tomorrow.

The woman smiled. "Thanks."

Emma smiled, too. Passing out flyers had been a good idea.

She was starting back down the front walk, still saying good-bye, when a German shepherd came trotting toward her. The greeting committee. Where had he come from? Emma was about to bend over to offer her hand to smell when the animal lunged at her with a growl and chomped down on her calf. Hard. "Yow!" And just to make sure she got the message Doggie Dearest took a swipe at her hand, too. *Oh, pain. Oh, not fun.*

"Willie!" cried the woman. The dog lowered its ears and tail and slinked to her. "Bad dog! Get inside." She hurried to where Emma was trying to examine her leg. "I'm so sorry. He's never bitten anyone."

"I guess there's a first time for everything," said Emma.

Was she going to get rabies? What was it with her and animals these days?

"Are you all right?"

The woman looked so upset, Emma couldn't bring herself to admit that her leg was on fire. Her jeans were toast. "I'll be fine," she assured both the woman and herself.

"Are you sure? He's never done that before, really. He's had his rabies shot. God, I feel awful."

Not half as awful as Emma felt. "Don't worry. It's no big deal," she said, and started limping off. "Nice meeting you."

The woman didn't say anything. She was already retreating behind her front door.

Okay, that was enough of passing out flyers. They had the newspaper article coming out tonight. It would have to do.

She got home just in time to catch a phone call from her mother. "I stopped by the shop. You were closed," said Mom.

"I closed early to go invite my neighbors to the meeting tomorrow night."

"Now that was a good idea," Mom said approvingly.

"Not really. I got bit by a dog."

"Oh, no. Is it bad?"

Emma pulled off her jeans and examined the wound. There was a big, long scratch and another, smaller one above it. Bite marks. And lots of blood. She fell onto a kitchen chair, suddenly light-headed. "I'm bleeding."

"I'll be right over," said her mother. "We should take you to the clinic and get it looked at."

There was nothing good about going to the doctor. You were always getting probed at one end or the other. "I'm sure it'll be fine," said Emma. But she was bleeding and she hurt. She laid her head on the kitchen table.

"You should get a tetanus shot. It's been over ten years since you had one."

How did moms keep track of all that stuff, anyway? "I don't want a shot." Shots were the worst things in the whole wide world.

"You don't want tetanus, either," said her mother firmly. "It's a terrible way to die."

Die? "Okay, let's go to the clinic," Emma decided.

"Meanwhile, clean the bite with hydrogen peroxide," Mom commanded. "It's the best thing in the world for infection."

"Good idea." Emma hurried to the bathroom, hoping that as she walked she wasn't pumping germy tetanus bugs all through her bloodstream. Tetanus shots were supposed to really hurt. Shots, infection—boy, did no good deed go unpunished. Still, if people came out for the meeting it would all be worth it.

How quickly did tetanus germs spread? Hopefully, she'd be alive for the meeting.

Emma lived, and on November fourth, she drove to the Heart Lake Grange Hall, hoping against hope that she'd see a parking lot full of cars. Or even half full. Okay, a third. She'd settle for that.

The trees parted to reveal the old log building that had been Heart Lake's Grange Hall since the thirties, when much of the land had been taken up by strawberry and blueberry farms. Exactly two cars sat in its potholed parking lot. One she recognized as her mom's. The other was Sarah's. Where was everyone else? Where was the woman with the leg-eating dog? She should have at least come out of guilt.

Emma parked her car and checked her watch. Six fifty-five and the meeting was supposed to start at seven. She suddenly felt like she had a stone inside her, sinking fast from her heart to her stomach. They had failed.

The crunch of tires on gravel made her turn. Yay, another body. People would show. They were just running late. Jamie pulled up next to her. She sighed. Well, the organizers were here. And their mothers. She grabbed her platter of cookies from the front seat and got out.

"Big turnout," Jamie said in disgust as she got out of her car.

"We still have five minutes," Emma reminded her.

"Let's hope that everyone in Heart Lake is running late," said Jamie. She shook her head. "And after that great article in the paper—if this is all the turnout we get I'm going to be majorly pissed."

You and me both, thought Emma. Except Emma wasn't going to admit it.

They went inside to find Sarah had already decorated, hanging purple, pink, and red foiled hearts all over the walls. Emma's mother hurried over to greet her daughter, trailed by Grandma Nordby. It wasn't hard to tell the two women were related. Each one of them looked like Russian nesting dolls—with the same round face and body Emma had inherited. Mom's strawberry-blond hair was now shot with gray, well on its way to Grandma Nordby's solid white. Emma didn't need a magic mirror to see her future. All she had to do was look at her grandma and mom.

"We're so proud of you, dear," said Grandma.

Emma frowned. "It's not much of a turnout."

Her mother looked at her watch. "It's not seven yet. You still have four minutes."

Four minutes. Anything could happen in four minutes. Emma set the platter of cookies she'd bought on the little table Sarah had covered with a tablecloth. It already held a flower arrangement courtesy of Hope Wells the florist and a plate of ginger cookies. Next to Sarah's famous ginger cookies, Emma's grocery-store offering didn't look like much.

Sarah emerged from the kitchen, carrying two coffee carafes. "Are we all ready?" she greeted them.

Emma nodded. "I just hope more people come."

Car tires crunched on the gravel. "They'll be here," Sarah assured her. "Sure you don't want to do the talking? This was your idea."

Talk in front of people? No, thanks. "You go ahead."

At that moment Sarah's husband, Sam, joined them. He was a big man, still buff and good-looking in spite of the growing bald spot on the top of his head. "Don't forget to put this out," he said, and laid the newspaper article on the table next to their cookies. "Pretty good publicity."

It was. The headline read, *Heart Lake Angels Work to Put Heart in Heart Lake*, and in addition to the article, they'd gotten their pictures in the paper. It was the first time Emma had ever had her picture in the paper. She was going to frame it.

So, with all that great publicity, where was everyone?

The door opened and in walked Sarah's friend Kizzy Maxwell with her husband, Lionel. She saw Sarah and Emma, waved at them and started their way, her husband in tow. "This is a great idea," she said, giving Sarah a hug. "Was it yours?"

Jamie had joined them now. She pointed to Emma. "Hers."

"Oprah would be proud," said Kizzy. Her husband grabbed a cookie from the platter and she cocked an eyebrow at him. "Lionel Jefferson Maxwell."

He frowned and said, "I'm just having one."

"They're free," said Sam, digging in, "have two."

"Good idea," said Emma, and took two ginger cookies as consolation for their poor turnout.

As the minute hand inched toward seven, more people trickled in. There was Hope, and behind her Emma recognized Pastor Ed the gentle giant who gave pastors a good name; Kevin Dwyer, who ran the chamber of commerce; and Lezlie Hurst, the reporter from the *Heart Lake Herald,* who had done their story. Yay! Movers and shakers. And now here came . . .

"Oh, lucky us," said Sarah next to her. "It's the mighty Quinn. She looks happy."

Mayor Melanie Quinn was dressed to the nines as always in a gray suit accessorized with a string of pink pearls. Her highlighted blond hair was freshly styled and her face was perfectly made-up. And her smile was totally phony. Her eyes looked like blue ice as she walked toward them.

"What's she pissed about?" Jamie wondered.

"You can't guess?" Sarah said in an undertone voice. "This wasn't her idea. She can't take credit for it. Melanie," she greeted the mayor. "This is an honor."

Melanie Quinn was a good enough politician to ignore Sarah's sarcastic tone. "I'm glad to be here. Anything that involves Heart Lake involves me," she added sweetly.

"How lucky for us."

Sarah and the mayor had known each other for thirty years, but this was no time for old rivalries. "It's great to have your blessing," Emma gushed, trying to make up for Sarah's unusual lack of manners.

"I just wish someone would have come to me with this idea," said Mayor Quinn, still smiling. Her eyes narrowed. "Maybe I could have helped ensure a bigger turnout."

"Heaven knows you're good at manipulating numbers," said Sarah. "How many recounts did we have to have last election?"

"Um, how about a cookie," said Emma, grabbing the platter. "Fresh from the bakery."

The mayor came as close to sneering as a public official who sensed the approach of the media could possibly come. "I'll pass. After a certain age most of us have to watch our waistline."

Now Sarah's eyes narrowed.

"Mayor Quinn," said Lezlie the reporter, pulling out her trusty camera. "How about a picture for the paper?"

"Of course," said the mayor, slipping an arm around Sarah and Emma, and pulling Jamie in, too. "Sarah, you just get curvier all the time."

"Still jealous?" Sarah shot back.

Mayor Quinn unhooked herself from them the moment the picture was snapped, saying, "If you ladies will excuse me, I need to speak with Kevin."

"That woman," Sarah growled as the mayor hurried across the room to network.

"Nice shindig," said a voice at her elbow.

Emma took in the short man wearing black slacks and a shirt that looked like a leftover from one of the *Pirates of the Caribbean* movies. The shirt was open to show off a chest bristling with gray hairs. To top off the ensemble, he had a gold chain dangling around his neck.

He was checking out Sarah the way Kizzy's husband had looked at the ginger cookies. She did look cute in her jeans and V-necked black sweater. The V-neck stuff had become standard since Sarah heard the lines were better for middle-aged women, although Emma suspected the newcomer wasn't so much admiring the flattering neckline on her sweater as he was the highlighted cleavage.

Sarah took the plate of cookies from Emma. "Cookie, Leo?"

"I love sweet things," he said with a smile that made Emma think of the big, bad wolf.

"We should start," said Sarah briskly. "Excuse me." She moved up to the podium on the little stage. "If we could get you all to sit down," she called, "we'll begin our meeting."

Everyone obediently found a seat among the folding chairs Sam had set up—a few bodies adrift in a sea of chairs. It was a pretty unimpressive beginning, to say the least.

"Thanks for coming," Sarah said once everyone was settled. "We know you're all busy and we really appreciate you taking time to come out for this meeting tonight. I promise we'll make it brief."

"Don't hurry on our account," cracked her admirer. "We're here as long as the cookies hold out."

Sarah managed a polite smile. "I'm sure you all read the article in the paper," she went on, "so you know how this idea started. We're here because we love Heart Lake, and we want to keep it the great, friendly place it's always been. That can be hard with so many new people moving in. You lose your sense of connection. Those of you who are here are the heartbeat of this town. And you care. We might start small, but we can make a big difference. We can keep the heart in Heart Lake."

"Amen to that!" Pastor Ed called, and started clapping.

The other attendees joined suit, and suddenly Emma didn't see a small turnout for a big job. She saw a real movie moment. She smiled and wiped tears from the corners of her eyes.

"So how does this work exactly?" asked Hope after the applause died down.

"As simply as possible," replied Sarah. "Like Oprah's Angel Network, only without Oprah," she added with a smile.

She brought Jamie up to share how she and Emma had created their goody jars. "You don't even have to do that," Jamie concluded. 'You could let someone go in front of you in line at Safeway or at the four-way stop."

"We don't want to make this complicated," Sarah said as Jamie sat down. "Just do a good deed and tell the person you helped to pass it on. It won't work unless we talk it up. And, speaking of talking it up, we thought it would be good to get T-shirts made. If you're all willing to buy one and wear it that will help build interest. And we can donate the proceeds to the food bank."

"Great idea," approved Pastor Ed.

"We could sell them at the chamber," offered Kevin.

"I can sell them at Changing Seasons, too," Hope said.

"Heck, let's all sell them," said Emma. This could catch on. It really could.

Sarah nodded. "Good idea."

"You need a headquarters," said Madam Mayor, "someplace central to coordinate this."

Not hard to tell whom the good mayor envisioned at the center of the project.

"I'm not sure we need a central office for good deeds," said Sarah.

"Well, if you do, we'll give you a corner of our office," Kevin offered.

"Great," said Sarah in a voice that settled it.

The mayor pressed her lips firmly together and crossed her arms.

"I think that basically covers it," said Sarah.

"Do we want to meet again?" suggested Pastor Ed. "Share some of our experiences?"

"Oh, good idea," seconded Emma. "Let's meet next month."

"How about January?" Sarah countered. "People get pretty busy during the holidays."

"We'll all be busy being angels," said Emma, beaming.

"Speak for yourself," cracked Sarah's admirer.

"January sounds good," said Kevin.

"All in favor?" asked Sarah, and everyone said, "Aye."

"The ayes have it. Thanks for coming, everyone. Now, let's go start putting the heart back in Heart Lake."

"And if something extraordinary or heartwarming happens, call me," added Lezlie. "We'll put it in the paper."

After a word with Lezlie, the mayor exited. Emma barely had time to thank Hope for the flower arrangement before she followed suit, probably anxious to get home to her new husband. The others stayed and chatted for a while. Good energy, thought Emma, watching them.

Leo Steele was the last to leave, only taking the hint when Sam said, "Okay, ladies, time to lock up."

"I wish more people had come," said Jamie as Sam turned out the lights. "We only had thirteen here."

"That's my lucky number," Emma said, determined to stay positive. "Anyway, look what Jesus did with just twelve disciples. And we have thirteen, a baker's dozen."

"I didn't see Jesus here tonight," Jamie said grumpily.

"I did," said Sarah. "And I think He's pretty happy about this." She gave Emma a hug. "It was an inspired idea. Good things are going to come of this. You wait and see."

"Yeah, for everybody but your poor, ignored husband," cracked Sam, coming up behind her.

Sarah ignored him. "If nothing else, we'll all be better people," she told Emma. "And that's worth something."

Of course, she was right, but Emma wanted more than that. She wanted everyone in Heart Lake to become better people, not just them. This had to work. They'd make it work.

Hopefully.

"All right," Sarah said as she and Sam drove out of the Grange Hall parking lot, "what did you mean by that remark?"

"What remark?"

"You know, the one about the poor ignored husband."

"Oh, that. I was just being a smart-ass."

Okay, good.

"But you do have this way of getting involved with projects," he added.

She frowned. "The kids are grown. What am I supposed to do when you're off at the station for days at a time, sit on my hands? I have to do something."

"I know."

And she knew that tone of voice. "But what?" She could already predict what was coming.

"It's just that I have a feeling I'm going to drop to the bottom of the priority list. Again."

"Sam Goodwin, for such a generous man you sure have a big selfish streak."

"Only where you're concerned." He shrugged, keeping his eyes on the road. "Sometimes I just think I come in last, that's all."

"Well, you don't," she assured him, and laid a hand on his thigh.

He let the subject drop, but she kept stewing over it the rest of the night. Okay, sometimes she was either too busy or too tired or too . . . not interested when he wanted to do something, especially when he wanted to do something naked. What did he expect? She hardly had a hormone left in her body, and, anyway, their sex life had become as routine as the rest of their life. And she had a business to run. And they had children, and responsibilities. You couldn't stay newlyweds forever. Anyway, Sam should have been happy that she was finding a way to salve her hurting grandmother's heart. She'd tell him that, first thing in the morning.

Except first thing in the morning she had to get to the bakery, and he was busy at the station. Well, she'd tell him . . . when she got time.

NINE

Selena Morrison, one of Emma's favorite customers, came into the shop on Thursday, bearing a small gift bag and wearing a large gauze bandage on her index finger. She held it up. "You should have warned me that quilting could be hazardous to my health."

"What happened?"

"I was cutting along the edge of my ruler and the blade slipped and went over my finger." Selena shook her head. "I should have been paying closer attention to what I was doing. But that's not why I'm here." She nudged the little gift bag across the counter. "You're my good deed for today."

Someone was already doing good deeds, and for her? "Really?"

"Absolutely. You go above and beyond for your customers, and I wanted you to know how much I appreciate it."

Emma reached inside the bag and pulled out a gift certificate for Eagle Harbor Books. "Aw, Selena. That's really sweet."

"You deserve it. By the way, the quilt you donated for

the fund-raiser for the new church kitchen went for two hundred dollars. You really are an angel. Keep up the good work. I love this idea and I hope it catches on big-time."

"Me, too," said Emma.

Wow. A gift. Out of nowhere. It was such a movie moment that even though nobody else came into the shop, Emma felt good all the rest of the day. Still infused with good vibrations, she stopped by the Safeway on the way home and stocked up on canned cat food. By the time she pulled up in front of her little duplex, it was raining cats and dogs. Had the storm deposited a certain cat by her doorstep?

Yes, there it was. Its pitiful yowl greeted her as she hurried up the walk. "Hang in there," she told it as she fumbled for her keys. "I've got something for you."

It poked its black head out from under the juniper bush and gave her an angry meow that probably translated into, *Hurry up, will ya?*

She had barely opened the door when a four-legged, wet black body raced in past her. "Well, come on in. Make yourself at home," she called after the animal as it darted down the hall to the living room.

She caught a glimpse of a wet cat bottom disappearing under the crazy quilt she had draped over the couch. The poor thing was probably freezing.

"I'll turn up the heat," she offered. She cranked up the thermostat, then went to the kitchen and pulled one of the cans of cat food from her grocery bag. "Since you're now officially a guest I guess we'd better put this in a bowl," she said, taking a dessert bowl from her cupboard. The sound of the lid popping open brought her visitor back, and it wound around her legs in anticipation. That was when she noticed the flea collar. No regular collar, though. No tag of any sort to tell her anything about the cat. "Did someone dump you?" she asked it.

The cat rubbed against her calf.

"Maybe you're lost."

The cat meowed.

"You poor thing," she cooed. "You're not a bad kitty, are you? You're just alone in the world and scared."

She set the little bowl on the floor and the cat hunkered down in front of it and began to eat like Emma's offering was its last meal.

"I know how you feel," she said, watching it. "Not that I'm really alone. I've got my parents and my grandma. But sometimes . . . well, never mind about that. And I do feel scared a little. About the shop. I'm not exactly making money hand over fist. If this shop tanks . . ." She sat back on her heels, suddenly disgusted with herself. "I'm telling my life story to a cat." Next she'd be talking to her plants. She had to get a grip.

She changed into her sweats, pulled some leftover salad out of the fridge, and went to check in on Tess. "No land auctions," she vowed as she logged on. "We're on a budget and it looks like we've got another mouth to feed."

Wait a minute. This little guy was going to need more than food. He needed a litter box, and probably a new flea collar. The flea collar she might have been able to wait on, but not the litter box. "Sorry, Tess," she said, putting her computer to sleep. "You're on your own tonight. I've got to run to the store." Thank God for credit cards.

Friday was soppy and cold—not pleasant weather for shopping, thought Jamie. Not good weather for coming in to work, either, obviously, since Clarice decided to call in sick.

"That is the phoniest cough I ever heard," Jamie informed her.

"No, I'm really sick," Clarice croaked.

Jamie heard a male voice whispering in the background. "Is Borg home sick, too?"

"Uh. Yeah."

"Hmmm. What a coincidence. Never mind," Jamie said. "I'll let you get away with it just this once because I don't exactly think we're going to be swamped today."

She was right. Only the most determined chocoholics came into the Chocolate Bar, which gave Jamie time to work on ideas for the Web site she was building for the shop. And to clean up the kitchen area. And wipe down the counters. And . . . what next?

Her eye caught on a leftover Mason jar sitting by the counter. Maybe this would be a good time to deliver a good deed. The only way to get this movement going was to do something to inspire people. She filled the jar with truffles. Now, who to give it to? She decided the next customer who walked in would get it.

At four-thirty the lucky winner arrived. Actually, it was winners, and she immediately recognized the lost fairy and her distraught grandpa from Halloween. And there was her older sister, too. No tears today, though. The two girls came bouncing into the candy shop bringing in a gust of rain-washed air and high-pitched squeals.

"Girls, you're going to break my eardrums," the man protested. "I promised them a treat," he explained to Jamie.

"How about some white-chocolate-covered apples?" Jamie suggested.

"Fine. We'll take three," he said.

"Grandpa, there's only two of us," pointed out the oldest girl.

"Lissa, honey, counting me, there's three, and I need a treat, too." To Jamie, he added, "My wife stayed home with our kids and made it look so easy. I don't know how she did it."

Jamie picked up her jar of goodies and handed it across the counter. "Well, here's something to help you. I made this to give to the next customer who came in and you're the lucky winner."

"Yeah?" He took it, looking pleasantly surprised.

"Yeah."

"Naw. I can't take this." He set the jar on the counter and pulled his wallet from his back pocket. "I'll pay for it, though. What do I owe you?"

"Nothing. It's my good deed for the day."

"Good deed?" He snapped his fingers. "I get it. You're doing that 'put the heart in Heart Lake' thing." Then true understanding dawned. "Wait a minute. You're one of the organizers. I saw your picture in the paper."

Jamie smiled. "That's me."

"I'm hungry, Grandpa," said Mandy the Fairy, pulling on his coat sleeve.

"Let's take care of that right now," said Jamie. She got two apples from the tray behind the glass counter and handed them to the man, who, in turn, gave one to each girl.

"You girls can sit at the table there and eat them," he said, and the girls obediently plopped down at the nearest table. "I *am* going to pay for these," he said.

"That's a deal." She took his money, then gave him change and another apple.

He took a bite and smiled. "Oh, man, that's damn . . . er, darned good." She grinned, and he lowered his voice and added, "Got to watch my language now that I'm the lady of the house. I'm up here helping my son. Name's George Armstrong."

Jamie took the offered hand and shook it. "I'm Jamie Moore. How long have you been in Heart Lake?"

"Just a few months. My son Josh got a job here, but they put him on swing shift and he needed help. He's a single dad, trying to raise these girls on his own." George's expression turned just the slightest bit sneaky. "So, you run this place with your husband?"

"No. All on my own. I mean I run it all on my own." She caught him checking out her left hand and whipped it behind her back.

He nodded and took a thoughtful bite of his apple.

"So, where is your wife?" Jamie asked, giving him a taste of his own nosy medicine.

His smile went taut and the laugh lines around his eyes flatlined. "Lost her six years ago."

Jamie immediately regretted her question. "I'm so sorry. But you've come to the right place to start over. This really is a great town."

He nodded. "I can see that. Lots of friendly people; just what I need. Just what my son needs."

The shop door opened and in blew Emma and Sarah, ready to make up for their missed Wednesday chocolate binge and debrief on the big kickoff meeting. George looked at them speculatively. Then he smiled and nodded, saying a polite hello.

Jamie made the introductions and it didn't take long for George to let it be known he was in the market for a wife. For his son, he added, after seeing the wedding ring on Sarah's hand.

"If your son is as nice as you I'm sure you'll have no problem," said Sarah. "We've got some great single women here in Heart Lake," she added, her gaze drifting back and forth from Jamie to Emma.

Emma's cheeks got pink, and she turned suddenly tongue-tied.

Next thing they knew Sarah would be running a dating service right here in the Chocolate Bar. "Yeah," Jamie added, "that's what Ginger says."

Sarah glared at her.

"Ginger?" George was looking hopeful.

"Not your son's type," said Sarah quickly.

"Would you mind flipping the sign?" Jamie asked her sweetly.

Sarah turned the sign on the door to CLOSED and George got the message. "Well, you ladies have a good afternoon. Come on, kids. We'd better shove off. Time to go home and make dinner."

"I don't want chicken nuggets again," Mandy whined.

"Okay. We'll stop at the store and get hot dogs," he said, ushering them out. "Nice to meet you."

"I swear," Sarah said after the door shut, "if you haul out your imaginary girlfriend one more time any man shows an interest . . ."

"He's too old for me," Jamie said.

"His son's not."

"I'm not in the market. That leaves you," Jamie said to Emma.

"Well, Emma didn't even have a chance to put her best foot forward with your subtle 'put the CLOSED sign up' comment," Sarah said in disgust.

"If I hadn't he'd have stayed here all night. And fed the kids truffles for dinner."

That put Sarah's thoughts on a new track. "I never thought I'd hear a child complain about having chicken nuggets for dinner." She shook her head. "Chicken nuggets and hot dogs—those poor girls. No wonder he wants to find his son a wife. They obviously need someone who can cook in that household. And how do you know you're not in the market?" she added. "You haven't even seen his son."

"Yes I have."

"Wait a minute," said Emma. "Those kids—they belong to the policeman I saw here Halloween night, don't they?" She didn't wait for Jamie to confirm it. "Oh, my gosh. He is . . ." She let out a breath and started fanning herself.

"I don't care how hot he is," Jamie said. "He could set my thong on fire and I still wouldn't be in the market."

Emma threw herself into a chair. "I'm in the market all the time. All I ever get is broccoli."

"Maybe you need to find a new market," Sarah told her.

Emma shrugged. "Oh, well. I have a new love in my life so I don't need no stinkin' policeman."

"Who?" demanded Jamie.

"Yeah," said Sarah. "Spill."

"He's black. And he has four legs."

"The cat," Jamie said in disgust, and Emma nodded.

"When did you get a cat?" asked Sarah.

"I didn't. He got me."

"I'll say," said Jamie, handing Emma her drink and sitting down at the table. "Didn't you see the scratch on her hand the other night?"

"He was just scared," Emma explained.

"Or demon-possessed," suggested Jamie.

"No, he's a good boy. He's moved in." She pulled her cheapie digital camera from her purse and brought up an image of the new baby on its screen. "Look at that. Isn't he cute?"

Jamie gawked at her. "You let that animal in your house?" They really did have to find someone for Emma. She was getting desperate.

"He let himself in. Anyway, deep down he's really a sweet little guy. I'm going to name him Pyewacket, after the kitty in *Bell, Book, and Candle*."

"Good choice, since he's probably some witch's lost familiar," Jamie scoffed. "You don't know anything about this cat. In fact, do you know for sure he's a boy?"

"Well, no," Emma admitted. "But he's so big I figured he must be a boy."

"You don't know where it came from," Jamie continued. "It could be feral."

"He had a flea collar."

"Maybe it's lost," said Sarah.

"I put a notice in the paper," Emma told her. "Hopefully, if he is lost his owner will claim him. If not, he can have a home with me."

"That way he'll always have someone to torture," Jamie teased.

Emma frowned at her. "Don't be making fun of my good deed. I want to always believe the best about people, even when they're cats."

"A good way to live," agreed Sarah.

Easy for you two, thought Jamie, you've never had your bubble burst. *Or your jaw broken*.

Emma didn't stay much longer. "I have to get home."

Jamie was tempted to tease her about running home to her new man, but judging from Emma's frost-tipped voice, she decided it would be wise to resist temptation. "I didn't mean to rain on her parade," she said to Sarah after Emma left.

"She'll get over it," said Sarah. "But let's not tease her. I know she's worried about the shop. This cat could be just what she needs to distract her."

"Mommy's home," Emma called as she came through the door. "Time for dinner. Where are you?" She threw her coat on a kitchen chair and got a can of cat food out of the cupboard. "Seafood delight, Pye. Come and get it." She popped open the lid.

A second later the new man . . . or woman . . . or it . . . in her life came trotting in. "There you are. Did you miss me? Did you use your cat box?" She set Pye's dinner down and the cat raced to the bowl and began to chow down.

"With those manners, you are definitely a boy," she decided.

She checked the bathroom where she'd set up his litter box to see if he'd been a good boy. Sure enough, he had. All right. She hung up her coat, and then made herself some pasta for dinner.

She had just started eating when Pyewacket jumped up on the kitchen table to investigate, nearly knocking over her vintage Fiesta pitcher. "You can't be up here," she told him. She reached to pick him up and remove him from the no-kitty zone, but before she could touch him he hissed at her and jumped down. "Whoa," she said. "Excuse me. Someone has some trust issues here." But they'd work through them.

Alone again, she ate her dinner and looked through her latest issue of *Quilter* magazine. By the time she'd finished, she was inspired to work on the quilt she'd promised Kerrie for the wildlife shelter. But first she needed to water her plants.

She was almost to the living room with her little ceramic watering can when she noticed the drapes. The shredded drapes.

TEN

Oh, no," wailed Emma. "What have you done?"

She went to the drapes and examined them more closely. Fringe. He had turned the drapes Mom had given her to fringe.

Pyewacket was nowhere to be seen now, probably looking for something new to wreck. She hurried to the bedroom to check on her pink sheers. Thank God he hadn't gotten to those yet. She decided that, for the time being, she'd go with a minimalist décor and use only the shade. She took the curtains down, storing them on the top shelf in her closet. The ones in her workroom came down, too.

She turned to find Pyewacket sitting on the pile of fabric on her worktable, watching her. Great. She'd taken in an animal with a fabric fetish.

"That is not a bed for you." She moved to shoo him off and he hissed again and stood his ground. Or, rather, sat it. "Okay, fine. You win for now. But if you wreck my quilt strips I'll hang you from the ceiling fan."

That scared him. He began to clean one of his front paws.

She squatted in front of where he sat enthroned on her quilt material. "Okay, what we have here is a failure to communicate. You've been in the wild for a while and it looks like you've forgotten how to be civilized. So, let me just bring you up to speed. You can't go around wrecking things. It doesn't make you a very nice houseguest."

The cat looked at her.

"Does that make sense? Am I getting through?"

He blinked once.

Blink once for yes. "So, why did you do that? Were you bored? Lonely? Did you think your claws need sharpening? Trust me. They don't."

The discussion was interrupted by a call from her mother. "How's the new baby?" she asked.

"He scratched up my drapes."

"This is not a good beginning," observed Mom.

"That's an understatement."

"You'd better run out and get him a scratching post or he'll start on the furniture next," Mom advised.

Emma looked at the vintage floral couch that had been Grandma Nordby's and felt the blood drain from her face. "I'm going out right now," she decided.

So, back out into the cold she went with her trusty charge card. She had to drive all the way to the mall where the pet superstore was to get her scratching post, but it was worth every drop of gas. She not only got a scratching post embedded with catnip that would make her new roommate very happy, she also found something to spray on furniture which would keep Pyewacket and his busy claws away. Purrfect.

Back home, she treated the couch and set out his scratching post while her new baby watched from a distance. "You'll like this," she told him. She wiggled it. "Want to come try?"

He remained where he was and blinked. *Blink once for no.*

"Okay, fine. Your loss," she told him. That scratching post was supposed to be irresistible to cats. If she had Pyewacket's willpower she'd be a size eight. She jiggled it one more time. "Just remember, this is for you. Let's try to stop scratching other things." She thought of her hand. "Especially living things."

All weekend Sarah found herself thinking of George Armstrong and his son. Two single men raising little girls. Those poor girls. She wished she'd found out where they lived so she could take them a casserole or a potpie.

They couldn't be that hard to find. How many Armstrongs were there in the Heart Lake phone book anyway? On Sunday, while Sam was busy at the fire station, she decided to look. Sure enough. There was a George Armstrong and a J. Armstrong, both with the same phone number. She picked up the phone and called.

A male voice answered, younger sounding than the man she'd met in the Chocolate Bar, and frazzled. She could hear little girls squealing in the background. "Girls, stop. I can't hear."

"Is this Josh Armstrong?" Sarah asked.

"That's me. Mandy, I said stop. Now."

"I'm sorry to get you at a crazy time," Sarah began.

"Every time is crazy," he said.

"Well, you don't know me. My name is Sarah Goodwin and I met your father the other day at the Chocolate Bar."

"Oh, you want to talk to Dad."

Sarah started to say no, but Josh was already calling, "Dad, it's for you."

A moment later George Armstrong was on the phone.

Sarah started again. "Hi. I'm Sarah Goodwin. We met the other day at the Chocolate Bar."

"I remember," he said, sounding pleased. "What can I do for you?"

"Actually, I'm calling because I'd like to do something for you. And your son," she added quickly, not wanting to pick up a second Leo Steele. "I think you boys could use a little help in the cooking department."

"Well, now, that's really nice of you," said George.

"If you like, I could swing by later with a chicken potpie."

"Chicken potpie? I haven't had that in years," he said.

Sarah could almost hear the drool in his voice. She smiled. "Well, then, give me directions to your house and I'll be happy to deliver one."

"It's a deal," said George.

"And how about some cookies?"

"We'll eat them, just to be polite," he said.

"All right," said Sarah. "I'll throw in some of my famous ginger cookies." And that would be her good deed for the day.

"You got a date?" Josh asked as his dad hung up the phone.

"Naw, she's married."

"What's a married woman doing calling you?"

"I think she's saving the girls from my cooking," Dad said, and told Josh about meeting the women in the chocolate shop.

"Well, that was nice and all," said Josh, giving his chili a stir. "But I'm home on the weekends. I can cook."

"Yeah, but you're not around on the weekdays and I can't," said Dad. "Anyway, that chili can wait till tomorrow. Even you can't make potpie."

Like they couldn't fend for themselves? Josh shook his head. "Geez, Dad, you're a mooch."

"I'm not a mooch. The woman wants to do a good deed. I'll let her."

"Just so she doesn't make a habit of it," Josh warned. "We don't need charity."

Now Dad was the one shaking his head. "There's nothing wrong with letting people help you, son."

"I know," said Josh. "But next thing you know she'll be wanting to match me up with some woman."

"Yeah? And what's wrong with that? You stopped liking women or something?"

"No. I just don't like people trying to match me up. Have you forgotten some of the women those church ladies tried to sic on me after Crystal died?"

Dad let out a bark of laughter. "You had some real winners there."

"Yeah, one with more five o'clock shadow than me, another who weighed just as much."

"I kind of liked the babe who sang opera," said Dad.

Josh frowned. "Thanks to her I've only got five wineglasses. And don't forget the green card hunter and the woman who wanted to get married and pregnant all in the next year."

"There were a couple of nice ones, too," Dad said, sobering.

"I wasn't ready," Josh said with a shrug. He still wasn't sure he was. Oh, he was ready in body. More than ready, especially when he thought of a certain pretty girl who specialized in chocolates and rescuing lost kids. But in spirit? The jury was still out on that. One thing he did know for sure, he didn't want other people running his love life for him. "Anyway, I can pick my own chick."

"Like the one who owns the chocolate shop?"

"Maybe."

"She's friends with this Sarah, you know."

"I still don't want to be matched up. I can get my own woman."

A high-pitched squeal followed by tears stopped the conversation. A moment later Lissa was in the kitchen holding half a necklace. "Mandy broke my Hannah Montana necklace."

"You wouldn't let me wear it," protested Mandy. "I just wanted to try it on."

"It was my favorite necklace in the whole world," Lissa continued, in tears. "You didn't even ask."

"You know you can't take your sister's things without asking," Josh said to Mandy.

"She hit me," Mandy said back.

"You know you're not supposed to hit your sister."

"She took my necklace. Without asking."

Josh was getting dizzy. "We'll go to the mall and get you a new necklace, okay?"

Lissa sniffed and nodded. "Okay."

"I want a necklace," cried Mandy.

"You, too," said Josh, and then both girls were jumping up and down and squealing. He looked at his dad. "We need more estrogen in the house, dontcha think?"

Still, he was nice to Sarah when she came over later, and the girls were on their best behavior. "You didn't need to go to all that trouble," he told her as she set the food on the kitchen counter.

"It wasn't any trouble. I like to cook," she said. "And bake, of course," she added. "Do you girls like cookies?"

Lissa and Mandy nodded vigorously.

"My mommy used to make cookies," said Mandy. "She's in heaven now."

For a second Josh could see that their visitor was taken by surprise, but she recovered quickly. "I'll bet she's baking cookies for all the angels. What do you think?"

Mandy smiled and nodded.

"You come by the bakery sometime soon and I'll make

sure you girls get a peanut butter cookie. How does that sound? Maybe we can even find a cookie for your daddy and grandpa."

"It won't be hard," said George. "We never met a cookie we didn't like."

"That's what we bakers like to hear," Sarah said.

Her mission accomplished, she left. The minute the door closed Dad leaned over the potpie and inhaled deeply. "Now that's what I'm talkin' about, home cookin'."

Josh had to admit the pie was good. So were the cookies.

Simply looking at them took him back in time to the days when life was perfect and he'd come home to the smell of chocolate chip cookies baking in the oven.

Chocolate. Chocolate shop. Chocolate babe. She sure looked tempting, but the vibes she put out said, *Keep away, sucker.*

Too bad Sarah Goodwin didn't have a daughter who was just as friendly as she was. And who looked like Jamie Moore.

The bakery was busy Monday morning, with throngs of people. They were going to run out of Sarah's herbed bread before closing. Her scones were about to be history, too, she thought as she slid a fresh batch of orange oatmeal cookies onto the tray behind the glass counter.

"Hi, there," said a friendly male voice from the other side of the counter.

She looked up to see Leo Steele.

"What's good today? Besides the baker."

"Just about anything," said Sarah. She managed to find a smile for him. After all, he was a paying customer. And a neighbor. And he was just trying to be friendly and fit in.

"How about a couple of those oatmeal cookies? Those look good."

Sarah nodded and slipped two in a little bakery bag. "Chrissy, you want to ring these up?"

"Sure," said Chrissy, taking over the transaction.

"How are the good deeds going?" Leo asked Sarah, obviously not ready to get passed on to someone else.

"Going good. How about you, Leo? Have you been paying it forward?"

"You betcha," he said. He caught sight of Sarah's new little friends skipping up to the counter, their grandpa right behind them. "Hey, girls. Do you like cookies?"

George had a hand on each girl's shoulder in a heartbeat. "Yeah, they do, and we're here to get them some."

Leo·stuck out a hand. "Leo Steele. I'm new here. Looking for my good deed for the day. These look pretty good. I thought I'd share."

"We don't let the girls take treats from strangers," George said, but he shook the man's hand.

"Oh, yeah. A different world from when our kids were little, huh? How about I give them to you and you can pass them on?" Leo handed him the bag.

George nodded. "Thanks."

Leo turned back to Sarah. "Guess I'd better buy some more."

"I guess you'd better go to the end of the line," snapped the middle-aged woman in back of him.

"No problem," said Leo easily. "But I've got a better idea. How about you let me buy you something?" he asked, giving Sarah a wink.

The woman gawked at him.

"We're trying to put the heart back in Heart Lake," he told her, "like it said in the paper."

"I read about that," she said. She looked speculatively at Leo. Sarah noticed she didn't have a ring on her left hand. "Well, okay. That's really nice of you."

The woman made it worth her while, ordering a dozen

ginger cookies, a loaf of the vanishing herb bread, and a piece of lavender cake.

"Make that two pieces," said Leo. "Want to join me?" he asked the woman. "I'm new here."

So many women, so little time, Sarah couldn't help thinking.

"Well, I do have to run some errands. But I can do them later," the woman added quickly.

Leo paid for the goodies as well as a couple of mochas and they moved off down the line.

"That was smooth," said George. "I'll have to tell my son about this place. It looks like the best pickup joint in town."

"Do we still get a peanut butter cookie?" Lissa asked him.

"Of course," Sarah answered, and passed two cookies over the counter.

Lissa took a big bite.

"Good?" asked Sarah, and she nodded.

"I guess we'll have to learn to make cookies, girls," said George.

The chicken nugget king making cookies, Sarah couldn't quite picture it. But after they left a new picture began to form in her mind. By the end of the day it was crystal clear.

ELEVEN

"What's this?" asked Dawn Schoemaker, one of Sarah's best customers, pointing to the flyer advertising Sarah's new brain baby. "A baking class for girls? You must be going through granddaughter withdrawals."

"I am," Sarah admitted.

Steph and the girls checked in on a regular basis, but the regularity had gone from daily to a couple of times during the week and once on weekends. Hardly surprising, considering their schedule. Steph was already working part-time, and the girls were busy with their new school. Then there was church, ballet lessons, and Katie had joined Camp Fire.

That news had given Sarah's heartstrings a wistful tug. She had enjoyed a brief stint as a Camp Fire girl, and acquired a nice collection of colorful beads for her vest by the time her dad got transferred and they had to move. She remembered the fun of earning those home craft beads, especially baking in the kitchen with her mother. She had been anticipating holiday baking with her granddaughters this year. Helping some other little girls had seemed like the perfect solution to her lonely grandma blues.

"That's some way to put the heart back in Heart Lake," Dawn said. "Are you going to hold the class here at the bakery?"

Allowing a group of little girls to run around the bakery kitchen wouldn't go over well with the health department. "No, I'll have it at my house."

"Boy, are you brave," Dawn said in a tone of voice suggesting that Sarah's bravery teetered on the edge of insanity.

"It will be fun," Sarah insisted. Of course it would be fun. How could it not? "Do you know anyone who might be interested?"

Dawn thought a moment. "Actually, I do. The mom's a nurse, and she works nights a lot."

"Is she a single mom?"

"No, but she might as well be. Her husband works construction on and off. When he's in charge, the kids pretty much run wild."

"How many kids are in this family?" Sarah suddenly had a vision of children running wild all over her house.

"Two boys, teenagers, and a girl about nine."

Nine was the right age. "What's she like?"

"A bit of a handful," said Dawn. "Last year she helped herself to my peonies to make a bouquet for a mock wedding she and some of her friends were having."

"Creative little thing," Sarah said diplomatically.

"She is a character," Dawn admitted. "Her mom doesn't seem to have the energy to keep up with her."

Sarah was pretty sure that meant she wouldn't, either. She'd never done anything like this before. Maybe she should start out slowly, with well-behaved, quiet children. Then, if all went well, she could branch out.

"Anyway, I'll have her mom give you a call," said Dawn. Before Sarah could voice her decision to ease into the baking class business, Dawn had taken her box of teacakes and sailed out the door.

Oh, well. By the time the woman called the class would be full, Sarah would make sure of it.

That very afternoon she recruited her first students. "Does it sound like something they'd enjoy?" she asked George Armstrong after she'd explained her idea to him.

"Would they! Sign 'em up. What do I owe you?"

Sarah smiled. "Nothing. This is something I want to do."

"Well, it works for me," said George. "I'm sure my son will think it's a great idea, too."

Okay, she thought as she hung up the phone, there were two. She'd start with six, a nice manageable number. She should have no trouble finding four more little girls like the Armstrongs. The class would be full before you could say "Cookie Monster."

"You got another taker," Sam said when she came home from the bakery the next afternoon.

All right. She knew it.

"Betty Bateman just signed up her grandkid."

Sarah's excitement melted faster than butter on a hot burner. "Betty? Oh, no," she moaned. "Just feed me rhubarb leaves right now and be done with it."

"You said you were taking the next four who called," Sam reminded her as he poured himself a mug of coffee. "Anyway, what's wrong with Beano?"

"Beanie," Sarah corrected. She took the mug from his hand and downed a big gulp. "And nothing. It's just that every time Betty brings her over I'm going to get Betty-ized. I'll be lucky if we can get anything done with Betty at the door wanting to talk all afternoon."

"There is that," Sam said. "You should have warned me."

"It's not your fault. And if it had even occurred to me that Betty would jump on this I would have, believe me."

"Doesn't her son live in Seattle? That's a long way to come for a baking class."

Sarah shook her head. "They moved to Lyndale this summer. That's close enough for Betty to pick up Beanie after school and run her here."

Sam gave Sarah a sympathetic shoulder rub. "Sorry, babe." And then he ruined his good deed by adding, "But you asked for it."

She turned and frowned at him. "Now, what is that supposed to mean?"

He shrugged. "You were the girl who wanted to change the world."

"Just Heart Lake," she corrected.

"And you will, one pain in the butt at a time."

"Oh, very funny."

The phone rang. "It's probably for you," Sam said, heading for the living room.

"There has to be a reason I married you," she called after him.

"Great sex," he called back.

She almost retorted that it wasn't that great, but decided Sam wouldn't see the humor in it, so she kept her mouth shut. That would be her good deed for the day.

Sam was right. The call was for her, another woman wanting to sign her daughter up for baking lessons.

"We'll be having four after-school classes, Monday afternoons, starting November sixteenth," Sarah explained. Only four classes. She could manage four weeks of Beanie, dirty fingernails and all. Betty was another matter altogether.

"This sounds perfect," said the woman. "I work swing shift a lot and my daughter could really use more girl time. What are you charging?"

"There's no cost," said Sarah.

"No cost?" The woman sounded shocked.

"It's my contribution toward putting the heart back in Heart Lake."

"I read about that. Oh, my gosh. You're the baker from the article."

"That's me." *Changing Heart Lake one pain in the butt at a time.*

"It's such a great idea. And it's really awesome of you to do this. I never bake, so this will be a good learning opportunity for Damaris. I know she'll love it."

Sarah hoped so. The thought of shaking Betty off her doorstep every week had only momentarily dampened her enthusiasm. She'd mentally sent Betty packing, and now she could envision herself in the kitchen, surrounded by sweet little girls with rosy cheeks and sparkling eyes watching as she took their freshly baked cookies from the oven. The vision sat in her brain like an old magazine ad from the fifties, looking good enough to frame and making her smile as she took down the necessary information.

"Now all I need is an emergency contact number," she said.

"If my husband's not home you can call me at the hospital," said the woman. "I'm a nurse."

Words began to swirl around the back of Sarah's mind: nurse, neighbor, peonies. *Oh, no. Say it isn't so.* "Do you, by any chance, live near Dawn Schoemaker?" Sarah asked, and held her breath.

"As a matter of fact, we do," said the woman. "She's wonderful. Well, I'd better go. My break is over."

Okay, Sarah decided as she hung up, the cooking class was now closed. She only had four girls, but this four would be enough. It will be fun, she told herself. Dawn had probably exaggerated.

Business had been a little slow at the Chocolate Bar the last couple of days. Jamie was sure it was due to the torrential rains pummeling Heart Lake. Who would want to go out in this? she thought, looking out the window at the downpour.

"It's awful out there," said Clarice. "I'm going to have to swim home. In fact, if it gets any worse I bet I won't even be able to drive. Maybe you should let me go home early."

Hope Wells had warned Jamie about Clarice's tendency to come in late and want to leave early, but Jamie was made of sterner stuff than Heart Lake's mild-mannered florist. No way was Clarice leaving until Jamie had squeezed every ounce of work out of her.

Still, there wasn't much work to do at this point without customers, and it was almost four. "Okay," Jamie decided. "First clean the kitchen area while I'm doing my paperwork, then you can scram." There was no point paying for help when she didn't need it.

Fifteen minutes later Clarice was ready to scram. "You know, I think that fudge is starting to get stale."

"Hint, hint?"

Clarice smiled shamelessly. "Soooo?"

"So, go ahead and take a bag home."

"Sweet," Clarice said, and bounced over to the fudge.

"Yeah, we'll see if you're still saying that when the scale goes up," Jamie teased.

"It never does," said Clarice.

Another minute and she was out the door, probably with a good two pounds of fudge. Oh, well, Jamie told herself, there's your good deed for the day. If getting rid of stale fudge counted as a good deed.

It was winter dark when she closed up and dashed for her car. She was pooped. Like Sarah, she had to get up early on a regular basis to make her inventory, and the long days coupled with the gloomy weather were making her feel like a bear ready to hibernate.

Heavy raindrops gave her windshield wipers a fight and

deepened puddles in the road. The night sky left the lake looking dark, like a perfect home for the Loch Ness monster's cousin. As she drove, all Jamie could think about was getting inside her cabin, building a fire in the woodstove, and heating up some of the homemade chicken soup Sarah had given her.

And then she saw the car with the flat tire hunched along the narrow shoulder of the road with its hood raised like a flag. It was raining. It was cold. It was the perfect good deed, especially for her.

Jamie had always been the last one picked when her friends were choosing teams for softball or kickball, and she'd never been the one her fellow students fought over when it was time for a group science project. But she was always the one they called to hang out with when they wanted to attract boys. Or when they got a flat tire. Her dad had taught her how to change a tire when she got her driver's license, and had followed up the lesson with the occasional surprise drill. She could still change a tire in her sleep.

Or in the rain. As she pulled in front of the car she saw the driver behind the foggy windows: an older woman—probably not someone who had changed a lot of tires.

As Jamie went to the other car, a cold finger of water slipped down her neck. She did her best to ignore it and the shiver it produced and tapped on the driver's side window. The woman lowered it cautiously. "If you've got a spare in your trunk I can get you back on the road in ten minutes."

"That's sweet of you, but I'll be fine."

"Have you got Triple A or something?" asked Jamie. Although how she'd call them on this stretch of road with its zero cell phone reception was a mystery.

"I do, but I don't have one of those portable phones. I'm sure some man will come along soon and help me."

"Well, there's no need to wait for a man," said Jamie. "I've been changing tires since I was sixteen. Pop your trunk."

"It's so nasty out," protested the woman.

Tell me about it. "It sure is, and you don't want to sit here any longer than you have to," Jamie informed her, and started walking to the trunk.

It popped open and she pulled out the spare along with the tire jack. By the time she had them the woman was out in the rain with her, her gray hair quickly sopped and flattened to her head, her coat collar pulled up around her neck.

"You can wait in the car," Jamie told her. "No sense both of us getting wet."

"What if it tips?" the woman fretted. "No, I'll wait here with you."

Jamie had no desire to get wetter and colder arguing with the woman, so she got to work. There were no street-lights out here, but she managed with the help of her car headlights and the little flashlight on her key chain. She had the car jacked up and the hubcap off and was just wrestling with the second lug nut when a car pulled up behind her, its headlights shining on her work. Flashing red and blue lights added extra color.

She knew, before she even looked over her shoulder, who was getting out of that patrol car, ruining her perfect, undiluted good deed.

TWELVE

*J*amie ignored the crunch of heavy male feet on the gravel of the road shoulder and unscrewed another lug nut.

"Could you ladies use some help?" rumbled a deep voice.

"Oh, Officer, thank you," breathed the older woman.

"I think we've got it under control," said Jamie, maintaining her position in front of the tire.

"Obviously, you do," said Josh Armstrong, squatting next to her.

Those big hands of his drew her gaze like a magnet. They were large, capable hands with squared-off fingers. Once upon a time she'd been a sucker for a man with strong, capable hands like those, but no more. And who cared if he had big shoulders? What was so sexy about big shoulders, anyway? His legs were massive. (Why was she looking?) There was probably nothing small anywhere on Josh Armstrong.

With that last thought her sex drive took over, driving her crazy. I am not attracted to this man, shouted her brain, trying desperately to call her wandering hormones back to the reservation. And now her nerves were getting into the act. Here it came. *No, no, no!* She clamped down an upcoming hiccup and about tore apart her esophagus.

"That's a nice coat you're wearing," he said, pointing to her light green raincoat. "Do you really want to get it dirty to prove a point?"

She was being stupid. She stood up and stepped away from the tire. "Have at it." To the woman she said, "I'm leaving you in good hands now." That sounded hokey, but it was probably true. This man really did seem like one of the good guys.

Except you never knew with people. Grant had seemed like a good guy, too. And he was, except when he was stressed, when he was drinking, and when he lost his temper, which added up to about ninety-eight percent of their time together.

"Thank you so much for stopping," the woman said to her. "You're proof that there are still good people in the world. You, too, Officer," she added.

"All in the line of duty, ma'am," he said. He pulled off the tire as if it were no more than a bottle cap. *The Incredible Hulk.*

"I hope you don't catch cold," the woman said to Jamie.

"I won't," Jamie assured her. "I'm tough. Good night."

She got in her car and drove off. Josh the cop wouldn't be stopping her for anything tonight. By the time he got done with that tire, she'd be home and in a hot bath. A sudden image of two bodies in a steamy shower popped into her head. She kicked them out to go freeze in the rain.

"Before I take off," Clarice said to Jamie as she settled in for her weekly chocolate fest with Emma and Sarah, "I've got something for you." She laid a small, green envelope on the table and nudged it toward Jamie.

"What's this?" asked Jamie, picking it up.

"Well, remember how Borg's boss was gonna fire him?"

How could she forget? Only the promise of extra hours if she needed them had kept Clarice from self-medicating with all the chocolate in the store.

"He gave Borg one last chance. He said Borg could thank you guys." Clarice beamed. "So, thanks from Borg. And that's from me," she told Jamie.

Jamie opened the envelope and found a gift card for Something You Need, her favorite local gift shop.

"Wow," breathed Emma as Clarice went out the door. "This is working. Slowly but surely, it's working."

"Maybe," Jamie said thoughtfully, and took a sip of her chocolate tea.

It would be nice. She'd never been much of a mover and shaker. In high school she'd been more of a good-time girl, sneaking off to parties where parents cultivated blindness while their teens cultivated a taste for beer, hanging out at the mall, or trying her best to be a surfer girl—not easy when you were a klutz, but she managed to work the bikini part. The way she stuffed a bikini had earned her a string of well-muscled boyfriends who liked fast cars and fast times. By the end of her twenties she'd outgrown her bad-boy phase, but she still remained a sucker for a nice sixpack.

Grant had possessed a superb set. He'd been a real man's man and she liked his toughness as much as he liked her smart mouth—both things they hated about each other when their relationship soured.

Emma was saying something. Jamie pulled herself back to the present. "What?"

"I saw one of your truffle goody jars yesterday. A woman was at Safeway walking up and down the check-stands, handing the candy in them out to the checkers."

"No way."

Emma nodded. "Way. Someone had given it to her and she decided to share. I asked her what she was going to do with the jar when it was empty and she said she was going to fill it with bubble bath and take it to her neighbor who's just about to get a cast off her foot. The neighbor has been counting the days till she can have a bath again. Is that awesome or what?"

Jamie had to admit it was. "You know, this is the best time of my life. I mean, I'm actually doing something with it." She smiled at Emma and Sarah through eyes suddenly teary. "It feels good." Emma opened her mouth, and Jamie pointed a warning finger at her. "And don't you dare turn this into one of your movie moments with some sappy quote."

Emma shut her mouth and frowned.

"Well, I'm almost wishing I'd thought of something like your gift jar instead of what I'm about to do," said Sarah.

"I think your baking class for girls is a great idea," said Emma.

"We'll see," said Sarah. "Some things work better in your head than in reality."

"You don't exactly sound excited. What happened?" asked Jamie.

"Oh, nothing really," Sarah said with a half shrug. "Betty Bateman signed up her granddaughter."

Both Jamie's eyebrows shot up. "The motormouth from down the street? Oh, my gosh. Does her grandkid talk as much as she does?"

Sarah sighed. "I hope not. As it is, I'll be lucky if I can get Betty off my doorstep so I can start the class." She took another long drink from her cup. "And I think I may have a problem child."

Jamie made a face. "Lucky you. You should've said you were full."

"Oh, well, it's only four weeks," said Sarah. "If I can't

handle four little girls for a couple of hours a week I've got a serious problem."

Jamie didn't say anything. She just got up and made Sarah another mocha.

Sam called Sarah from the station on Monday. "So, are you all set?"

"I think so." In honor of Thanksgiving they were going to make Sarah's raisin pie cookies—sugar cookies pressed together tart-style over a raisin filling. It was an ambitious recipe for a first project (what had she been smoking when she decided to attempt it?), but she had premade the filling and had all the ingredients for the cookie dough standing ready. She hoped that would make the whole process easier.

Now, all she had to do was get away from Betty and into the kitchen. "Are you sure you have to stay at the station?" she pressed.

"Sorry, babe, but yes."

"What good is it to be the guy in charge when you can't get away when you want to?" she grumped.

He gave a snort. "Who says I want to?"

She sighed. "That's what I thought."

"Everything'll be fine," he assured her. "You going to save me some cookies or are they getting scattered to the winds?"

"As if you never get anything."

"The cobbler's children," he retorted. "And sometimes the baker's husband. For a guy whose wife runs a bakery I don't get much."

"Come by in about an hour and you can be sure you'll get something," Sarah suggested.

"Nice try, babe. Gotta go." And with that, he hung up, leaving her to her fate.

"It will be fine," she assured herself as she put the

cordless phone back in its recharge cradle. She looked around her kitchen, checking out the stations she had set up. One end of the granite-topped island counter would be for rolling out the cookies after they made the dough. She'd station two girls there. The other end of the counter would be the filling station where two other girls could work on assembling their creations on cookie sheets. Everything was laid out and she had background music already going—Miley Cyrus to make the day girl-friendly. Let the games begin.

She poured herself a cup of coffee for energy and snagged the ringing phone. "Hi, Nana," piped Katie.

The good feelings that spread through Sarah were better than a sugar buzz. "Katie, my little cupcake with the cherry on top. How are you doing?"

"I'm good, Nana. We got a new puppy. Guess what we named it?"

"I can't imagine," said Sarah.

"We named it Nanacakes."

"Nanacakes?"

"Uh-huh. She's white and black. She's a girl."

"Well, that's great," said Sarah. *Nanacakes.* She smiled.

"Nana, I miss you so much."

Now she was going to cry. Phones were great. It was almost like having the other person in the same room. Almost, but not quite. You couldn't hug a child through the phone.

"Mommy's going to e-mail you a picture of Nanacakes," Katie said. Then, to a persistent voice behind her, "No, I'm talking to Nana."

The doorbell rang. Sarah walked to the door, saying, "Katie, put Addie on so I can say hi, okay?"

"Okay," Katie said grudgingly.

"Addie, my little sugar dumpling."

"Nana, we have a new puppy."

"So I hear," Sarah said, opening the front door.

There stood George Armstrong, Lissa and Mandy next to him. Lissa was beaming and Mandy was bouncing up and down as though the front porch had suddenly turned into a trampoline. "Are we too early?" he asked.

She shook her head. "Come on in." To Addie she said, "Nana has to go, sweetie. I love you. Be good for Mommy and tell her I'll call her later. Okay?"

"Okay."

And then the grandchildren were gone and she had new children to attend to.

"We're ready to make cookies," Lissa informed Sarah.

"Can we eat them?" asked Mandy.

"Of course," Sarah said, smiling down at her.

The two girls exchanged squeals and jumped up and down.

"Are you sure you're up for this?" George asked dubiously.

"Absolutely," Sarah replied firmly enough to convince both of them. She'd offered this class, and, by gumballs, it was going to happen.

George left, and Sarah ushered the girls into the kitchen to wash their hands and then had them don the little aprons that Emma had generously made as her contribution to the Sarah Goodwin Baking School for Girls.

They were drying their hands when the doorbell rang again.

Betty Bateman and two little girls stood on the front porch.

"Oh, and here's our heroine," said Betty, beaming at Sarah. "Beanie, you remember Mrs. Goodwin, don't you?"

The redheaded child next to her was dressed in a dirty parka, torn jeans, and tennis shoes that looked like she'd dragged them through a pasture in the rain. She held up a grimy hand in greeting. "Hi."

"We've just been so excited about this," said Betty. "Haven't we, Beanie?"

Beanie opened her mouth to speak.

"Oh, and I have some wonderful cookie recipes if you need any. The kids just love my sugar cookies. Don't you, Beanie?"

Beanie tried again, but she wasn't quick enough.

"And I have a lovely oatmeal cookie recipe. Of course, it can't compare to those cookies you make at the bakery. Are you going to teach the girls to make those?"

"I think we're going to concentrate on something a little more seasonal," Sarah said, smiling at the other girl. "And you must be . . ."

"Damaris," said the girl.

Sarah looked around. "Your mother?"

"She's at work. My dad dropped me off. He said to call when we're done. Are we gonna make Christmas cookies?" she asked, her voice powdered with disgust. "It isn't even December."

"Which is why we're going to make something else today," Sarah replied with a determined smile.

"Are we having snacks?" asked Damaris.

"I'm hungry," said Beanie.

Actually, Sarah hadn't thought of that. Of course, she'd figured they'd sample the cookies, but snacks—where had her brain been? Was she that far removed from motherhood? Or even grandmotherhood, for that matter. "We'll find something." she said, and hoped she sounded like a woman with a plan.

"Oh, snacks. I didn't even think of snacks," said Betty. "You know, I could have brought something," she added as Damaris slipped past Sarah and down the hall with Beanie following her lead.

"Go ahead and wash your hands," Sarah called after

them. Now she had four little girls in her kitchen, unsupervised. That wasn't good.

"I could run home and grab some chips," Betty offered. "We always keep Doritos on hand. They're Beanie's favorite. Oh, and let's see, I might have some Chips Ahoy."

Store-bought cookies at a baking class? That was just sick and wrong. "That's sweet of you, Betty, but we'll be fine." What did she have in the fridge? Milk to go with the cookies, of course, a couple of yogurts, salad makings, tofu to make up for her vanishing estrogen—nothing that would get a group of grade-school girls excited. *Come on, Sarah, think.*

"Well, it's no problem," said Betty. "Except, let me see. Did Beanie eat the last of the Doritos? I wonder if we have any cookies left. Well, no problem. The store isn't far. And we have our little hybrid. Let me tell you, that gets the best gas mileage."

"Don't worry. We'll be fine," Sarah assured her and started to move the door toward shut.

Betty leaned around to keep her face in view. "If you're sure. I don't mind."

"No, not a problem, really. We'll see you at five. I'd better go get the girls started."

She shut the door while Betty was still babbling. New sounds were coming from the kitchen. Little girls squealing. What were they into?

Sarah hurried to the kitchen to find her baking class chasing each other around the island counter. "Okay, ladies," she said, catching Beanie. "Let's settle down. Have we all washed our hands?"

"Yep," said Beanie.

Sarah lifted one of Beanie's hands for inspection. "Let's do it again."

"Do we have to wear these stupid aprons?" Damaris asked, holding up one made with red checked material.

"Actually, yes. That way you won't get your clothes dirty."

"My grandma doesn't care," said Beanie.

Damaris had tossed aside her apron and was now fingering Sarah's vintage miniature milk glass Hen on Nest figurine. "Let's not do that," Sarah said sweetly, removing it from the child's hands.

"I was just looking at it," said Damaris.

"Let's look with our eyes, shall we?"

"I like these," said Lissa, pointing to the wooden Dutch girl and boy with holes in their rounded bellies for shaking out salt and pepper.

"Those are older than you," Sarah told her. "Older than me, even. They were my mother's."

"This is boring," said Damaris.

"I'm starving," wailed Beanie.

Oh, yes. This had been a great idea, positively inspired.

THIRTEEN

$\mathcal{P}$izza," Sarah decided. "We're going to send out for pizza."

"Yay!" said Beanie. "I love pizza."

"Me, too," said Lissa.

"Me, too," echoed Mandy.

"We have pizza all the time," said Damaris in a bored voice.

The other girls looked at her, at first like she was from Mars, then like maybe they were. "Pizza's okay," said Lissa with a shrug. She saved herself from becoming a Damaris clone by adding a polite, "Thank you."

"You're welcome. I'll call in the order," said Sarah, wishing she could order a gag for Damaris.

"Pepperoni," Beanie requested.

"That's nasty," said Damaris. "Let's have Hawaiian. Hawaiian is better than stupid pepperoni."

"Yeah," said Lissa.

"Yeah," said Mandy.

"Pineapple. Gross," said Beanie, making a face. Beanie was obviously her own woman.

"We can do half pepperoni and half pineapple," Sarah said.

Damaris shrugged, but Beanie smiled gratefully at Sarah, and Lissa said, "Then we can have some of each."

"Have you ever seen a whole pepperoni?" Damaris asked the other girls as Sarah was looking up the phone number for Pizza Heaven.

All three shook their heads.

She lowered her voice. "It looks like a giant weenie." It wasn't hard to tell from the hand motions that accompanied her words that the girl wasn't talking about hot dogs.

Lissa and Beanie giggled and Mandy asked, "What's a weenie?"

"She doesn't know. She's a baby," explained Lissa.

"I am not a baby!" Mandy cried hotly.

Sarah's junior bakers needed to refocus. "Okay, girls, let's check to make sure we have all the ingredients while I'm ordering pizza."

The squabbling was instantly forgotten and the girls clustered around the counter, each one randomly grabbing for salt, baking soda, measuring spoons, and cups.

"I'll get you started," Sarah said, pushing between them. She pointed to the recipe sheet. "Here's the recipe we're using. Lissa and Damaris, you can measure the dry ingredients." She showed them how to tap on a filled measuring cup, then cut across it with the flat side of a knife to get the exact amount of flour.

"That's easy," said Damaris, grabbing the cup.

Fine, go for it. Sarah turned her attention to the other girls. "Mandy, you can put the sugar into the mixing bowl, and Beanie, use this knife to put the shortening into the measuring cup. Like this." She demonstrated and Beanie nodded eagerly. "As soon as I'm off the phone I'll show you how to do the raisin filling."

Okay, that should keep them busy while she ordered pizza. She moved to the counter where the phone sat and picked it up, giving one final admonition. "Remember, it's important, when you're baking, to follow the recipe exactly so your cookies turn out well."

"I already knew that," bragged Damaris, dipping her cup into the flour canister.

Maybe she was too advanced for this class. Maybe Sarah could suggest she go learn how to hang glide or something.

"I knew that, too," said Lissa, not to be outdone. She smiled at Sarah. "I want to be a baker like you when I grow up. Then I can eat all the cookies I want."

"My mom says eating too many cookies gives you a big butt," Damaris said as Sarah punched in the number for Pizza Heaven.

Sarah was suddenly conscious of four pairs of eyes checking out her own big butt. She turned and leaned against the counter, hiding it behind her.

"I don't want a big butt like Mrs. Goodwin's," said Damaris. "I'm going to go on *America's Next Top Model* and become a supermodel." She struck a sex-laced pose that sat oddly with her nine-year-old body.

"Pizza Heaven," said a bored teenage-girl voice. "Heaven's what we deliver in every sliver."

Sarah needed a little heaven right now, and pizza alone wasn't going to do it.

After the girls got busy baking, moods improved. Even Damaris forgot she was a pill and began to have fun.

But once the pizza arrived and Sarah insisted they eat at the table she reverted to pillhood. "We always eat on the couch and watch TV," she informed Sarah. "*High School Hitters* is on right now," she explained to the other junior bakers. "I looove Seth."

"I'm going to marry Bo," Beanie announced.

"You can't marry Bo," Damaris said. "You have to be totally hot. Anyway, him and Kirsten are breaking up today. Can we watch it?" she asked Sarah.

Sarah didn't watch much TV, but even she knew about the new teen soap that was luring kids to the small screen after school on a daily basis. "Not today," she said, sweetly but firmly. "Today we're too busy living real life to watch pretend life."

"I hate real life. Real life is boring," said Damaris.

"Only if you're a boring person," Sarah retorted.

Damaris shut up and took another bite of her pizza.

"I was a fairy for Halloween," Mandy announced.

"I'll bet you were a very pretty fairy," Sarah told her.

"I was a pirate," said Beanie, her voice full of swagger.

"Girls can't be pirates," scoffed Damaris.

"Yeah, they can. Didn't you see *Pirates of the Caribbean*?"

"She wasn't a pirate. She was just a pirate's girlfriend."

"Well, I was a real pirate. I get to take fencing when I'm older. My grandma said," Beanie bragged.

"I'm going to take acting lessons," countered Damaris. She dove to beat Beanie to the last piece of pizza and tipped what was left of the Coke that had come with it.

And I'm going to take an Excedrin, thought Sarah, reaching for a sponge.

"Sorry," said Damaris, and stuffed the pizza in her mouth.

"That's okay. Accidents happen," said Sarah. *It's only pop, nice, sticky pop.* "Okay, girls, time to get back to our cookies."

By five o'clock a miracle had occurred. Everyone was

smiling and each girl was loading up a paper plate with cookies to take home.

Damaris pronounced the cookies good and the other girls agreed. "That was fun," she said to Sarah.

"I'm glad you enjoyed yourself," Sarah said. Maybe "relieved" would have been a better word. *One cooking lesson down, three to go.* "Do you need to call your dad to come get you?" *How soon can he get here?*

Damaris shrugged. "There's no hurry. He doesn't live far."

"Well, let's call him now," said Sarah. *The sooner the better.*

Damaris was dialing when the doorbell rang. George Armstrong stood on the doorstep, holding a bottle of white wine. "I thought maybe you could use this."

Sarah smiled. "You have no idea. Come on in. The girls are getting their cookie plates ready to take home."

George stepped inside. "My hat's off to you. I sure couldn't do this. You women must have some extra gene that makes it so you can cope."

"As a matter of fact, we do," said Sarah, leading the way to the kitchen. "It's called the insanity gene."

"Grandpa!" squealed both girls at the sight of him. "Try our cookies," said Lissa, holding up her plate.

The phone rang. Sarah answered it to find Sam on the other end of the line. "I'm just checking to see if you survived."

"I did," she said.

"Did you save me a cookie?"

"Ah, now we're getting to the real reason you called," she teased.

"No, I really wanted to know how it went," he insisted.

"It went great. George is here right now, so I'll call you later."

"George?"

"He's here picking up the girls. I'll call you back," Sarah said, and hung up. Or better yet, she'd run a care package over to the station as soon as she'd gotten everyone out the door and Betty off her doorstep. Which meant she'd get there around midnight.

"So, are you going to do this again next week?" asked George as the girls got their coats.

They had survived this first class somehow, and everyone was happy. That was a good sign. Surely she could manage this three more times. Anyway, Sarah had already planned the next week's baking challenge. "Of course we are. We're going to make pumpkin cookies for Thanksgiving."

"Sounds good," he said with a nod. "That way if I burn the turkey we'll end the feast with a good taste in our mouths."

"You're cooking Thanksgiving dinner?" She'd already figured out that George Armstrong was no Emeril. His poor family.

"Not me. My son's a pretty good cook. He'll probably do most of the work."

"He'll do no such thing," Sarah said firmly. "You tell him you're all coming here for Thanksgiving dinner. I insist."

"Naw, we couldn't do that," George protested.

Sarah could tell it was halfhearted. "Please do. It's my first Thanksgiving without my daughter and her family, and having children in the house would really help me get through it."

"Well. Twist my arm," he said with a grin. "But you'd better assign us something to bring or my son will kill me."

"You tell him to bring his best dish, whatever it is. Oh, except dessert. Between my niece and me, we'll have it covered," Sarah said. "I'm sure she'll bring a ton of chocolate."

"Your niece?" George's expression turned speculative. "The one who owns that chocolate shop?"

"That would be the one," said Sarah. "She's alone, and she'll be with us this year."

George nodded, and Sarah could tell by the glint in his eyes that they had successfully gotten on the same wavelength. "Sounds good."

"What are we going to make next week?" Damaris asked.

"One more thing for Thanksgiving. Then, the week after I'll teach you how to make candy cane cookies."

"Cool," said Beanie.

"Yum," said Damaris.

"Come on, girls. Time to go home," George said to his granddaughters, ushering them out of the kitchen.

"Do we have to go already?" asked Lissa.

"Yep. Tell Mrs. Goodwin thanks."

"Thank you for having us," said Lissa. The phrase came out well rehearsed but heartfelt.

Mandy did her one better. She hugged Sarah fiercely.

Sarah suddenly thought of Addie, her youngest granddaughter. Her eyes misted and she reached down and touched the child's head. "You were very good."

Betty arrived to pick up Beanie just as George and company were leaving.

"Beanie, your grandma's here," Sarah called from the doorway, determined to keep Betty corralled on the front porch. Beanie thundered down the hall, followed by Damaris.

"Oh, look at those lovely cookies!" Betty cried when Beanie showed her the plate of goodies. "And you made those all by yourself?"

"We all made them together," said Damaris, but Betty didn't hear her. She was still raving about the cookies and Beanie and Sarah's big heart. Damaris shrugged and set her plate on the porch, then skipped onto the front yard to do cartwheels. "Can you do that?" she taunted Beanie.

Beanie trotted onto the lawn and did a back flip, making Damaris gawk.

"She just loves gymnastics," bragged Betty, following Sarah's gaze. "And soccer and climbing trees and anything that gets her dirty." Betty lowered her voice. "This is so good for her. I understand that she's athletic and all but I want her to be well rounded. I want her to remember she's a girl." She looked at Damaris in her hip jeans and jacket. "This little girl who is with her is awfully cute."

So were baby tigers. "Beanie is fine just the way she is," Sarah said. "And she did enjoy the baking. I think she's perfectly well rounded."

"Well, it's good to see she's making some nice, new friends. A girl can't have enough friends, you know. We moved around so much when I was little I just didn't have that many," Betty confided.

Sarah had moved a couple of times herself as a kid, but she'd had trouble leaving friends, not making them. Betty's difficulty probably had more to do with her mouth than her physical location. Or maybe that was why she talked so much now. Making up for lost time?

Betty kept Sarah freezing on the front porch for a good ten minutes while the two girls chased each other around the front yard and Sarah continued to check the street for some sign of Damaris's father.

"Damaris, did you get ahold of your dad?" Sarah finally asked.

"The line was busy," said Damaris, who was now twirling in circles.

"You don't have voice mail?"

"We have an answering machine," Damaris replied. "My dad likes to screen calls."

At this rate the child would be here all night. "I'll take

you home," said Sarah. At least it would get Betty off her porch.

"No, that's okay. I'll call." Damaris rushed back into the house.

"We could give her a lift," offered Betty. "I have to take Beanie home anyway. And besides, I haven't done my good deed for the day yet." She wagged a playful finger at Sarah. "Can't let you outdo me."

That worked for Sarah. She could get rid of everyone and go collapse with a nice glass of wine. "Thanks, Betty. I appreciate that. Damaris, tell your dad never mind," she called. "Mrs. Bateman is going to take you home." No reply. "Damaris?"

Damaris came walking down the hall a moment later. "It's too late. He's on his way."

"Let's go, Grandma," said Beanie, tugging on Betty's arm. "I have to go home and learn my spelling words."

"They give these children so much work," Betty said with a shake of her head, but she let Beanie lead her away.

And that left Sarah alone with the baby tiger.

FOURTEEN

*B*ack inside the house they went. "I'm thirsty," Damaris decided. "Do you have chocolate milk?"

"We can make some," said Sarah, resigned to her fate.

Damaris fingered the wine bottle while Sarah poured her milk. "My dad drinks beer."

"A lot of people do," Sarah said.

"I had beer once," said Damaris, dumping in enough spoons of chocolate to turn her into fudge.

Somehow, Sarah wasn't surprised to hear it.

"My dad let me have a drink of his." Damaris wrinkled her nose. "It was nasty."

"It is," Sarah agreed.

"What does wine taste like?"

Nice try, kid. "Just as nasty," Sarah told her. "Chocolate milk is better."

"I like chocolate. Can we learn to make candy like what they sell in that chocolate shop?"

"Maybe."

Damaris made a face. "That means no. My mom always says maybe."

The doorbell rang and Sarah heaved an inward sigh of relief as she went to answer it.

Damaris's dad looked to be somewhere in his thirties. He was dressed in jeans and a Huskies sweatshirt, which proclaimed him a fan of the University of Washington's football team. His stocky frame betrayed him for an ex-football player, probably high school, Sarah guessed.

He gave her a polite nod. "I'm here to get Damaris."

"Damaris, your dad's here," Sarah called.

"I'm finishing my drink," Damaris called back.

"Dam, quit screwing around. We gotta go," her dad yelled. "We have to pick up her brother from soccer practice," he explained. A moment later Damaris sauntered down the hall. "Come on, Dam," he cajoled, "we're late."

She shrugged and skipped out the door past Sarah. "Bye."

"Bye." . . . *Dam*. If ever there was a fitting nickname for a child—this kid was Dennis the Menace in drag.

"Thanks for having her," said the man. Then he turned and followed Damaris down the walk.

Sarah shut the door and went to the kitchen and opened the wine. Sam could have the cookies she'd saved for him tomorrow. By the time she was recovered from her first baking class she'd be in no condition to drive.

"There's someone in here. This time I'm sure," hissed Mrs. Kravitz.

"I'll check it out," Josh promised, and entered her house to look for burglars. For the third time in one week.

Martinez had taken to teasing Josh that Mrs. Kravitz had the hots for him. "Pretty soon she'll be wanting you to stop by for a cocktail."

"Yeah, well, you should talk," Josh had retorted. "At least she's not requesting a ride along every week like your romance babe does with you."

"That woman's a writer. She's doing research."

"Yeah? What's she researching? She want to know how big your gun is?"

"Maybe. At least the romance writer is under fifty. And she is a babe."

That was more than Josh could say for Mrs. Kravitz. She was a sixty-something widow with gray hair. And she was paranoid.

Who did Mrs. Kravitz think was going to burgle her house at eight in the evening? And why would anyone pick this place? It was a funky, old, two-story farmhouse with battered shingle siding, and it screamed no money. The floorboards creaked under Josh's feet as he walked through the living room on his way to the back bedroom.

"He's upstairs," Mrs. Kravitz whispered, right on Josh's tail. If Josh stopped suddenly she'd bump into him.

A door off the bedroom led to a staircase the width of a pencil. Josh motioned for her to stay put, then started up the stairs.

"There he is. I hear him," she whimpered.

Mrs. Kravitz needed to get her hearing checked. Or her head.

Josh stopped on the stairway and listened. And then he heard it, too. His adrenaline came on duty and his heart rate picked up. He pulled his gun and started up the stairs, ready for an attack. A small hallway and landing was flanked by two large rooms. He chose the one to the left and entered gun first. No one in the room itself.

He took a deep breath and approached the little door in the corner that probably led to some sort of crawl space alongside the room. Now he had his flashlight and his gun. He opened the door cautiously, gun ready, and shined the light into the cobwebby dark. He heard the noise again and leaned in further.

Then he saw it and about dropped his flashlight. It was a rat the size of King Kong.

Shit! He backed up so fast he knocked his head on the rafters. Once out, he slammed the door shut and rubbed his head, swearing under his breath.

Okay, it was just a rat. A giant, killer rat with fangs the size of daggers. Nonetheless, he was glad none of the guys had been present to witness this little scene.

He took a deep, restoring breath while he holstered his gun and flashlight. Then he went downstairs to tell Mrs. Kravitz that she was safe. As long as she didn't open that door.

"Rats!" she cried. She looked in disgust at the fat, white cat sleeping on her bed. "Really, Princess. What good are you?"

"At least it's not a burglar," Josh told her.

"I'm calling an exterminator first thing tomorrow," she said as she walked him to the door. "Thank you for coming out, and thank you for believing me. I'm sure I sounded crazy."

He hadn't, and she had, but he sure wasn't going to tell her. "We're here to serve, ma'am," he assured her. And sometimes the best way to serve was to be willing to listen.

He couldn't help wondering if this widow had anyone to listen to her these days. On his way out he noticed that the shutters on the living room windows were hanging loose. Did Mrs. Kravitz have kids? And if she did, where the hell were they?

He got back in his car and drove downtown for a quick patrol before going to run radar over by the high school. Driving by the Chocolate Bar gave him a hankering for some candy. Too bad it was closed for the night. Maybe he'd pop into Safeway and get a Snickers.

As if what he really wanted could be found in Safeway. You're a fool, he told himself. No guy in his right mind would stoke the hots for a woman who continually sent buzz-off vibes. Well, he hadn't been in his right mind since Crystal died, so no surprise. Maybe he never would be again.

Life had been perfect before a drunk driver plowed into his wife's car as she was coming home from a Tupperware party. A damned Tupperware party. She'd wanted extra containers to store her Christmas cookies in and some asshole with fresh divorce papers wanted an escape. He'd escaped all right, staggered out of the wreckage with nothing more than a broken arm.

Josh stopped the patrol car with a sigh. He knew that life wasn't fair, that bad things happened to good people, but what happened to his family was beyond unfair. It was wrong. His girls shouldn't have to grow up without a mother.

There was only one way to fix that problem.

Except finding the right woman to help him fix it was a daunting task. Don't be in a hurry, he counseled himself. *The girls don't need any more grief and neither do you.*

And he sure didn't need to eat Thanksgiving dinner with a bunch of strangers. "Why the hell didn't you ask me?" he demanded when his dad told him the next morning about their dinner engagement.

Dad scowled at him, the same scowl that used to scare the shit out of Josh when he was ten. "What are you getting so damned pissed about? We've got to eat."

"Yeah, with our own family. That's what Thanksgiving is for."

"So? There'll be families there."

"I don't want to go out," Josh said. He knew he sounded like a sullen fifteen-year-old, but hell, he had a right. "You know, it's great you came to live with us, but I'm the dad in this house. I get to make the big decisions."

The scowl deepened. "You may be the dad in this house, but I'm still your father. And I want to go to the Goodwins' for Thanksgiving."

"So go. No one's stopping you," Josh snapped. He turned his back on his father and poured himself another cup of coffee.

A moment later he felt a big hand on his shoulder. That hand on the shoulder had been a comfort when his team lost the championship game, when his first girlfriend dumped him, when he stood bewildered in the church foyer, trying to think of what to say to people after Crystal's memorial service. Now it called up a lifetime of memories: his dad swearing over a leaky inflatable boat that ended their fishing adventure on an ill-fated camping trip, his dad holding him on his lap while they watched a scary movie, his dad in trouble when Mom came home and discovered Dad letting him watch a scary movie.

"Oh, hell. If you want to go, we'll go," he said.

The old man was smart enough not to gloat. "Sarah said bring whatever you want as long as it's not dessert."

Fine. He'd bring something. But not his enthusiasm.

By four o'clock in the afternoon exactly three customers had come through Emma's shop door. The first was Shirley, who had managed to skip off with two yards of fabric she'd never pay for. Emma had chalked it up as her good deed for the day.

But these last two—well, one, really—were enough to drive her to close up early. She'd been trying not to eavesdrop as the women talked in a corner over by the hundred-count fabric, but the shop wasn't exactly buzzing with activity.

"This is nice," said the short, middle-aged woman with the dark hair.

Her friend, a tall, frosted blonde with perfect makeup and expensive clothes, took the cloth between well-manicured fingers and inspected it. "It is. Overpriced, though. You know, you can get the same thing at the Savemart for fifty cents a yard less."

"Really?" said the short woman.

"All my quilting friends shop there."

So that was where all Emma's potential customers were. Panic and defeat began to play ring-around-the-rosy in her stomach.

"Still, it's nice to support local shops," said the short woman.

"I suppose," said her friend, who could obviously afford to do the same.

"I think I'll buy this," the short woman decided. "And this."

Bless you, thought Emma. She set aside the work she was pretending to do and donned her cheeriest smile as the two women approached the counter. "How are you ladies doing today?" she asked, trying to sound cheerful.

"Fine," said the short woman.

Her friend just stood next to her and said nothing. Emma was willing to bet she hadn't gotten that fancy suede jacket at Savemart.

The short woman laid two bolts of cloth on the cutting counter. "Can I have two yards of each of these?"

"Of course," Emma said, and cut the cloth. She wished she could think of something else to say, something friendly and inspiring that would prove to these women that shopping with her was worth an extra fifty cents a yard. But all she could think of was how she wasn't going to be able to make her rent either here or at home this month unless her fairy godmother or the patron saint of quilters showed up. And then there was the small matter of the eighty-thousand-dollar bank loan she'd taken out to buy her inventory. Her parents had matched her savings with another ten thousand and cosigned for the loan. With all of forty-six dollars left in her savings account, she was in very deep doo-doo.

Didn't these people understand about community loyalty? Hadn't they ever watched *It's a Wonderful Life?* "Are you ladies new to Heart Lake?" she asked. They couldn't be from around here. Otherwise they'd understand the importance of supporting their local merchants.

"I've been here for ten years," said the woman in the suede coat.

Even though by Heart Lake standards that made her a newcomer, ten years was still long enough to figure a few things out. But judging from what Emma had overheard, a lot of people in town were just as clueless.

"I'm new here," said the short woman, "and I love it. Everyone is so nice and friendly. And I love the idea of doing good deeds. I saw the article in the paper," she added, beaming at Emma.

"Well, you've just supported a local business and done your good deed for the day," Emma said as she rang up the purchase.

"You do know you're overpriced," said the other woman. Did she consider sharing that information to be her good deed for the day?

Her friend blushed, and Emma felt a sizzle on her own cheeks. "I try hard to keep my prices competitive. Unfortunately, I can't always offer the same discounts as the big chains. But I make up for it in service." She slipped a flyer announcing her upcoming quilting class in the bag along with the fabric and handed it to the short woman. "Classes are free when you buy your fabric here."

"Now, that's a good deal," said the woman.

"And there's something to be said for shopping right here in town," Emma continued. "Think of the money you save on gas."

The short woman nodded thoughtfully. "You're right."

But as they walked out the door, Emma heard the tall one say, "Savemart's not that far away, and the amount of money I save on everything there, including my groceries, more than makes up for what I spend on gas."

Emma wanted to scream after them, "But does Savemart care about you? Do they care about the community? DO THEY OFFER FREE QUILTING CLASSES?"

After the depressing encounter she felt too sick to keep the shop open. She closed up and went straight home. Pyewacket was her welcoming committee. He came trotting out from her bedroom and followed her into the kitchen, rubbing against her legs as she dialed her mother. "In a minute," she told him. "And what were you doing in my bedroom?" She could have sworn she'd shut the door.

"Hi, sweetie," said her mom. "Why are you calling me from home?"

"I'm sick. I'm not coming over for dinner tonight."

"Oh, no. What have you got?"

A bad case of discouragement. "Nothing really, I'm just . . . my stomach's upset. I'm going to have some tea and then go to bed." *And consider smothering myself with a pillow.*

"Do you want me to bring you some chicken soup?" offered her mom.

"No, thanks. I'll be okay."

"Maybe it's a simple case of exhaustion. You've been working too hard."

She wished. If she'd been working hard it would have meant she had customers and could pay her bills.

"Get a good night's sleep," said Mom. "And if you're still sick tomorrow I can man the shop."

The ghost shop. The last thing Emma wanted was her mother there all day, seeing no one coming in and nothing happening, but she murmured her thanks. Then she hung up and went to see if her bedroom had survived a day of Pye.

The quilt on the bed was her first concern. She'd made it when she was thirteen, and Grandma Nordby had helped her. Her parents had been busy building their house on the lake and she had stayed with Grandma. She'd been convinced she'd be bored with no friends around, but Grandma had introduced her to the magic of creating beautiful patterns out of bits of fabric, and between that and watching old movies together, the summer had flown by.

Now, seeing the quilt, she wanted to cry. "Oh, Pye!" She held it up to survey the damage. One whole side looked like Freddy Krueger had gone on a binge.

The cat had followed her in, probably to remind her that he expected his food dish to be filled immediately, as always. She glared at him. "Look what you've done!"

He could have cared less about looking. He already knew. Unlike a dog, who would have realized how he'd disappointed his master and come slinking over to her to offer an apology, Pyewacket simply scatted.

Emma slammed the bedroom door after him. Then she fell on the bed and indulged herself in a good cry. No good deed went unpunished. She was living proof.

FIFTEEN

Jamie had enjoyed a great week. The shop had been busy and so had the town. It really looked like Heart Lake was rediscovering its small-town spirit and getting into doing good deeds. She and Emma had finished their design for the T-shirts, adding a red heart with an angel perched on top to their KEEP THE HEART IN HEART LAKE slogan, and a shop in Seattle was printing their first batch of shirts. Now one of her customers who had gotten into the gift-jar idea was in buying chocolates to fill another Mason jar.

"I started a game of front porch tag in my neighborhood," she reported.

"I was always It when we played tag," Clarice said. "That sucked."

"This is much more fun," the woman assured her. To Jamie she said, "I left one of your truffle jars on my neighbor's porch along with a note to go tag someone else, and I just saw a jar at a house at the end of the street on my way here."

"If it meant getting chocolate, I wouldn't mind getting tagged," said Clarice.

Like she needed to. Clarice was a two-legged chocolate mouse. If she didn't stop sneaking into the inventory Jamie was going to have to hide a mousetrap in the display case among the white chocolate–blackberry truffles.

"That is awesome," Jamie said to their customer.

"Looove in a jar," crooned Clarice. "Hey, that almost sounds like a commercial."

"Or at least a headline," said Jamie. "Want to be in the paper?"

"Really?" The woman was grinning like a jack-o'-lantern.

"I think that would be a yes," said Clarice, so Jamie sicced Lezlie Hurst on her.

On Wednesday the paper's Lake Living section ran an article dedicated to the art of goody jars with all kinds of suggestions for turning a Mason jar into a good deed.

"Those gift jars are really catching on," Sarah said when the three friends met.

"I'll bet the baking classes are, too," said Emma.

"They are," Sarah said, "but I'm not sure the real thing is matching up to what I envisioned."

"Reality sucks," said Jamie cheerfully. "What happened?"

"Nothing that bad. The girls are a handful, that's all." Sarah stared into her empty mocha cup. "I may not have had the purest of motives when I started this baking class."

"You? You're joking, right?" scoffed Jamie.

Sarah shook her head. "I think I was expecting those girls to magically turn into granddaughters. I was doing it more for me than to help someone."

"You shouldn't be so hard on yourself," said Emma. "Of course you miss your granddaughters, but part of why you miss them is that you don't have anyone to do nice things for. Isn't that why you really started the baking class?"

"Yeah," put in Jamie. "You weren't being a selfish grandma. You were a good deed looking for a place to happen."

"I don't know," said Sarah. "I hope you're right." She looked at her watch. "I should get going. I've got a lasagna to deliver to the firehouse."

"You spoil those guys," Jamie told her.

"Maybe, but guess who gets a free calendar every year," Sarah retorted.

The fire department's fund-raising calendar, featuring hot firefighters from the local stations, always sold out.

"I need to start taking lasagna over there," cracked Jamie. She regretted the words the minute they were out of her mouth. Sarah would take them as permission to start matchmaking.

Sure enough. "We've got a couple of new guys," said Sarah. "Both single."

"Give 'em to Emma."

"Hmm. What can I set on fire?" Emma said with a smile.

It wasn't a typical Emma smile, though. Her eyes were sad. "Are you okay?" asked Jamie.

"Me? Sure. Why wouldn't I be?"

"I don't know. You tell me," said Jamie.

"Life is great. Well, except for the fact that I have no customers. And do you know why I have no customers?"

Emma's chipper voice had taken on an edge. "Uh-oh," said Jamie. "Why?"

" 'Cause they're all going to Savemart where they can save fifty cents a yard on fabric," Emma said, her smile determined, her voice brittle.

Jamie scowled. "Beatches."

"Are you going to make your rent okay this month?" asked Sarah, cutting to the chase.

"I'm sure I will," said Emma, sounding far from sure. "If worse comes to worst I can close and move back in with my parents," she added in an attempt at humor. Her eyes were tearing up now. She stood suddenly. "I'd better go, too. I'll see you guys next week."

"Wait," called Sarah, "let's talk about this."

Emma shook her head violently. "There's nothing to talk about."

Jamie could think of a few things, like how Emma was going to pay off her business loan and how they were going to drum up customers for her. But while she sat there in shock, Emma was already to the door.

"Emma," said Sarah, going after her.

"I'll be fine, really," Emma said, holding up a hand. "Things will work out. Don't mind me."

And then she was gone, leaving Jamie sitting stunned in her seat and Sarah standing in the doorway.

"What are we going to do?" asked Jamie.

"I don't know, but we'd better think of something before the end of the year," said Sarah, "or there's going to be new retail space to rent on downtown Lake Way."

That quilt shop was Emma's baby. Jamie couldn't imagine what she would do if she lost it. Somehow, they'd have to find a way to make sure she didn't.

To do her part, she left Clarice in charge on Saturday and slipped off to purchase some fabric.

Quilting wasn't her thing. When it came to arts and crafts she preferred shorter projects with more immediate results. But what the heck? It was always good to learn a new skill.

She found Sarah already there, buying fabric like it was the end of the world.

"Not you, too," Emma greeted her.

"What?"

Emma smiled at both of them and took a swipe at her eyes. "You guys are the best. You know that?"

"Yes, we do," said Jamie, and went to browse the little book section over by the window. She found one full of holiday gift crafts. "You should definitely push this," she said, holding it up for Emma to see. "You could have a Christmas gift-making class."

"By gumballs, that's a great idea," said Sarah. "I'll sign up for it."

"Me, too," said Jamie. "Put an ad in the paper."

"I will," said Emma with a decisive nod. "It can go right next to the one I just put in."

"Oh, for what?" asked Jamie.

"I'm going to have a Thanksgiving sale: forty percent off. Tell everyone."

"Whoa, that's quite a markdown. Don't you want to wait and do that in January?" suggested Jamie.

Emma's perky smile faded. "Not if I want to still be in business in January."

"You will be," Sarah said.

"You really think so?" Jamie asked her as they left the shop, laden with fabric.

"I hope so."

"We need to find her a sugar daddy," Jamie said.

"A man isn't always the answer. You know that," said Sarah.

"Not for me," Jamie agreed. "But Emma's different. She's a believer."

Jamie was once, too. Sometimes she wished she could

turn back the clock and start her love life over again. Would she have been any wiser in the choices she made? Who knew? One thing she did know for sure, she was going to be smart from now on.

Whatever her motives for starting her girls' baking class, Sarah was determined to finish it with a big heart and a big smile.

Big heart, big smile, she repeated to herself on Monday afternoon as she dealt with spilled pumpkin on the floor, Beanie dropping a hot pad on the heating element and catching it on fire, and Damaris declaring their finished product, pumpkin cookies, "Okay."

The only silver lining in the afternoon's cloud was that Sarah would be getting rid of Damaris on time thanks to a dinner invitation from Lissa. "Go with God," she said to George.

"Thanks," he said. "I survived Desert Storm. I should be able to survive this. If I'm lucky."

"Just remember how fast they grow up," Sarah told him. "It will all be over sooner than you think."

They were still talking when Leo Steele sauntered over from across the street. "Looks like a party over here," he said with a wink. "Thought I'd join in."

"I wouldn't call having a bunch of kids running around my place a party," said George. "More like a bad case of insanity."

"We've been having a cooking class," Sarah explained. "George is here to pick up his granddaughters."

Leo stuck out a hand. "Nice to see ya again."

George shook hands with him, but Sarah could tell by his cool reception that he had no desire to become buddies with Leo. That made two of them.

"I came over to see if you had a can of tomato soup I could buy," Leo said to Sarah. "I'm all out."

"I do. And you certainly don't need to pay me. I always keep extras on hand to use in my spaghetti sauce."

"I should get going," George said. "Come on, girls," he called. "Time to go get hamburgers."

That was all it took to send the girls squealing to his car. He gave a casual wave and followed them. He was just driving away when a familiar white truck pulled into the driveway. Out stepped Sam. Her husband's easy, sanguine nature had earned him the nickname Smilin' Sam, but today he wasn't smiling.

"Hi," she called. "What are you doing here?" He'd made it abundantly clear he wouldn't be stopping by on baking-class day.

"Just came home to check on a few things," Sam said, looking at Leo.

"I guess I'll shove off," Leo said.

"Wait. Your soup," said Sarah.

"Oh, yeah. Thanks."

She hurried into the house and fetched soup from the pantry. Both the men remained on the porch. It wasn't like Sam not to invite someone in. She was glad he hadn't stayed true to form today, though. She was pooped.

"Well, I got my money on the Seahawks," Leo was saying. "Ah, there's what I need. Now I can eat tonight. Tomato soup and grilled-cheese sandwiches."

That was all he was having? She had leftover pot roast in the fridge. She opened her mouth to offer him some, but Sam was already bidding Leo good-bye and towing her into the house. What was going on? Was her husband suddenly sex-starved?

"Okay, why are you here?" she demanded as soon as the door shut behind them. If it was bad news of some sort, she wanted it now.

He frowned at her. "I just thought I'd come by and see how you were doing."

"An in-person visit instead of a phone call? What's with the new-and-improved you?" she teased.

"I want you to stop being so friendly to that clown across the street," Sam said firmly. "Every time I turn around the guy is on our porch. And now you've added this George Armstrong."

"George!" she protested. "What do you think I'm going to do with George with his granddaughters running around?"

"They're not around all the time," said Sam. "All these men over when I'm gone, it doesn't look right. Especially Leo."

"Oh, Sam, for heaven's sake," Sarah said in disgust. "Please tell me you didn't decide to stop by to check up on me."

If he hadn't been so serious, she would have laughed. The expression on his face was a mixture of chagrin and anger. "No. I just needed to get something."

Did he really think she was buying that? Sam never bothered to come home to get anything. He was always suckering her into dropping things by the station for him. "Yeah? What?"

"This." He grabbed her and kissed her. Hard.

He hadn't kissed her like that in years. "Sam." *Where have you been hiding?*

Who cared? She grabbed his face and kissed him back, the memory of her frustrating afternoon completely forgotten.

Sam's unneighborly attitude also went forgotten when she came home from the store the day before Thanksgiving, loaded with groceries, and found Leo Steele at her side, offering to help her lug them into the house. Leo was going to be alone on Thanksgiving.

"The boys are going to their mom's." He shrugged.

"She's a better cook. But what the hell?" he said cheerily. "I've got one of those TV dinners—turkey, stuffing, and all the fixings, and there's the football game to watch."

A TV dinner? That was pathetic. The football game would be on here at their house, too, and there would be other men to watch it with. "Come here for dinner," she urged.

"Nah, that's okay. I wouldn't want to impose."

"Don't be silly. Dinner is at two."

"Well, okay. If you're sure," said Leo.

"I'm sure," she said. Sure that Sam would probably not be happy about this newest guest. She should have thought before she spoke. But no one should be alone on Thanksgiving, and making Heart Lake a better place to live meant reaching out to everyone in the community, including Damaris and Leo.

He was barely gone when Sarah heard the front door open, followed by her husband's voice. "Hey, babe. I'm home."

"Out here," she called, and began sorting through possible options for how to tell him about their newest guest.

He came into the kitchen, carrying a newspaper and wearing a smile. "Dad's coming over tonight to play some cribbage. I figured you'd be too busy baking and messing with the table to do anything."

"That's fine," she said, "but first will you help me put the leaf in the table?"

"Sure. How many are coming, anyway?"

"Mom, Dad, us, Jamie . . ."

"Your friend and his family," Sam added. "That makes nine."

Sarah wasn't sure she liked the way he'd said "friend" when referring to George Armstrong. It didn't bode well for Leo. "Actually, we'll have one more," she said, keeping her voice light as meringue.

"Oh, yeah? Who?"

"Leo Steele." This would be a good time to put away the eggs. She opened the refrigerator and hid behind the door.

From the other side she heard her husband's voice, angry and incredulous. "Who?"

SIXTEEN

$\mathcal{M}$y ears have got to be broken," said Sam. "I can't have heard right. You're inviting that clown over when I told you I didn't want him hanging around here?" He walked around the fridge and positioned himself on the other side of Sarah where she could have a good view of his angry face.

She shut the door and went back to her grocery bags, hauling out sugar and flour. "That look may work on those kids at the station," she informed him, "but we've been to-gether too long for it to scare me."

He downgraded from angry to exasperated. "Damn it, Sarah. You're carrying this good deed thing too far."

"How could I not invite him?" she protested.

"Easy. Keep your mouth shut. I don't like the guy."

"Well, I don't, either," said Sarah, "but he's alone. And by gumballs, no one in my neighborhood is going to eat Thanksgiving dinner alone as long as I can stand at a stove."

Sam heaved a long-suffering sigh and pulled her to him. "Okay, you win."

She slipped her arms around his neck and offered him a teasing smile. "You know I'm right."

"You always are," he said, and kissed her. "But if Steele gets too friendly with you I'm going to stuff him like the turkey he is."

"He'll have to catch me first, and I wish him luck with that." On holidays she was always either busy in the kitchen, surrounded by other women, or taking food and plates to and from the table. Leo would be no problem. "It will be fine," she assured Sam. "I just wish the kids were going to be here."

"We'll have 'em both back at Christmas." He shook his head. "What an invasion. Your sister and her family . . ."

"Your folks, half the fire department."

"Ain't it grand?" he said with a grin.

She grinned back. "Yes, it is." And they were on the same page again. It never took long, because she was always right. And Sam knew it, which was what made him the world's best husband.

Jamie arrived early at Sarah's house on Thanksgiving Day, bearing a plate of truffles and the chocolate mint pie that had always been her mom's specialty. "Put me to work," she said. "What do you need done?"

"How about setting the table for me?" suggested Sarah as she popped a tray of herbed biscuits in the oven. "I only got as far as putting on the tablecloth."

"You got it. How many plates this year?"

"Just ten."

"Just ten?" Sarah amazed her. "Who are the extras this time, half the fire station?" asked Jamie.

"Odds and ends of Thanksgiving orphans," said Sarah, "including our neighbor across the street."

"You mean the lech who keeps coming to the bakery?"

"I think he'd use the term 'ladies' man.' "

"Ladies' lech," Jamie corrected. "So, who else?"

Sarah dumped a cube of butter onto a silver butter dish. "John and Edna. Here, you can take this out to the table when you go."

Jamie didn't leave. There was something mildly evasive about Sarah's behavior. "Okay, it's not like I was missing when the brainmobile came. Who else have you invited?"

"Just George Armstrong and his son and grandkids."

George Armstrong. The name didn't ring a bell at first. But it didn't have to. Son, two kids, no wife mentioned. This was a setup. And then she remembered. "The cop," she said, narrowing her eyes.

Sarah stopped mashing potatoes long enough to point the masher at Jamie. "Now, look. I've already had to whip your uncle into shape. Am I going to have to do the same with you?"

That shit didn't work on Jamie. "I already have a mom. Remember?"

"I'm not being your mom. I'm being your aunt—your sweet, loving, taking-you-in-on-Thanksgiving—"

"Matchmaking, meddling aunt," Jamie finished for her.

"Look," Sarah said, switching from combat to negotiation, "they were two men alone for Thanksgiving. I'd have invited them anyway. And the girls need a mother figure."

"Just so it's you they're looking at," Jamie said. She grabbed the butter and marched to the dining room to take Sarah's Wedgwood plates out of the china hutch. Sarah could say what she wanted, but she wasn't fooling anyone. She was matchmaking.

Jamie sighed inwardly. There was a time when she'd have enjoyed flirting with a man, especially a hunkalicious one like Josh the cop. In her twenties, flirting had been her specialty. Then she'd met Grant and decided to specialize. He had seemed like the perfect man, good-looking and generous. And the money he spent on her while they were dating—it made her feel like a princess. She'd envisioned a perfect future with kids, backyard barbecues, and family vacations, but it was too late for all that now. The old flirt muscle had dried up from lack of use, just like other parts of her. Sex was overrated anyway. That's what she heard. Somewhere.

She had just finished setting the table when Sam's parents arrived. John had the ancient-lizard skin of a longtime smoker. He was as thin as the cigarettes he loved and smelled like an ashtray. Edna still kept her hair dyed crayon yellow and was as skinny as her husband.

"Hey, kid, how're ya doin'?" he greeted Jamie in his gravelly John Wayne voice, and gave her a one-armed hug. Then, without waiting for an answer, he ambled into the living room where Sam already had the TV on with the football game playing.

Edna handed over a pie to Sarah and asked, "What can I do to help, dear?"

"How about keeping the boys under control?" Sarah said. "We'll put you to work when it's time to dish up."

Edna nodded, pleased with the arrangement, and followed her husband into the living room.

"They're going to be fighting over that," Jamie cracked, nodding at the pie when she and Sarah were back in the kitchen. Edna's baked goods always smelled like cigarette smoke and tasted worse.

"Sam and I will eat a piece," said Sarah. "And John. He's got no sense of smell."

The next to arrive was Leo Steele, who came bearing a can of black olives and a bouquet of fall flowers from Changing Seasons Floral for Sarah. "I never like to show up empty-handed," he explained. "Want me to put these olives in something?" he added, his gaze sneaking to Sarah's boobs.

Mr. Disgusto. "I can do that," said Jamie, pulling the can out of his hands.

"Why don't you go make yourself at home and watch the game," said Sarah.

"You're sure you don't need any help?" he asked.

"Leo, I had the distinct impression that you don't cook," Sarah teased.

"I don't. But I'm good at doing what I'm told," he retorted.

"Wow, that makes you quite a catch," said Jamie sweetly. "How is it you're single?" Sarah gave her a look that threatened a spanking with a wooden spoon. She just smiled.

"This is my niece, Jamie Moore," said Sarah.

"Nice to meetcha," said Leo genially. Obviously, a man not easily offended. Or else too thickheaded to know when he was being offended. "Guess I'll go check out the game."

"Try to behave yourself, will you?" Sarah scolded when she and Jamie were back in the kitchen alone.

"I'll try. In fact, if you want I'll make up for my rudeness right now and go invite Mr. Steele in here to open these olives. You can show him where the can opener is. I'm sure he'd like to get in your drawers."

"Keep this up and I'll tell Josh it was your idea to invite him here," Sarah countered.

"Okay, okay. I'll be good," Jamie promised. "What do you want me to do next?"

"Whip the cream. That should keep you out of trouble for a couple of minutes."

Jamie was at the sink, whipping cream, when the doorbell rang, announcing the arrival of the last guests. A tingle of excitement threaded its way up her spine. She told herself it was dread.

The low rumble of male voices, accented by the little-girl excitement, drifted in to the kitchen. A moment later, two little girls were entering alongside Sarah, who was saying, "I'll bet you're just in time to lick the beaters."

Mandy the Fairy had taken Sarah's hand and was skipping beside her while the older girl walked carefully, bearing a casserole dish in front of her as if it were frankincense. "We brought green bean casserole," she announced.

"You can put it right on the table," said Sarah, pointing to her old drop-leaf kitchen table.

She'd had that table ever since Jamie could remember. They'd played countless games of cards at it and probably eaten enough pizza to fill Heart Lake. Jamie and her sister, Krysten, had sat there opposite each other, licking beaters laden with everything from chocolate frosting to whipped cream. She stopped her whipping and pulled out the beaters. "You're just in time," she said, and handed one to each girl. "Make yourselves at home. That's what I did when I was a kid."

"Yum," said Mandy, taking hers with eyes as big as her smile.

"Are you Mrs. Goodwin's daughter?" asked Lissa.

"Almost," said Jamie. "I'm her niece."

"Our mommy's an angel," said Mandy, taking a big lick of whipped cream.

It was a good thing Jamie wasn't holding the beaters anymore, she'd have dropped them. Dead? His wife was dead? She'd assumed he was divorced, screwed up.

Like he wouldn't be screwed up from having lost his wife? The poor guy. The poor girls. Jamie felt a sudden nearly overwhelming desire to grab them both and hug them.

"Grandpa says maybe someday we'll get a new mommy," Mandy continued.

"Maybe you will," Jamie agreed. They were sweet girls. They deserved another mommy. She could see Emma as their new mom, teaching them to quilt, dunking them in hydrogen peroxide when that demon cat of hers scratched them. But she couldn't see Emma with Josh. Odd.

"Girls," said Sarah, "would you like to help us put the food on the table?"

"Sure," said Lissa as if she'd just been offered a special prize.

Maybe for a little girl who was being raised by men—rather like being raised by wolves—the company of women was a prize. It was easy to take family for granted. You never realized what you had till you lost it.

Sarah became a kitchen general, marshaling her troops. Edna and the girls were put to work hustling steaming bowls of mashed potatoes, savory stuffing, rutabagas, peas, and Sarah's biscuits out to the big mahogany dining table while Jamie served in the kitchen as her right-hand woman, dishing up from the stove and pulling things from the fridge. The array of dishes seemed endless: candied yams, cranberry sauce, fruit salad, pickles and olives, and, of course, the green bean casserole Lissa had so carefully carried in. Last of all came the turkey, big enough to feed a whole boatload of Pilgrims.

The guests gathered at the table and Sarah continued directing operations. "John, Edna, how about taking your usual places over there. And Leo next to them. Then George. Josh, you can sit next to Sam. Jamie, how about sitting by me. And let's put the girls between you and Josh."

So she and Josh could get some kind of subliminal message about what a great family they'd all make, of course. Boy, Sarah never missed a trick. But it was her party, so Jamie didn't argue. Some of the manners her mom had worked so hard to drill into her had stuck.

She couldn't help smirking when Leo pretended to have misunderstood and took George's seat, placing himself next to Sarah. Just punishment for her meddling.

But she put on her polite hostess smile and sat down.

Jamie sneaked a peek in Sam's direction to see how he liked the new seating arrangement. He looked like he'd just guzzled vinegar.

"Sam, would you say grace?" Sarah asked.

"Sure," he said grudgingly, and bowed his head with a frown. "Dear God, we thank you for all the good things you give us, for this feast, and for our family. For those who don't have family, we pray that you'd help them find some."

The sooner the better? Jamie thought as everyone said, "Amen." If that last sentence were meant to be some sort of message to Leo, it was way too subtle. Out of the corner of her eye, she saw Mandy looking up at her. She turned to smile at the child and found her sister also looking her way with an eager-to-please smile.

Josh caught it all. He quickly looked away and reached for the mashed potatoes as Sam set to work carving the turkey.

"Dad, dark meat for you," Sam said as his father passed his plate. "And white for Mom. What'll you have, George?"

"If nobody wants it, I'll take one of those legs," said George.

"How about you, Leo?" asked Sam.

"I like the breast," said Leo.

He got the other leg.

Sarah frowned at Sam, who said, "Sorry, the breast is all taken."

Leo shrugged. "No big deal. I like legs, too. These green beans are my favorite," he said to Sarah, dishing himself up a hearty serving.

"Don't get too excited," Sam told him. "Sarah didn't make them."

"My daddy made that," Mandy said proudly. "We helped."

"It's good," Jamie said to her, and was rewarded with a worshipful smile.

"So, you can cook, huh?" Sam said to Josh. "You're pretty self-sufficient."

"Between the two of us, Dad and I do okay," said Josh.

"That's all well and good, but there are some things a man needs a woman for," Leo said.

Sam frowned and Sarah blushed. She grabbed the bowl of biscuits and handed them to Jamie. "How about passing these around?"

Jamie bit back a smile. Poor Sarah. This was not going to go down in history as the most successful dinner party she'd ever had.

After the main course and kitchen cleanup, everyone settled in the living room to play charades. The grown-ups kept it easy, throwing in plenty of books, songs, and movies the girls would know. George earned applause for acting out *Kung Fu Panda,* and Jamie helped Mandy act out *The Cat in the Hat.* A few grown-up songs got thrown into the mix though, and Jamie drew Bryan Adams's "When You Love Someone." What a joke. But she gamely acted it out anyway.

After the last charade had been guessed Sarah sprawled in her chair and said, "I'm pooped. Jamie, how about taking care of the pie orders for me?" Edna opened her mouth to offer to help, but Sarah was too fast for her. "Josh, it's tradition for the men to help with dessert."

"Since when?" protested Sam.

"Since now," Sarah informed him.

"Can we help?" asked Lissa.

"Absolutely," Jamie told her.

In the kitchen, Josh asked, "Is she always this subtle?"

"Always. It's a family trait."

"I've noticed." He shot her a smile. "You still pissed at me for stopping you?"

"You never gave me a ticket. Nothing to be pissed about," said Jamie with a shrug. Just because she wasn't falling all over herself to snag him, he thought she was pissed? There was a bit of ego for you. She concentrated on lining all the pies up on the kitchen table. "Lissa, you can get the whipped cream out of the fridge. It's in that big yellow bowl."

"What can I do?" asked Mandy.

"As soon as I start putting the pie on plates you can carry them out to people." She handed a small tablet and pen to Lissa, who had now returned with the whipped cream. "Now, you can go out and take orders, see who wants what. We have apple, pecan, pumpkin, and chocolate mint."

Lissa nodded and scurried off.

"What should I do, boss?" asked Josh.

Go away. This man was stirring up hormones that had been hibernating for way too long. "You know, you really don't have to be out here."

"I know," he said. "I want to."

"Then I guess you can help me cut the pies." She found another pie cutter and handed it to him and he positioned himself next to her. Her head came up to his shoulder. What would it be like to lean her head against that strong chest?

What would a man this big be like in a towering rage? That last thought drenched the fire growing within her immediately. Of course he'd have a temper. All men had tempers.

"So, I guess I was just imagining that you were pissed when I stopped to help you change that flat tire the other day."

"You were ruining my good deed."

He nodded slowly. "Ah. So it's not that you don't like cops."

"I didn't say that. I was married to one."

"Not good?" he guessed.

"There's an understatement."

"We're not all pigs."

"Daddy is a pig," put in Mandy. "He eats a lot."

Josh rumpled her hair. "Is that so?"

Mandy nodded and smiled up at him adoringly. So maybe not all cops were created equal.

Or maybe this one simply hadn't cracked yet. Jamie couldn't help but remember the story of the Tacoma police chief who killed his wife and then shot himself. That could have been her if she'd stayed with Grant. An image crashed into her mind—Grant showing her his service revolver and telling her, "Just remember, baby, accidents happen." How did you ever know when the pressure would get to a man, when too much of the violence and the dark side of human nature would finally make him crack and turn him into something as dark as what he dealt with? It was a crap shoot.

Gambling was for fools.

"Are you cold?" asked Josh. "You're shivering."

She forced herself to come back to the moment at hand, cutting into the pecan pie. "No. I'm fine." Just fine, just as she was.

So when the day finally ended and they were all leaving and Josh said to her, "So, I'll see you around?" she made sure he got the message loud and clear.

"It's possible. It's a small town."

The shutters fell on his open smile. Good. He'd gotten the message.

Emma returned home from her family Thanksgiving feast with a special treat for the man in her life: turkey. Not the entire contents from the foil-wrapped packet Mom had sent home with her, but a nice-sized chunk.

"Pye, Mommy has something for you," she sang as she walked in the door.

Pyewacket immediately appeared, trotting down the hall, tail held high.

"Were you a good boy while I was gone?" she asked.

He rubbed against her legs like a normal cat, like a cat who loved his mommy. Like a cat who smelled turkey.

Baby steps, she told herself. Right now he loves me for my turkey. Someday he'll love me for myself. She set the foil packet on the table, opened it, and pulled off a piece of turkey from the pile sitting atop the mound of stuffing. "You're going to love this." She proffered the treat.

Pyewacket advanced and took it in one delicate bite. Then he squatted down and proceeded to enjoy the feast.

She put out a hand and petted her boy. He didn't hiss or scratch her. He simply took his turkey and left.

She stood and sighed. "Someday you're going to love me," she called after him. But when?

Winning the love of an orphaned black cat was the least of her problems, she reminded herself. If she didn't turn her business around pretty soon Pye would be homeless again and so would she. Well, okay. She wouldn't be homeless. She'd be living with her parents and looking for a job. And her baby would be at the animal shelter on kitty death row since Mom was allergic to cats. No one would adopt him because the little guy was about as far from lovable as a cat could get.

What was she going to do?

Be thankful, she told herself. *You got a free meal today and have leftovers for tomorrow. It's more than half the world's population gets.*

She could hear Mrs. Nitz's TV blaring through the duplex wall. What was Mrs. Nitz doing home? Didn't she have any place to go on Thanksgiving?

Emma looked at the foil-wrapped bundle of leftovers

sitting on her table. Nobody made stuffing like Mom. It would taste so good tomorrow.

It would taste even better today, and Mrs. Nitz probably loved stuffing. Who didn't? Emma slipped back out and went to bang on her neighbor's door. She'd already had her feast, and, after his stuck-up behavior, a certain cat sure didn't deserve any more treats.

SEVENTEEN

Josh couldn't get Mrs. Kravitz out of his mind. Had the woman been alone on Thanksgiving? Had she gotten rid of Godzilla Rat? Would anyone ever paint and repair those shutters?

The day after Thanksgiving was chilly but sunny—a perfect day to nail up shutters.

His dad agreed, so ten A.M. found Josh and his family on Mrs. Kravitz's front porch, Lissa holding out a plate of the cookies she'd learned to bake from Sarah.

"We thought you could use a couple of handymen," Josh explained.

Her face lit up like he'd just told her she'd won the Publishers Clearinghouse Sweepstakes. "Oh, how sweet!"

"These are for you," added Lissa, holding out the plate.

"They look delicious. Did you make them yourself?"

"My sister helped."

"Well, you're both very talented," said Mrs. Kravitz. "Come in, everyone. I'll make a pot of coffee."

Josh was ready to get to work, but he knew the

importance of the ritual cup of coffee. So he sat and drank, and let Mrs. Kravitz sing his praises to his dad and get their whole family history.

With the girls right there they brushed past the whole thing of Crystal's death at the speed of light and Mrs. Kravitz got the message and changed the subject. But the quick conversation opened the door to a corner of Josh's heart where he only got trapped late at night after the house grew silent and he'd crawled into bed alone.

Crystal. When he lost her it was like a psychic cleaver had cut off part of him, and the dark emptiness of night brought the ache back like a phantom pain. So he always turned on his radio and put himself to sleep listening to the late-night talk shows. He'd recently stumbled on a great program where the host interviewed scientists with far-out theories and people who claimed to have been kidnapped by aliens. And, if he was lucky, he'd only dream about UFOs and he'd wake up rested and ready to check off another day on the calendar. Checking off days, it was a shitty way to live, but he'd been doing it long enough now that he was good at it.

"You would have loved this town, babe," he murmured as he got to work with his hammer and nails.

And what would she have thought of Jamie Moore? Would Crystal have considered her good mother material? The girls sure seemed to like her. And they weren't the only ones. Jamie had made his radar in a big way. She was a little bit of a thing, the kind of woman a man felt compelled to protect.

But Jamie had made it pretty obvious that she didn't need protecting, at least not from him. The only woman he'd met since Crystal who even remotely interested him and she didn't like cops. It just figured. Well, he and the girls and Dad had a good life here. They were doing okay.

He gave the last nail in the shutter an exceptionally hard

pound. At the rate he was going, it was going to be a long time before his girls got a new mother. And it was going to be a long, long time before he got laid.

"Sarah and I are going in to Seattle on Sunday to hit the Thanksgiving-weekend sales," Jamie told Emma. "Want to come? I'll pay for your lunch."

Emma propped the phone between her shoulder and ear as she made the final touches on her Thanksgiving blow-out sign for her store window. "I can't. I'm going to be open on Sunday for my forty-percent-off sale."

There was a moment of silence on the other end of the line. Then, "Em, are you sure you want to mark off so much?"

It was an insanely drastic markdown; she knew that. "If I don't do something to move my inventory I'm not going to be able to pay my rent, let alone my small-business loan." Pulling up those words made Emma's voice tremble.

"I'm really sorry," Jamie said. "So many people quilt. I just don't get why you're not making it."

"Because people would rather get a bargain than support a local business," Emma said bitterly. It was a different world from when her grandpa did business. He and Grandma bought their washer and dryer from Anderson's Appliance, filled their prescriptions at Vern's, and supported the little local grocery store until the Safeway came to town and Pop's was finally forced to close its doors. "People just don't care like they used to." She sighed. "You were right to sell chocolate. You'll always be in business."

"Well, don't give up. The sale might be just what you need to prime the pump," Jamie said.

Who was she kidding? The well of human kindness in Heart Lake was running dry and no amount of priming was going to help. Emma hung up, thoroughly depressed. All these efforts to get people to do good deeds were a waste of time. The bottom line was, people didn't care.

You can't think that way, she scolded herself. People were basically good. They were just ignorant and had to be taught. A sale would lure in new customers. She'd talk up her quilting classes, drop big hints about the importance of shopping locally, and things would change. Quitters never win and winners never quit. She had to remember that.

She'd just hung up the sign when Shirley Schultz wandered into the shop. "You're having a sale?"

For Shirley, who would, of course, conveniently forget her checkbook, it would end up being a giveaway.

No, she had to be firm. "Cash or credit card only," she said in her sweetest, cheery voice, "so don't forget to stop by the bank."

Shirley frowned. "I don't like to carry cash. I'll try to remember my checkbook."

"I'm sorry, Mrs. Schultz, but I'm afraid, with such a deep discount, I'm going to have to take only cash or credit cards tomorrow," Emma said firmly.

Shirley's thin lips fell down at the corners. "Well, I would think you'd want to accommodate your loyal customers."

Accommodate? Shirley had probably absconded with enough free merchandise to set a record. "I try to accommodate all my customers," Emma said. She kept her smile only by sheer willpower. "So, is there anything I can help you with today?"

"No, I don't think so," said Shirley, her voice icy.

"Well, then I hope we'll see you tomorrow."

"Probably not," she said, and marched out the door.

"Well, there goes my best worst customer," Emma muttered, as she watched Shirley storm off down the street, her worn coat flapping behind her. Now she could see Shirley had run into Ruth Weisman. Shirley's mouth was going about a mile a minute, and with her stiff posture and glowering face, it wasn't hard to guess what she was talking about. "That's right. Go ahead and blank out on all those times you 'forgot' your checkbook and still walked out of here with a bag full of fabric," Emma grumbled. She probably shouldn't have rocked the boat with Shirley. Bad angel karma. But all her good deeds really hadn't done much good anyway. She was living with a cat who barely tolerated her, her business was on the verge of going belly-up, and she couldn't even afford to have any fun with Tess in *My World.*

Every heroine has dark moments, Emma reminded herself. *Think of Katharine Hepburn's character in* The African Queen. *She lost her brother and her home and nearly died. But in the end, she took out a German gunship and found true love.*

You're not Katharine Hepburn.

Well, that said it all.

Ruth was in the shop now. "I hear you've got a sale coming up tomorrow. I guess I'll wait to get my fabric then."

"You may as well," Emma said. She knew her voice was flat. She probably looked like a droopy, old basset hound, but she couldn't help it.

Ruth studied her a moment, then said, "What the heck. I need fabric today."

Bless you, thought Emma.

"And good for you for holding Shirley's feet to the fire. I haven't seen her so mad since the bank stopped giving away free toasters for new accounts."

Emma sighed. "I probably shouldn't have done that. Poor Shirley is just squeaking by."

"Like heck she is," Ruth said with a snort. "She lives

on the lake and I know for a fact she's got half a million in the bank. I heard her bragging about it to the teller just last week."

"But her clothes."

"She's proud of the fact that she dresses like a bag lady. That's one of her secrets to success, along with suckering local merchants into letting her get away with murder."

Emma shook her head. "I think I'm the world's biggest sucker."

Ruth smiled. "That's because you've got the world's biggest heart."

"Big hearts don't pay big bills," Emma muttered.

"No, they don't. Remember that," Ruth said sternly. "And don't give up. It takes time to build a business."

And a small fortune, which Emma didn't have, but she nodded and smiled gamely. "You're right." Things have a way of working out. That was what Mom always said. She hoped Mom was right and things would start working out tomorrow.

It looked like a good sign when Emma woke up to an overcast day. But no rain. That was the best weather for a merchant in the Pacific Northwest. When it was rainy and cold, people often opted for socking in with a fire in the fireplace rather than venturing out to shop. When the sun was out, potential shoppers played outside in their yards, went on picnics, drove to the mountains. But a day like today? Perfect for shopping.

All she had to do was sell enough fabric to make her shop rent. She was sure Mr. Pressman at the bank would be patient for his money. But hey, why think small? Maybe she would have tons of customers this weekend and she'd be able to make both her rent and her business loan payment. She hoped she wouldn't have to float another loan from Mom and Dad for her rent at home.

"It's hard to start a business," Mom always said. "We're happy to help you. You're going to get it all some-day anyway. We'd rather help you now, when you really need it." But they'd done so much already. She couldn't keep being such a drain on her family. It was do-or-die time.

Whoa, was that minicrowd of women outside her shop all for her? She gawked as she drove past the front en-trance on Lake Way and turned down the little cobble-stone alley that held more shops.

It was a cute little no-name street that housed a travel agency, real estate office, a day spa, and a hair salon. Re-cently, Kizzy's Kitchen had relocated there, too. The rent was cheaper than on Lake Way and those shops still had a Lake Way address. Many a time, as Emma had passed them to turn and park in back of her more expensive build-ing, she'd wished she'd opted for a less prominent and cheaper location.

At least you have customers today, she told herself. Maybe she would make her rent this month. She parked in back of the long building that housed her shop as well as Changing Seasons Floral and Something You Need Gifts, her heart skipping with excitement. Of course, it would have been nice if this many people came in when she wasn't having a lose-your-shirt sale, but oh, well. It was a beginning. Maybe some of them would sign up for her quilting class, maybe some would tell their friends. She'd get people started on her punch card. People loved punch cards that promised them a bargain after they had pur-chased so much merchandise.

She hurried into the shop, shed her coat, and ran to open the front door. "Welcome, ladies," she sang.

Smiling, they surged past her, with—surprise, surprise—Shirley in the lead. Emma recognized one of the women as the Savemart devotee who had sneered at her overpriced fabric. Well, she'd like to see Savemart compete with her prices now.

"Does the forty percent include patterns?" asked the woman.

"No, sorry. Only fabric," said Emma.

The woman frowned and made a beeline for Emma's most expensive fabric.

As Emma watched, her earlier euphoria evaporated. An image crept into her mind of buzzards picking at the carcass of some poor dead animal in Death Valley. You're not dead yet, she told herself firmly.

"Great sale," said her friend Kerrie, coming up to the counter with a couple of bolts of fabric. "I want to sign up for your quilting class."

"I thought you were too busy with Nesta to start quilting," said Emma, surprised.

"It's slowly dawning on me that I'm going to be busy with Nesta for a lot of years. I may as well start having a life. This will be something fun I can do when she's napping."

Emma was ringing up her purchases when Shirley came to the counter, practically lost under a pile of fabric finds.

"Wow, aren't you ambitious," Emma greeted her.

"A girl's got to take advantage of the sales," said Shirley playfully, her irritation from the day before forgotten.

Hopefully, she wasn't going to take advantage of the shop owner. Emma took Kerrie's money, gave her two punches on her punch card and her fabric, and then sent her on her way. She turned her attention to Shirley, who had heaved her finds onto the cutting counter.

"I want two yards of each," Shirley said. "Oh, and lets add two spools of white thread, too."

"Okay." Should she ask Shirley now if she'd brought cash or just trust that she had? Emma opted for trust and cut the fabric.

"And I brought my cash," Shirley said, scrabbling around in her purse as Emma worked.

Hallelujah.

But when Emma rang up her purchases Shirley's face fell. "I only brought a ten," she said, setting the bill on the counter.

And she'd spent almost thirty. Surely she hadn't expected to buy so much for so little. Very sneaky to announce her money shortage after Emma had cut the fabric. Emma was nearly overcome with a strong desire to wrap a measuring tape around Shirley's scrawny neck and squeeze.

"I'll come in tomorrow with the rest," Shirley promised.

Okay, Shirley could live another day. "Great," Emma said with a smile. She put the fabric in a bag and slipped it onto the little shelf behind the counter. "I'll hold it here for you."

Shirley gaped at her. "Oh, but I wanted to take it today."

Emma was suddenly aware of other women hovering nearby, listening. One of them was the Savemart woman. She should stand her ground with Shirley. Otherwise everyone would think she was a soft touch. Or maybe they'd think she was heartless.

But all this had nothing to do with heart. It had to do with running a business. Her big heart had been part of her problem. Big heart, little brain, bad combination.

She opened her mouth to say, "Sorry. No can do." Instead, she took the ten and handed over the bag, saying, "Go ahead and take the fabric."

Idiot. You deserve to go out of business. What are you thinking? Panic welled up in her the minute the words were out of her mouth. She'd be bankrupt or paying off her business loan until she was fifty. She lowered her voice. "But please, Mrs. Schultz, bring me the rest of what you owe me tomorrow. I really need to balance my books." *And pay my rent.*

Ruth was at the counter next. She gave Emma a pene-
trating look, the kind her mother always gave her when
she was pretending everything was okay. "Are you in
trouble, Emma?"

"What do you mean?" she stammered. Oh, this was not
good. A woman couldn't go around telling her customers
she was a failure. If only she were Tess L'amour, confident
and successful. She tried to get in touch with her inner Tess
and smile as if she didn't have a care in the world.

"You know what I mean," Ruth said sternly. "If you're
going to stay in business you can't keep letting mooches
like Shirley have a free ride."

"You're right," she said. "That's great advice." She
blinked hard to keep back the tears. Too bad the advice
was coming too late. She was going down the financial
tubes, forty-percent-off sale and all.

EIGHTEEN

$\mathcal{N}$ow, this is what I call a sale," Jamie said as she and Sarah sifted through a pile of women's sweaters stacked in front of a BUY ONE GET ONE FREE sign. It was Sunday afternoon and the mall was crowded with Thanksgiving weekend shoppers. So was this store. Did Emma have a crowd at her shop today? Jamie picked up a mint-green cashmere sweater. "Does this scream Emma or what?"

"I could see her in that," Sarah agreed.

"I think I'll get it for her for Christmas." Emma would, of course, love the sweater . . . if she didn't drown herself in the lake before Christmas. Jamie chewed her lip for a minute. "Do you think she's doing okay?"

Sarah frowned at the sweater in her hand. "No."

"You know, she actually lets people get away without paying? I'm worried about her. I think she's pretty much burned through her savings and she's got that big loan to pay off and I don't know how she's going to do it if her shop goes under."

Sarah shook her head. "I've thought several times of

suggesting she sell the shop, but I just can't bring myself to say something, not when she's so passionate about quilting."

"Make that *was* passionate about quilting," said Jamie. "These days it seems she'd rather watch movies or play on the Internet."

"Avoidance. Probably even working on her own projects reminds her of the mess with the shop."

"So, what are we going to do?"

Sarah shook her head. "I don't know. If I had a fortune I'd bail her out."

Jamie scowled. "Sometimes it sucks not to be rich."

"Sometimes it sucks to be in business for yourself," said Sarah. "We all take a chance. If she goes under we'll just have to help her the best we can."

"I'd rather find a way to help her before she goes under."

"Me, too," said Sarah.

They both stood there for a moment, staring at the sweaters. Finally, Jamie asked, "Could you use some fabric?"

Sarah smiled. "By gumballs, that's just what I need."

"Isn't that funny? I don't know how many times I've driven down this street and never noticed this shop," said the woman as Emma rang up her purchase.

With those Coke-bottle glasses her customer was wearing, Emma was surprised she could even see the street.

"My daughter wants to start quilting. This book will make a perfect Christmas present for her. I'll tell her about your quilting classes. Maybe she'll want to sign up in the new year."

Maybe Emma would be in business in the new year, but probably not. It was almost three in the afternoon and she suspected this woman was the tail end of her customers.

She'd made enough in the last two days to pay her rent, but the business loan hung over her like the sword of Damocles.

She forced a smile. "That's very kind of you. Quilting is a wonderful way to express yourself creatively."

"I agree," the woman said as the shop door opened. "It's so nice to find a shop right here in Heart Lake."

"It sure is," said Jamie. "Hey, are we too late for the sale?"

Friends were like a quilt for the heart, Emma decided, looking at their smiling faces. She suddenly felt warm from the inside out. "You're just in time."

"Good, 'cause we need to do some serious shopping," Jamie informed her, and aimed herself in the general direction of the batiks, her designer-knockoff boots clacking on the floor as she went.

"How did the sale go?" Sarah asked after Jamie's customer had found the door and left.

Emma pasted on a big smile. "Great. Lots of people. At least more than usual," she added honestly.

"Are you going to make your rent?"

"Absolutely." And please don't ask me about my loan.

"I've got a spare couple hundred."

That made Emma want to cry. If only everyone in Heart Lake were like Sarah and Jamie, it would be heaven. Or at least Bedford Falls.

Jamie dumped half a dozen bolts of fabric on the cutting counter. "How will these work for a wall hanging?"

Jamie's selection looked completely random. Emma raised a suspicious eyebrow. "What do you want your theme to be?"

"Um."

"Just as I thought. Go put those back." It hadn't been that long since both she and Sarah had been in the shop, buying merchandise they'd never use. She couldn't let them do it again.

Jamie laid an arm over the fabric in front of her to ensure it stayed put. "I will not."

"I know what you're up to," Emma informed her. And it was really sweet. But Jamie wasn't made of money.

"You do not. Now, are you going to help me or do I have to go to Savemart?"

Just the mention of her fabric nemesis was enough to make Emma want to throw up. "Don't use the S-word in my shop."

"I won't if you quit being a stubborn brat and help me," Jamie said sweetly.

"You may as well give up," said Sarah. "We're still in sale-shopping mode and we can't be stopped."

"You mean rescue mode," Emma corrected.

"You'd do the same for us," said Jamie. "Anyway, Christmas is coming. This is going to be a present."

Emma gave up. "Okay, let's take a step back. Who is it for?"

Jamie shot an uncertain look at Sarah. "My mom?"

"Does your mom like florals or modern colors? And what's her décor? Is she country, French provincial?"

Jamie's eyes were starting to glaze over.

"Country," said Sarah. "And maybe you should do something with a Christmas theme," she suggested to Jamie. "In fact, I think that's what I'll do."

Last Emma had heard Sarah hadn't even finished the quilts for her granddaughters. She raised an eyebrow. "Because you're just a quilting machine?"

"You know the expression: so little time, so much fabric," Sarah retorted. She moved from the counter to the fabric section. "Oh, here's a great Christmas green. Have you got any fabric with holly on it?"

"Have I got fabric with holly!" Emma joined her and pulled down two bolts. "And here's a fun Santa print."

Half an hour later, Sarah and Jamie had spent a small fortune and proclaimed themselves excited to go home and make wall hangings.

Of course, it was all a bunch of hoo-ha. "You guys are the best," Emma told them. She was going to cry.

"Not really," said Sarah. "This is a bargain basement opportunity to do something special for Christmas presents."

"But Christmas of what year?" teased Emma. "Maybe you'd better let me help you."

"Good idea. Let's start now. Come on over to my house and we can cut fabric," Sarah suggested. "I've got plenty of Thanksgiving leftovers."

It was exactly what Emma's flagging spirits needed. She closed up shop, got in her car, and followed her friends to Sarah's place. Sam was home and had built a fire in the fireplace and Sarah made them all turkey sandwiches while Jamie put on a Michael Bublé CD.

Eating at Sarah's dining room table, softly serenaded, Emma reminded herself how lucky she was. Okay, so her shop was in trouble. But she had friends, and no woman was really poor who had friends.

She stayed at Sarah's house for two hours, making sure she got Sarah and Jamie on the right track with their projects, and then left for home. Alone in her car, she couldn't escape reliving her day, and as she backed further up in time she remembered her mom's words when Mom and Grandma came into the shop. "Gosh, I thought you'd be swamped."

"That was yesterday," Emma had said.

It hadn't been enough to remove the worry lines from Mom's forehead. And now it wasn't enough to keep Emma from sliding back into the blues. "It will work out," she told herself as she unlocked her front door. Things had a way of working out. The sad part was that they didn't always work out the way you wanted them to.

She opened the door, juggling the goodies Sarah had sent home with her with the bag of groceries she'd gotten at Safeway. "Mommy's home," she called, forcing her voice to sound cheerful so she wouldn't upset the baby.

She barely made it in the door when her grocery bag burst, dropping cans of cat food like bombs. One bounced off her foot, making her yelp in pain. Another rolled down the hall.

As she bent to pick it up, something at the end of the hall caught her attention. Dirt. And sticking out from behind the archway she could just see the leaves of the corn plant Mom had given her lying lifeless on the living room floor like the telltale hand of a dead body.

She hurried down the hall to find her new plant had been knocked off its stand. The pot lay in pieces and there was dirt everywhere. And there, in the middle of the floor, cleaning himself, sat the culprit.

"Pyewacket! You are the worst cat ever!"

As if he cared. He loved being the worst cat ever, delighted in it. He combed a paw over his head, smoothing his silky black fur. No one had told him that pretty is as pretty does.

"Are you listening to me?" Of course he wasn't. She stamped her foot and clapped her hands together, making him jump and scoot out of the room. "That's it," she called after him. "I'm taking you to the animal shelter where you can never destroy anything again!"

Pye didn't stop to regard her with his usual look of superior unconcern. This time he kept right on running. A black cat behind disappeared out the front door, which she'd stupidly left open in her haste to get to her plant corpse.

Oh, no! He hadn't been outside since the day she brought him in. She hurried down the hall to the front door. "Pye?"

There was no sign of Pyewacket. She stood in the doorway, listening for a meow, a yowl, even a kitty growl. Nothing. "Pye? Here, kitty, kitty. Mommy's sorry. I didn't mean it about the animal shelter. Really." She stepped out onto the porch and peered under the juniper bush. No Pye. She hurried down the walk, calling his name. Nothing. It was freezing and a cold rain was misting down. Rubbing her arms, she turned and went back to the front door. She called his name one last time. Nothing.

He'll be back, she told herself as she shut the door. He'll get scared and cold and he'll come home.

She put away her food. Then she opened the front door to see if Pye was on the doorstep. He wasn't.

She cleaned up the mess, then spent a little time seeing what was new in *My World*. After that she checked her e-mails. A friend had sent her a cat picture from Cute Overload and she quickly closed it. She put her computer to sleep and opened the front door one last time. No Pye.

"Okay, fine," she yelled. "Stay out in the cold all night. I hope it rains dogs on you!"

She slammed the door and went and took a bath. Once she was comfortable in her jammies she fetched her quilt in progress, put on her DVD of *Sabrina,* and settled into her chair to do some basting. And just as the new and improved Sabrina was making her Cinderella appearance at the Larrabee family bash, she pricked her finger.

"Damn!" She dropped the quilt on her lap. "Damn!" she repeated because the first one had felt so good. Then, possessed by temporary insanity, she shoved the quilt onto the floor and stood up and swore one more time because, of course, the third time was the charm. But it wasn't. So she hooked a toe under the stupid, who-cared-if-it-ever-got-done-piece-of-poop quilt and kicked it. It lifted like a big bat and fell in folds at her feet. She stepped on it. Then she jumped on it. And stabbed her toe on a pin. She picked it up to rip to pieces with her bare hands and instead burst into tears.

Still crying, she dropped the quilt, turned off the TV, and went to bed and indulged in a good cry. By the time she was done she had a major headache going. "Stop it," she scolded herself as she went to the medicine cabinet for aspirin. "It's just a stray cat. A stupid stray cat."

She got into bed and burrowed under the covers. She hoped Pye would be okay. She hoped she would be okay.

NINETEEN

"It's my birthday on Saturday," Damaris announced at the next baking class. She gave invitations to the other girls much like a queen handing out gifts. "You can all come to my party. My mom rented *High School Musical Reunion* on Netflix. And I'm having a *High School Musical* cake."

"Awesome," breathed Lissa.

"And we're gonna make jewelry," Damaris continued. "My mom bought beads. You can all bring me *High School Musical* stuff."

"Very considerate," Sarah said, "helping your friends out with gift ideas."

Of course, her sarcasm was lost on Damaris. She was beaming. "Now that I'm ten Mom says I can have a cell phone, and I get to get my ears pierced."

"My dad won't let me get my ears pierced till I'm thirteen," Lissa grumbled.

"There's nothing wrong with waiting," Sarah assured

her. "And thirteen is a great time to get your ears pierced. You have a special way to kick off your teen years."

"My mom said she had her ears pierced when she was a baby," said Damaris.

Damaris was obviously going to grow up to be a lawyer. She had a comeback for everything. "Okay, ladies," Sarah said, "let's talk and work at the same time. Wash your hands and we'll get started."

Handwashing went without incident, but it was all downhill from there. Creaming together eggs, sugar, and butter should have been easy. Mash up butter and sugar. Crack the eggs in a separate bowl to ensure the cookie dough stayed free of shells. Then dump in with butter and sugar. But somewhere between bowls the eggs got lost, slurping down the side of the counter.

"Way to go," said Damaris, probably channeling one of her older brothers.

"It's okay," Sarah told Mandy, who was responsible for the mishap and looked teary. "We'll just clean this up and start again."

And that was when the phone rang. Caller ID warned Sarah that it was Betty, but she couldn't not answer, not when Betty's granddaughter was at her house. Maybe Betty needed to talk to Beanie.

"I just picked up some Cheetos," said Betty. "Do the girls need a snack? Should I bring them over?"

"Oh, I think we're fine here," said Sarah. She'd already filled the after-school empty corners with nachos. Hey, she could be taught.

"I'll get more eggs," said Beanie, opening the refrigerator.

"I can get them," said Damaris, crowding in next to her.

"I'll get them," Beanie insisted, her voice rising as Damaris grabbed for the carton.

"Are you sure?" asked Betty. "Because it's no problem to drop them by."

Now the girls were having a tug-of-war. "Girls," Sarah said, working hard to stay serene and patient, "just wait to take the eggs out of the fridge till I'm—"

Splat.

"Off the phone."

"You dropped all the eggs," Damaris accused Beanie. "Now we can't bake cookies."

"You made me," Beanie retorted. "I'm sorry, Mrs. Goodwin," she wailed, looking at the mess on the floor.

"It's okay," said Sarah. "It was an accident."

"Is everything okay over there?" asked Betty.

"I want to make cookies," Mandy said in a small voice.

"We will," Sarah said calmly. "Betty, have you got a couple of eggs I can borrow?"

"Oh, of course. I'll be right over," said Betty.

Goody.

"Hey, there's one that's not broken," cried Damaris.

"I'll get it," said Beanie, diving for the egg.

"It's okay, girls. I'll get it." Sarah went for the egg, anxious to head off a wrestling match on her kitchen floor. Her left foot made contact with something slimy. And slippery. Like a skater in trouble, she windmilled her arms, then went down on her bottom with an oomph to a chorus of squeals.

Damaris burst out laughing. "Oh, my gosh, Mrs. Goodwin. That was just like on AFV. If we'd taped that and sent it in you could have won ten thousand dollars."

Which she then could have used to pay the doctor to put her back together again.

The doorbell rang.

"I'll get it," said Damaris.

"It's my grandma. I'll get it," said Beanie, racing after

her down the hall. Both were probably tracking raw egg all over the carpet in the process.

Meanwhile, Sarah had her hands full focusing on getting off the floor. She tried to stand and found a fresh egg-white puddle to slip in. Down she went again. Oh, this was such fun. Who was the idiot who thought it would be a good idea to teach little girls to bake?

She finally grabbed the counter and hauled herself up with Lissa attempting to help her.

"Are you okay?" asked Lissa.

It could have been worse. At least she'd landed on her most padded end. But she had managed to wrench her back. It was going to be a two-Advil night. "I'm fine," she said, as much to herself as the child.

"Egads, what a mess." Now Betty was in the kitchen, holding a carton of eggs and a bag of Cheetos and gawking at the puddle on the floor.

"We had a little accident," said Sarah. "But everything's under control." Somewhere in the universe this was true.

Betty looked dubiously at Sarah's egg-slopped jeans.

"It's okay," Sarah assured her.

"Do you want me to help you clean this up?" Betty offered.

"No, no. We'll be fine. We'll be back on track in no time." Sarah took two eggs from the carton and cracked them into the mixing bowl. "Okay, girls. Have at it. I'll just walk Mrs. Bateman to the door." She slipped off her egg-drenched socks and started Betty moving toward the front door.

As they left the kitchen, Sarah could hear Lissa saying, "It's my turn to work the mixer."

"No it's not," insisted Damaris.

"You got to do it last time," said Beanie.

"You are a saint," said Betty.

Or else she was insane.

"If the girls need a break, they can have those Cheetos," Betty said. "Beanie loves Cheetos. And you can keep the whole carton of eggs. Safeway has them on sale. I got two cartons. Oh, they have rump roast on sale right now, too."

She was still talking about her grocery bargains as Sarah eased her out the door.

With Betty finally gone, she hurried back to the kitchen, where suspicious quiet now reigned. She found the girls gathered at the kitchen table, devouring the Cheetos. Well, good. It would give her time to change and clean up the mess on the floor. "I'll be right back," she said, and picked up her trashed socks and hurried off down the hall.

Another ten minutes and the cookie production was once more under control. Her junior bakers enjoyed looping the ropes of pink- and plain-colored dough into candy canes, and were pleased with their works of art. Damaris's father was actually on time to pick her up, mainly because they ran ten minutes over. He took Beanie, too, sparing Sarah from another never-ending conversation with Betty. Sarah breathed a sigh of relief as she waved George and the girls off, and then returned to put her kitchen back together.

"One more class," she told herself as she wiped down the counters. She sprinkled cleanser into the kitchen sink and scrubbed it out. Then she washed the counter on both sides and took a swipe at the windowsill, moving her knickknacks around. And that was when she noticed that her little vintage Hen on the Nest was missing.

She stood a moment, looking at the empty spot where it had been only . . . when? A day ago? A week ago? When had it gone missing? And how?

She thought of the times in the last couple of weeks that a certain child had been left unsupervised in her kitchen, remembered her conversation with the girls about her collectibles, and her eyes narrowed. She was going to kill that kid.

Except she had no proof that Damaris had taken her little hen, and, really, no way of finding out. She supposed she could confront Damaris, but if she did, the child would simply deny having taken it.

She could call the girl's mother. And Damaris would still deny having taken it. It was probably well hidden by now.

It looked as if Sarah would have to let this go, but she sure didn't want to. She had a silly sentimental attachment to that little chicken. "That will teach you," she scolded herself.

She took the salt and pepper shakers and stowed them in the top shelf of her dish cupboard, vowing not to leave her kitchen unguarded again. Next week would be the last baking class. And the last time she did something like this. Ever.

"Damaris's party is today," Lissa reminded her father Saturday morning. "You said we'd get a present."

He'd forgotten. In fact, he'd forgotten all about the party. Kid parties and presents for kid parties, he'd always thought that sort of thing would be handled by his wife. Well, that was Plan A. When Crystal died a lot of things got refiled under Plan B.

"Let me just finish my coffee." He'd need the caffeine.

He remembered the days of accompanying Crystal to the mall. Talk about an activity designed to sap the energy right out of a guy. Crystal had loved to shop. And compare bargains. And try on clothes. And make her poor man sit outside the dressing room holding her purse. He'd tried any number of ways to cope: bringing along a Tom Clancy novel, reciting baseball stats, watching for potential shoplifters. Nothing really helped. Shopping was for women. But a man in love did what he had to do.

Lissa had inherited her mother's shopping gene. Josh poured himself another cup of coffee.

"Daddy!"

"Okay, okay." He transferred it to a travel mug and followed the girls out the door with Lissa in the lead. A man did what he had to do.

An hour later they had combed Vern's for *High School Musical* paraphernalia and come up empty-handed. There had been plenty in August, the clerk informed him, but they'd had a run on the notebooks and pencil boxes at the beginning of the school year, and once school supplies were gone at Vern's they were gone until the next school year. *You snooze, you lose.*

"Hey, how about this?" Josh suggested, picking up a game.

Lissa made a face. "Daddy, that's boring."

"Since when is Operation boring?" Josh demanded. They'd played it just a few months ago.

She didn't answer him. She was too busy examining the wares in front of her. Judging from the frown, none of them were measuring up.

He picked up some kind of Barbie doll. "How about this?"

"She doesn't play with dolls."

"I want that," said Mandy. "Can I have it, Daddy?"

"Sure," he said, and wondered how much other stuff he'd get suckered into buying before they got around to getting birthday presents. "Come on, Liss, there must be something here." At the rate they were going the party would be over and they'd still be standing in the toy aisle deciding on a present.

"There's nothing," Lissa said in disgust.

Josh scratched his chin, hoping for inspiration. None came. If they were shopping for a boy they'd have been done by now. He'd have gotten that cool Airzooka or the ant farm.

Lissa turned from the toy aisle and Josh trailed her, calling over his shoulder, "Come on, Mandy."

Mandy reluctantly put back the coloring book she'd been looking at and joined the parade.

They passed an aisle already brimming with Christmas things and Mandy snagged a little snow globe with a Santa inside it. "I want to give this to Damaris."

"That's nice," he said. Good. *One down, one to go.* "See anything here?" he asked his oldest daughter hopefully. "There's a lot of cool candy."

Mandy fell for it. She picked up an M&M's novelty candy dispenser complete with candy. "I want to give this to her, too."

"Okay, that should do it for you," Josh said after looking at the price. Someday, before they got much older, he'd have to explain to the girls about budgets.

Meanwhile, Lissa was striding down the aisle like a girl on a mission. She didn't stop until she got to the makeup section. There she began to pull bottles of nail polish off the shelf.

Nail polish? "How old is this kid?" Josh asked.

"She'll like this," Lissa said, ignoring his question and adding a bottle of blue polish to the black, red, and pink ones she already had.

What did he know? "Okay."

Lissa would have opted for a dozen bottles of polish, but he stopped her at five. The stuff wasn't cheap.

"Hey, guys, we did good, huh?" he asked, checking the rearview mirror as they drove away.

"Yep, we did," agreed Mandy, who already had her new doll out of the bag and was looking at it.

Lissa sat regarding her purchase, frowning. "It's not very much."

"At thirty bucks? It's plenty."

"Everyone else is going to be giving her *High School Musical* stuff," Lissa said.

"Well, Liss, we can't help it if there isn't any left in the store," Josh said reasonably.

"Can't we go to the mall?" she begged.

"I want to go to the mall," said Mandy, always up for more fun.

Josh checked his watch. "I'm not sure we've got time." He looked in the rearview mirror to see how Lissa would take the news.

She looked downright despondent. Her present hadn't measured up, even though she'd tried. That was pretty much his fault. He should have remembered about the party, had Dad take the girls to the mall where Lissa could have scoured the stores till she found something she'd been really happy with. That was what Crystal would have done. Damn. He should have remembered about the party.

They were at the four-way stop at the end of Lake Way now. To the left and down that road lay Valentine Square, and a certain chocolate shop. "Want to get her something from the Chocolate Bar?" Josh suggested. No hidden agenda there.

Lissa brightened. "Yeah." She hopped out of the car as soon as Josh had parked and ran into the shop ahead of him, Mandy hot on her heels. She and Jamie were already deep in conversation by the time he walked through the door.

Jamie reminded him of the doll he'd bought Mandy: slim, pretty, dressed to kill. It was only a sweater and jeans, but the way they showed off what was under them was killing him. Her hair was pulled back and little gold earrings glinted in her ears.

She smiled at him. Was it just a friendly smile or was there a hint of wanting in there somewhere? He couldn't be sure. At least she wasn't frowning at him. And no nervous hiccups. That had to be progress.

He flashed his best grin at her. "Did you hear? We've got a present emergency."

"I did, and I think I can help you. It's going to take a few minutes, though." She slid three cups of hot chocolate across the counter. "Here's something to drink while you wait."

"Thanks," he said, and took it.

"Thank you," said Lissa, smiling as she reached for her drink, and her sister echoed her.

Josh took one look at the little tables and chairs and opted to remain standing. So did the girls. They hovered by the counter, watching with big eyes as Jamie nested the bottles of nail polish and a variety of truffles in metallic white shredded paper inside a gold gift box.

She wrapped the box in gold ribbon, then slid it across the counter to Lissa. "There you go."

"It's so pretty," Lissa breathed.

"I think your friend will like it," Jamie said.

"What if she doesn't?" Lissa worried.

Jamie shrugged. "Then she'll pretend, because real friends try hard not to hurt each other."

A good bit of wisdom thrown in as a bonus. It sounded like something Crystal might have told their daughter.

"Thanks," said Josh, stepping up to the cash register. "What do I owe you?"

"Five dollars."

He raised an eyebrow. "That barely covers the drinks."

"The drinks are on the house." Josh tripled the amount, but she shoved the extra bills back at him. "Don't be ruining my good deed again or I'll have to report you to the Heart Lake Angel Patrol."

He gave up and gave the counter a playful rap. "Okay, thanks. You're a lifesaver."

"All in a day's work for a chocolate superhero," she said.

He was tempted to ask if chocolate superheroes ever changed into average small-town girls and went on dates on a Saturday night, but asking her in front of Lissa didn't seem like a good idea, so he kept his mouth shut and ushered his daughters out of the candy shop. And once he was out in the cold, fresh air and could think clearly he remembered that asking her out wouldn't be a good idea. Period. Jamie was not in the market for a man, at least not the law-enforcement variety. Much as he would love to serve and protect her twenty-four/seven, he'd be crazy to let himself keep falling for her.

It looked like his daughters already had. The girls talked about Jamie the whole way home.

The present was ready to go a lot faster than his oldest daughter. They had about half an hour until they had to leave and she took every minute of it. "Where's your sister?" he asked Mandy when she came out of the bedroom.

"She's putting on a different top," Mandy said with a shrug.

The all-important preparty what-to-wear phase. Lissa was just a little girl. What was she doing in that phase already? And then it hit Josh. This was like clouds on the horizon, heralding a change. He wasn't ready for his little girl to grow up, for boys to start following her with just one thing on their minds. For her to start wanting bras and buying maxi-pads.

His mind shied away from this new mental trail. He couldn't go there. But he was going to, probably sooner than he wanted. And so far, the only person he had to go with him was his dad.

Lissa was hurrying down the hall now. "Let's go, Daddy."

They needed a woman who understood girls, someone they could look up to.

A woman who had blond hair and made chocolates.

Maybe he and Jamie could date just as friends. Would she do that? Would she want to even hang out with him as friends? She seemed to like her life with no complications. And he sure came with complications.

Still, the more Josh thought about the woman who rescued lost kids, who loved her family, and played charades and laughed with his daughters, the more he became convinced that he really owed it to his family to date her.

Now he just had to convince Jamie Moore that she owed it to herself to date a cop with a banged-up heart who came with two kids and a dad. That could take a lot of convincing.

TWENTY

$\mathcal{E}$mma was in Sarah's bakery Monday morning, hanging up a lost-cat poster. In addition to the cat's picture, Emma had provided both her phone number and address. At the bottom of the poster, she'd added in big bold letters: LIKES TO HIDE UNDER BUSHES.

"I've been putting them up all over town," she told Sarah. "I hope he's okay. It's getting really cold out."

Sarah was more worried about Emma than the cat. "I'm sure you'll find him waiting on your porch when you get home tonight," she assured Emma. "He probably just had a yen to go catting around."

Emma's eyes got teary. "He ran away. I yelled at him. And he didn't get his dinner last night."

"He's been well fed. He could probably afford to live off his fat for a week," Sarah assured her. She didn't look assured, so Sarah handed her a ginger cookie. "Here, this will make you feel better." *Sort of.*

"Nothing's going to make me feel better," Emma

declared, and took a big bite. "I'd better go. I've got to put up some more posters and then get back to the shop."

Sarah watched her leave and sighed. Poor Emma was in a major slump. First her shop and now her cat. Not a good way to go into the holiday season. Sarah understood how hard it was to lose something—or someone—you cared about. If only a grandma could put up posters and have someone bring back her granddaughters. But at least she had granddaughters. And kids, and a husband. Emma needed more in her life than a cat. There had to be somebody at the fire station that she and Sam could hook Emma up with.

"She looks like her best friend died," said Amber Howell as she restocked a tray with a fresh batch of orange oatmeal cookies.

"Just about. Her cat ran away."

"Aw, that really sucks."

"It does. That cat was her big love."

"Maybe she needs to find a bigger love," said Amber.

"It's hard to find Mr. Perfect. And easy to just give up and settle for what you're stuck with."

"But you can't give up. That never gets you anywhere." Amber smiled at a new customer.

"Sometimes I think I should just be sneaky and put an ad in the paper. 'Perfect man wanted,'" Sarah said, and turned to greet whoever it was Amber was smiling at.

"What looks good today?" asked Leo Steele, giving her his lounge-lizard grin. "Besides the baker." Leo's greeting was getting as stale as his aging-lothario clothes. Today he was wearing slacks and a shirt that he'd left open halfway down his chest and his leather bomber jacket.

"Everything's good here. You know that, Leo," Sarah replied.

"That's for sure. I guess I'll have one of those cinnamon rolls," he decided.

"Good choice. Amber, you want to get Mr. Steele a cinnamon roll?"

"I'll take a cup of coffee with that, too. Sarah, you look tired. Take a break, lemme buy you a cup of coffee."

"I'd love to, Leo," Sarah said, backing toward the kitchen. "I've got too much to do today. Thanks for the offer, though."

"Okay," he called after her. "Take it easy."

Take it easy, ha! After work she had her junior bakers to contend with, and Lezlie Hurst from the *Herald* was coming over to do a story. "This is a perfect story to start December and get people in the mood to do good deeds," Lezlie had assured her.

Sarah just hoped the girls behaved. For their last baking class they were making snowball cookies—hard to screw up and no eggs involved. And she'd already made the dough for the frosted sugar cookies. The afternoon should go smoothly. Lezlie was coming toward the end of class so she could get a picture of the girls and their finished product.

"What are we making today?" asked Damaris as they washed their hands.

"More Christmas cookies. After this, you'll all be experts." *And I'll be free.* Not that she wanted to be free of all the girls. Just one.

The afternoon went without mishap if not without mess. Four little girls and a bowl of frosting and jar of sprinkles was a recipe for disaster, Sarah realized as she chased stray bits of colored candy with her broom. But the frosted cookies were a huge success. After they had rolled the last batch of snowball cookies in powdered sugar, making a fresh mess, she said, "Now, to celebrate the end of class, we have a special guest coming."

"My grandma?" guessed Beanie.

"She's not special," said Damaris. "She was here last week."

"Of course Mrs. Bateman is special," Sarah said. In her own weird way. At least Beanie thought so.

Beanie gave Damaris a so-there smile, basking in her moment of one-upsmanship.

"But Mrs. Bateman is not our guest. Miss Hurst from the *Heart Lake Herald* is going to do a story on our baking class and she's coming to take a picture of us for the paper."

The girls looked at each other, then let out squeals of excitement.

"Oh, my gosh. My hair!" cried Damaris, and ran for her backpack.

"Mine, too," said Lissa.

"Mine, too," Mandy parroted.

"Beanie, you need to let me do your hair," said Damaris as they all stampeded for the bathroom. "Mrs. Goodwin, do you have hairspray?"

FCA—future celebrities of America, thought Sarah, following them down the hall.

But she got into the spirit, too, digging out some of the ribbons, bows, and barrettes she always kept on hand for her granddaughters.

"This is so cool," said Damaris. "I've never been in the paper before. But someday, when I'm famous, I'm gonna be. A lot."

Hopefully she wouldn't be in there as a criminal mastermind, Sarah thought. She couldn't help smiling, though, as she watched the girls primping in front of the mirror. Every little girl should have a chance to feel special once in a while.

Hmm. So should every grown-up. She grabbed a brush, saying, "Pass me that hairspray, Beanie."

Lezlie arrived to find them all properly primped and the

cookies displayed on one of Sarah's best Fitz and Floyd cookie plates.

And the girls were perfect angels during Lezlie's interview.

"What were your favorite cookies?" she asked.

"I liked the pumpkin ones," said Damaris.

The cookies she'd thought were just okay? Sarah felt her mouth dropping.

"I like these," said Lissa, pointing to a frosted tree decorated with sprinkles.

"And what was your favorite thing about doing this baking class?" Lezlie asked.

"Eating the cookies," crowed Beanie.

"Baking," said Damaris. "My mom works. She never bakes."

"It was like having a mommy," said Mandy softly.

Mandy's testimonial caught Sarah by the heart. Emma would have called this a real movie moment.

Lezlie smiled admiringly at her from across the table, as though she were the Mother Teresa of the kitchen. She jotted down Mandy's words, then shut her tablet, saying, "Okay, how about a picture?"

It was what the girls had been waiting for. Eagerly, they gathered at Sarah's kitchen table in front of the plate of cookies, with Sarah standing behind them like a mother hen.

As Lezlie snapped away with her trusty camera, Sarah couldn't help wishing she'd changed her clothes. She was in her jeans and top from work and still wearing the apron she'd donned for the baking class, which made her look like a fat snowwoman. And her stubborn hair had already forgotten to stay where the hairspray put it. Oh, well. At her age, she didn't need to look like a sex symbol. She would look exactly like what she was: a grandma.

"Are we gonna do this some more?" asked Damaris as Lezlie was gathering up her things.

The heartwarming Mandy moment was quickly cooled by memories of mess, irritation, and a certain missing knickknack. "We'll see," Sarah said noncommittally.

Damaris fell back on her kitchen chair with a frown. "That means no."

"This is going to be a great story," Lezlie predicted as Sarah walked her to the door. "And how has the experience been for you? Will you do this again?"

Sarah felt like a last dab of cookie dough caught in the bowl with a giant hand coming after her. "I think I've learned as much as the girls," she said, choosing her words carefully.

"Like what?" Now Lezlie had her pen and pad out again.

"Well, I think I've come to realize that it really does take a village to raise a child." And in the case of some children, it probably took several villages. From the kitchen, Sarah could hear hoots and raucous laughter. Who knew what they were up to in there now. "It sounds like the natives are getting restless," she said. "I'd better go check on them. Thanks for coming. I know the girls will love seeing their picture in the paper."

Lezlie nodded and said a quick good-bye, okay with getting shooed out the door.

Sarah got to the kitchen just in time to stop a food fight from turning into a war. "All right, let's clean off the table," she said, producing a sponge. "Damaris, I'll call your dad and tell him we're done."

"There's no hurry," said Damaris.

That's what you think. Sarah smiled politely and grabbed the phone.

Ten minutes later all her little bakers were gone and the house was quiet. She almost wished Sam would come by for a surprise visit. The place felt empty. She remembered Lezlie's probing question. Would she do this again?

It was like having a mommy.

And, she had to admit that once in a while, when things were going well, her weekly afternoons with the girls had felt like having granddaughters.

But not quite, Sarah reminded herself. No one could take her granddaughters' place in her heart.

Which meant that her heart was going to be empty for a long time to come. She suddenly felt like crying. She wished she hadn't sent off all the cookies with the girls. A good dose of sugar would have been just what she needed right now.

Her doorbell rang again. Who could that be?

She opened the door to find Leo leaning in the doorway. "Hiya."

"Leo. Um, did you need to borrow something?" Thank God Sam hadn't decided to come home. How would she explain Leo Steele on her porch, a bottle of wine dangling from one hand?

"Just a couple of wineglasses." He stepped inside and began to saunter down the hall. "I saw all the brats left. Figured you might want to wind down."

Yeah, but not with him. She trailed him into the kitchen. "Leo, I've got a lot to do. Maybe we could have drinks some other time. When Sam is home."

He set the bottle on the counter and took a step closer to her. "Come on, Sarah, you don't have to lie to me. I've seen it all since the first day you brought me that coffee cake."

"What? Seen what?"

"We're both adults here," he said, and ran a hand up her arm, raising goose bumps.

She jumped back. "Leo, I think you've gotten the wrong idea."

He shook his head at her. "Why play coy? I overheard you talking in the bakery. You've been settling for years, waiting for the right man to come along. Well, baby, he's here."

"What! What did I say in the bakery?" This man was insane. She took another step back.

He took a step, too, reaching for her as if they were doing the tango. "Come on. All that talk about wanting Mr. Perfect—I'm it, Sarah. I know how to appreciate a woman like you. And believe me, I wouldn't keep you in the kitchen all the time." He looked her up and down. "A woman like you belongs—"

"That's enough," she said firmly, swatting his hand away. "I'm sorry if I've given you the wrong impression, but I'm a happily married woman."

"Who are you kidding? Your man's never here. Everything about you says lonely."

Lonely for grandkids, not some crazy middle-aged wolf. "Really, Leo—"

"Sarah, Sarah," he cooed. "No need to put an ad in the paper, not when the man who gets you lives right across the street."

"Ad in the paper?" she echoed. And then she remembered. Oh, good grief. "I wasn't talking about me."

He gave her a "yeah, sure" look. "You need someone who appreciates you, someone who pays attention to the signs." Then, before she could tell him that he was delusional, he hooked an arm around her waist, tugged her against him, and latched on to her lips like a giant leech.

"Leo," she tried to protest. He took advantage of her moving mouth and stuck his tongue inside it.

Okay, no more Mrs. Nice Guy. Where was that wine bottle? She put one hand behind her and groped around on the counter, determined to grab it and club Leo. She just hoped she didn't kill him. *Mrs. Goodwin did it in the kitchen with a wine bottle.* It beat doing it with Leo, that was for sure.

Suddenly, a male voice rumbled behind her. "What the hell is this?"

TWENTY-ONE

$\mathcal{L}$eo's tongue immediately vacated Sarah's mouth and then his body spun away from her.

"Sam," she stuttered.

Sam was too busy socking Leo in the face to hear her. Leo staggered back against the counter with such force he tipped over the wine bottle. It rolled off the counter and landed with a glassy crash on the floor, spraying wine all over the trio's feet.

Leo put a hand to his cheek and another up to ward off a fresh attack. "Hey, that's assault. I could sue you."

"Yeah? You just try that and we'll talk about how you assaulted my wife."

Assaulted? Sarah's legs suddenly felt weak.

"I wasn't assaulting her. I was giving her what she wants. She obviously hasn't been happy with you in a long time," Leo added.

Okay, Leo Steele was definitely a lunatic. Sam was a big man, and now, puffed up with anger, he looked like the

Incredible Hulk. No man in his right mind would want to make him madder than he already was.

"Get out of here, you little cockroach," Sam snarled. "If I ever catch you on my property again I'll have you arrested for trespassing."

"Fine," Leo spat. "Your loss," he told Sarah. Then he turned and stalked out. A moment later the front door slammed after him.

"I should have thrown that little pissant out the door," Sam growled.

Sarah slumped against the counter. That was not an experience she wanted to repeat ever again. Thank God Sam had come home when he did.

She opened her mouth to thank him for riding to the rescue, but before she could say anything, he glared at her and snapped, "What was he doing over here? Is he your latest good deed?"

"What? Sam, he just walked in."

"You honestly expect me to believe that?"

"Yes, actually, I do." Sarah yanked a handful of paper towels off their rack and began blotting up the spilled wine. "I opened the front door and there he was with his little wine bottle and his big ego."

"And you said, what? 'C'mon in. My dumbshit husband's not home.'"

"I didn't say anything. He didn't give me a chance." This was not how they should be acting. Sam should be holding her in his arms, comforting her, asking her if she was all right. She marched to the pantry and grabbed the broom and dustpan.

"You had to have done something to encourage him," Sam insisted.

Had her husband actually just said that? "Well, I didn't. He overheard me talking about trying to find a man for

Emma and somehow, in his oversexed little brain, he thought I was talking about him. Really, Sam, how could you even think I'd have the bad taste to encourage a lech like that?"

"Oh, so it's 'cause he's a lech that you didn't want to take up with him. If he'd been somebody else, no problem."

A long day topped by a close encounter with Leo the Tongue had left Sarah like baking soda in the drain, just waiting for someone to come pour vinegar on her. She put a hand on one hip and gave Sam the universal welcome-to-the-doghouse look that any husband married longer than six months could recognize. "For such a smart man that was an incredibly dumb thing to say."

Sam had the grace to look chagrined. "I'm sorry, babe. I just saw him kissing you and went berserk. I thought maybe." He stopped and shrugged.

"You thought maybe what?"

"I just thought maybe . . . well, between this guy and George Armstrong, you've had men hanging around here for weeks. I thought you'd had enough of being married to me," he added with a shrug. "It happens, you know."

"Not to us." She came to stand in front of him. "Sam, we've been lovers and best friends since we were nineteen. I would think, after all these years, you could trust me."

"What was I supposed to think when I saw you kissing that moron?" Sam threw up his hands in a helpless gesture. "I don't want to lose you. I don't want some clown to come and sweet-talk you away."

"Oh, really, Sam. As if that's ever going to happen."

"You don't think it could? You haven't been happy since the girls left, and I'm gone a lot. You're still a good-looking woman. And, I'll admit it, I'm a selfish bastard," he added. "I get jealous of how much of you everyone else gets. I have to share with the bakery, the neighborhood, and every little girl in town, but, damn it, Sar, I draw the line at a lech like Steele." He drew her to him. "After all these years, I'm still crazy about you. I guess I'm crazy. Period."

"I guess you are," she agreed, lessening the sting with a smile. "You know you're not off the hook for not trusting me. It's going to cost you for a long time to come. So you'd better plan on taking me out to dinner on Saturday."

"Dinner," he repeated.

"And I was looking through the park and rec catalogue. I want to take the dance class that starts in January. Salsa."

"Dancing?" He looked like she'd just asked him to lop off an arm.

"You really did hurt my feelings, Sam. The surprise visits, those accusations . . ."

He held up a hand. "Say no more." Then he kissed her and whispered that he loved her. "Thanks for putting up with me all these years. You really are the best thing in my life."

"And you're the best in mine," she assured him. Her husband had all the qualities a woman wanted in a man. He was kind, generous, and blind. Every day the mirror showed her a woman with expanding hips and falling breasts and a waistline the size of a tree trunk, and yet Sam still thought she was beautiful and guarded her like treasure.

As she shut the door after her departing husband, though, she wasn't thinking about how lucky she was. She was remembering something he'd said. Did Sam really feel neglected?

Yes, she was busy with the bakery, and when Steph had lived nearby she'd done a lot with the girls. But now that they were gone . . . she was still busy, doing good deeds for everybody in town but her best friend. Maybe instead of putting the heart back in Heart Lake she needed to focus on putting a little more heart in her marriage.

With that thought in mind, she went to the garage where the spare freezer hummed away, preserving her extra meat, bread, and freezer jam, along with the stash of berries she kept to make pies in the winter. She pulled out a carton of blackberries, took it to the kitchen, and got to work.

An hour later she called the station and told the fireman who answered to tell the chief to get home. His wife needed him ASAP.

Exactly seven minutes later Sam burst through the front door, calling her name.

"Out here," she called from the dining room.

He charged down the hall and into the room, skidding to stop. His jaw dropped at the sight of her low-cut black dress. He watched as she set the freshly baked pie on a trivet. "Babe, what's going on?"

She walked around the table and laid a hand on his chest. "Nothing. Yet."

He smiled. "Okay. How about the pie, is that for us?"

"Nope," she said, and enjoyed watching his face fall. "It's for you."

"Yeah?" He was grinning now.

"Want a piece?"

He slipped his arms around her. "Maybe later."

"That's like something out of a sitcom," said Jamie after Sarah told her and Emma about her close encounter with Leo when the women met for chocolate.

"It is now, but, believe me, I wasn't laughing at the time," Sarah said, and took a sip of her mocha. "The nerve of the guy."

Jamie shuddered dramatically. "What would make Leo think you wanted him, insanity?"

"Conceit," said Sarah. "It makes me think of the old fart in *Tootsie*. 'They call him the Tongue,'" she intoned.

"Now, there's a great classic movie for you girls to watch," she added.

Jamie nudged Emma, who was at the table with them, but only in body.

"I'm sorry. What?" she said.

Sarah and Jamie exchanged looks.

"You guys, that snow is starting to stick," Emma said. "I'm going to go."

"Do you want to spend the night at my house?" Jamie offered. "If the power goes out we can build a fire in the woodstove."

"Thanks, but no. I should be home in case Pyewacket comes back."

"Call if you need anything," Sarah told her.

She nodded and stood, grabbing her coat and leaving her hot chocolate unfinished. "I'll see you guys."

"There must be something we can do to cheer her up," Jamie said, watching Emma trudge off down the street. Poor Em. First her business, now her cat. A cat, of course. "I know! Why don't we get her a kitten for Christmas? That will cheer her up."

"That's a great idea. It won't save her business, though."

"I don't know what to do about that," said Jamie with a sigh. "I can afford a cat. I can't afford to finance another shop."

"If worse comes to worst and she has to close, I'll hire her," said Sarah.

"At least she won't starve then."

Now Sarah sighed. "Maybe not physically. Poor Emma. She's invested so much of herself in that shop."

Jamie got up and took her mug and Emma's over to the little sink in her work area. "You know, with all the nice things she's done for people, you'd think they'd be a little more loyal. How many quilts do you think she's donated for raffles and auctions in the last year?"

"I've lost count," said Sarah.

Jamie frowned. "This whole Heart Lake Angel thing is a bust as far as I can see."

"Don't give up yet," said Sarah. "People—"

"Are not basically good," Jamie finished for her. Sarah should have figured that out by now.

"I wasn't going to say that," Sarah said patiently. "But I was going to say that people have a lot of good in them, and this time of year tends to bring it out." She glanced out the window. "Oh, that is really starting to stick. Do you want to leave your car here? I can take you home."

It was a kind offer, especially since Sarah hated driving in the snow. "I'll be fine," Jamie assured her. Her tires would be more like skates than tires but she'd make it if she went slowly.

"You're sure?" Sarah pressed.

"Absolutely."

"Okay. Call me when you get home."

"Yes, mother," Jamie teased.

Sarah pointed a scolding finger at her. "I'm the closest thing you've got up here so don't give me grief." With that parting shot, she hugged Jamie, then hurried off.

Jamie didn't dawdle over her closing-up tasks, but by the time she got out of the shop there was a good two inches of snow on the ground and the dark sky was thick with falling flakes. *Oh, boy.*

Hoards of snowflakes hurled themselves at her windshield as she drove away from the shop. A car eased past her, the snow softly shooshing under its tires. Farther up she saw another car already in a ditch. No surprise. With its mild Pacific Northwest weather, Heart Lake didn't get enough snow to turn its residents into expert drivers. Living in California hadn't turned Jamie into an expert, either. She clutched the steering wheel and forced herself to breathe. *Just ten minutes. You'll be home in ten minutes.*

Who was she kidding? At the speed she was going she'd be lucky to get home in thirty. If she managed to stay on the road. Was it getting slipperier?

"You're fine," she assured herself. She'd have been finer if she'd taken her trusty charge card to Big Ben's Tires and gotten all-weather tires when she first heard the weather forecast. But she'd thought she had another day. This wasn't supposed to hit till tomorrow. That was what she got for trusting the weatherman.

She crept around the lake. Just a little farther and she'd be in her cabin, feeding the woodstove and heating up a can of chili. Just a little farther and . . . *Whoa. Slipping here. Okay, turn into the slip. Except there's a car coming! Panic. Scream. Turn the other way. Slide sideways. Hit the ditch, tip to the right.*

Swear.

The other car swooshed on by, its red taillights disappearing behind a rooster tail of snow.

"Okay, don't panic," she told herself. "It's not like you're in the middle of nowhere." It only felt like it. She grabbed her purse from the floor and pulled out her cell phone. No bars, of course. Why had she bothered? She knew there was no cell reception on this stretch of road.

What should she do? Should she get out and walk? She had no parka, no boots. Maybe that wasn't a good idea. She did have a blanket in the trunk. She'd get that out, then put up her car hood as a distress signal.

She popped the hood, pulled the old blanket out of her trunk, and then hustled back inside her car and huddled under it. Mom had always lectured her about having an emergency kit in her car: flares, blanket, water, and some sort of food. Well, she had the flares and she had the water. She wished she'd remembered to replace the stash of Pringles she'd eaten a few months back when money was tight.

Where were Emma and Sarah? Had they made it home okay? They should have all stayed together, just gone to Sarah's and had a big slumber party. It was too late for that, so what to do now? What would Emma do if they were stuck here together? Sing some dopey Christmas song, of course.

Jamie took a stab at it. " 'On the first day of Christmas, my true love gave to me . . .' " Oh, this was dumb, and it wasn't making her feel any better. She hunched down farther under her blanket and began rewriting the old carol. "Oh, the first thing I'll get with my trusty credit card: four brand-new tires."

Speaking of tires, did she hear the crunch of tires on snow in back of her, the crunch of slowing tires? It was a truck, a big, kick-ass, who-cares-if-it's-snowing truck. Sarah was right. People did have good in them.

Not people. Person. Big, hunky, not-right-for-her Josh Armstrong. What was he doing out of uniform? Who cared? For the first time since they'd met by the side of the road she was glad to see him.

She let down her window. "If you're wondering why I'm stuck here, it's because I saved a life."

He bent over and leaned an arm on the car. "Yeah?"

"I decided to slide away from the other car rather than into it."

He smiled. "That was thoughtful. I guess that counts as your good deed for the day."

"Maybe even for the week."

"Want a ride?"

She made a face at him. "No, I kind of like sitting here feeling my toes freeze." She grabbed her purse and scrambled out.

He chuckled and followed her to his truck. Once there, he reached around her and opened the door. She clambered inside the cab to the welcome embrace of warmth and Brad Paisley on the radio singing about waiting on a woman.

"You can call a tow truck when you get home," Josh said. "Although I imagine it will be a while before you get your car back."

"Oh, well," she said. "If this stuff sticks I won't be going anywhere tomorrow."

"From what I hear about how you all handle snow up here, nobody will," said Josh. "I hope it's gone by the weekend. Isn't that the big Christmas Festival?"

"Yeah. A lot of our local artists really depend on it. It's where they make most of their money for the year." It was an effort to keep her voice sounding casual when she was fighting off a pheromone zing.

"I hear Santa shows up."

"Oh, yeah," she said, trying to distract herself with the memory of all that kid excitement.

"My girls are counting the days," said Josh.

"So did I when I was little. By the way, why aren't you in your trusty patrol car, handing out tickets and changing tires?"

"I'm on days for the next three months. Kind of nice to have a normal life," he added.

He was a widower with two little girls. She wondered if his life was ever normal.

When she came back to her childhood roots, she'd come hoping that in the familiar soil of Heart Lake she could grow a new beginning. The new life was still a work in progress, but it was looking better all the time. What was life like for Josh Armstrong? When someone you loved died how did you fill that black hole?

"What are you thinking?" he asked.

She blinked at him. "How normal is your life?"

He rubbed the back of his neck. "You don't waste time

cutting to the chase, do you? It's as normal as I can manage to make it."

She understood about managing. She nodded and looked out the window. It was a blizzard out there. "We are all going to be snowbound tomorrow."

"Unless we have a truck and four-wheel drive," he corrected her with a grin. "Poor Dad. He's going to have the girls home all day."

They pulled up in front of her cabin and she turned to him. "Thanks. That was really nice of you." Josh did seem like a nice guy.

So had Grant when she'd first met him.

He smiled. "You're welcome." Then, "You got food?"

"I'm okay."

"Woodstove?"

As if he couldn't see the chimney. "Yes. And wood." The landlords had left her half a cord.

"Got somebody to make a fire for you?"

"Yes."

"Who?"

"Me. I wasn't a Girl Scout for nothing."

He smiled, undeterred. "I could use a cup of coffee before I drive back out onto those cold, snowy roads."

She smiled back sweetly and opened the door. "You've got a four-wheel-drive truck. Remember? A little thing like snow isn't going to stop you."

"I take it gratitude isn't your strong suit?"

Of course she was being rude. "I am hugely grateful," she said as she slipped out of the truck. "Come by the store and I'll give you a fortune in free chocolate. I promise."

"I'd rather have a cup of coffee."

She gave up. "Okay, fine." She took a quick step back, but not in time to hide the sudden hiccup.

"I won't bite, you know," he said as he followed her up onto the porch.

She looked over her shoulder. "So you say. For all I know you could be a vampire."

He leaned over and gave her a good look at his teeth. "See? Perfectly safe."

She felt a sudden shiver and unlocked the door. Inside, she flipped on the light.

"You'd better call the tow company while you've still got power," he suggested, walking over to the woodstove.

She already knew that. She didn't need Josh the cop to tell her. *You are being a total beatch. Isn't it nice to have somebody care?* She had plenty of people who cared, she argued. She didn't need a man. At least not this one.

As she dialed she heard the iron squeak of the wood-stove door as Josh opened it, followed by the crumpling of paper. By the time she got off the phone he'd found the matches in the little tin cookie box she kept by the stove and a flame was licking up the paper and kindling.

He put a small log on the fire, and then gave her wood box a careful examination. "Got more wood?"

"I'll bring some in later."

"Out back?"

"Look, you don't have to—" He was already on his way to the door, his big boots clomping on the old hardwood floor. "Okay, suit yourself," she muttered, and got busy making coffee.

The phone rang just as she finished. Caller ID reminded her that she was supposed to let Sarah know she got home safely.

"Good," Sarah said as soon as she answered. "I was getting worried."

"Sorry. I just got in," Jamie said, and decided that was all she was going to tell her aunt. Sarah didn't need to hear about her little accident with the car. She'd insist on buying tires for Jamie, and she'd done enough already. "Have you heard from Emma?"

"She made it in twenty minutes ago."

"Any sign of the hellcat?"

"No."

"It definitely looks like a kitten for Christmas for Emma," Jamie said.

"I think so. Are you sure you're going to be okay?" Sarah asked.

Josh came back in, his arms loaded with wood. He seemed to fill the doorway. He dumped the firewood in the wood box and then disappeared outside again.

"I'll be fine," Jamie assured Sarah. Josh Armstrong was making sure of that. "Hey, don't try to go in to work tomorrow. The snowplows won't be out at four A.M."

"Don't worry. I went by the bakery on the way home and hung a CLOSED FOR SNOW sign in the door. I've already given my girls the day off. I'm going to stay home and tuck in with my new issue of *Bon Appétit*. And you stay warm over there. Remember, if you need anything, give a holler."

What Jamie needed was protection from this uncomfortable feeling of attraction that was coming over her like the flu. "Are you ready for that coffee?" she asked as Josh deposited his second load of firewood in the wood box. She hoped her tone of voice relayed the message that she would be friendly but not friends. There was no percentage in friendship. Guys always wanted more.

"Sure." He shrugged off his coat and hung it over a chair, then joined her at the little kitchen's breakfast bar. He leaned on the counter and looked around. "Cool place."

She got down a mug and poured coffee in it. "I like it."

It wasn't much, really: two bedrooms, a bathroom, this little kitchen, and the not-so-great great room. But with its cedar paneling, old wood floors, and vintage throw rugs it was cozy. Her furniture consisted of the buttery yellow leather couch she'd saved for a year to buy, a vintage rocking chair that had been her grandma's, the old hope chest her mom and dad had given her for her eighteenth birthday, and an ancient cedar picnic table with accompanying benches that she'd gotten at a garage sale and restained. The table sported her newly made pinecone wreath, which held a scented pillar candle. Her one piece of art was a giant painting of sunflowers that she had bought from a local artist during the Fourth of July festivities.

That was it for the decorations, other than a picture of her family, which sat on the kitchen counter. When a girl had a view like the one she had outside her living room window, pictures were superfluous.

"So, you own this place?" Josh asked as she poured his coffee.

"I'm renting, which is fine. I'm happy renting."

"I like owning my own place," said Josh. "It makes me feel like I'm in charge of my life. Not that I am," he added, and took a big slurp of his coffee. He saluted her with the mug. "This is good."

"It's pretty hard to screw up coffee."

"I don't know. My wife was pretty good at it." Suddenly his smile wasn't so easy.

"You still miss her?" Why was she asking? Now she'd made him uncomfortable. Heck, she'd made them both uncomfortable. "Sorry. That's so none of my business."

"That's what everybody thinks," he said. He put his coffee mug down and stared into it. "People don't like talking about things like this. They tiptoe around it or just stop talking about it. But then it's like the person never even lived and that doesn't seem right. My wife was great. I wish she was still alive. I wish my girls still had a mom. But, like they say, wishing don't make it so." He took another drink of coffee.

"It doesn't seem fair," Jamie mused. She stopped short

of asking if he ever thought of getting remarried. Not only was that a nosy question, it could very easily be misinterpreted.

"We're doing okay," he added. "I've turned into a pretty good wife myself."

"So, you got in touch with your feminine side," Jamie teased.

"Yep. It was a disaster at first, though. You probably know why you shouldn't wash colored and white clothes together. I didn't. And I thought you always put bleach in the laundry."

"Don't tell me, let me guess. You wound up with pink underwear."

"I look pretty in pink," he quipped. "I never did laundry when I was a bachelor. Always took it home to Mom or sent it out to be cleaned. Then I got married and Crystal did the washing. And the cooking." His voice trailed off as he looked at something Jamie couldn't see. He forced himself back into the present. "I'm one self-sufficient dude now," he finished, and went to put another log on the fire.

He turned and stood with his back to the fire, regarding her. "So, what about you? Your aunt seems to be busy on your behalf."

Jamie suddenly felt the need to check the kitchen clock. It was almost six. Didn't Josh the cop have to be home for dinner? She should offer him dinner. It was the least she could do after he'd rescued her from being snowbound. But if she did he'd get the wrong idea.

Maybe they could make a pact to adopt each other as brother and sister. Brothers and sisters didn't risk their hearts, didn't give their bodies and their souls—didn't get hurt. *Hic.*

He frowned. "Why do I make you so nervous?"

Before she could answer, the lights went out.

TWENTY-TWO

A power outage should have been the perfect distraction, offering them something to talk about besides her nerves, like, "Where are the candles?" And something to do, like fetching candles, instead of fighting off the little pheromones Jamie felt zinging around her like bees. The way the flickering firelight silhouetted Josh's tall frame when he bent to snag a book of matches from the cookie tin made her think of romance novels, all the good parts. He returned and lit the candle on her table.

She should get her extra candles out of the kitchen cabinet. *Come on, feet, let's move. The cabinets are that way.* But her feet betrayed her, standing perfectly still.

Now he was next to her. He was so big. *Look at the size of those pecs. Wouldn't it be fun to touch them? No!*

"Do you have some more candles somewhere?"

Who asked about candles in such a seductive voice? A hiccup escaped her as she yanked open the cupboard door. *Candles, candles. Romantic candlelight, candlelight dinners. Stop it!*

Now he was behind her, so close they were almost touching. "So, why do I make you so nervous?" he asked softly.

"Because." There. That explained it all. She pulled down another pillar candle. The one on the table was already doing its job and the room was starting to smell like apple pie. Josh took the other from her hand. Their fingers touched and she felt like he'd lit a fuse. It burned all the way up her arm and exploded in her chest.

"Because?" he prompted. He struck another match and touched it to the wick. Light blossomed between them, showing her the hard planes of his face, that strong angular chin, now stubbled with five o'clock shadow.

Fear flooded her—fear of what he'd do, what she'd do if he did it. One kiss and she'd be trapped. She couldn't be trapped again. She took a step back. "Because I don't like cops. I told you, I was married to one."

That should have offended him, brought back a sharp retort. He should have stalked off in anger. Instead, he nodded thoughtfully, studying her. "The ex-husband. Did he beat you?"

She bit her lip and nodded. She could almost feel that horrible pain again; feel the emotional shock and betrayal. She shut her eyes.

"So, we're all like that. Is that what you've decided?"

He made her fears sound so irrational. But they weren't. Her wounds had taught her it was better to be safe than sorry. She turned her back on him. "I'm a dead end for you."

She heard him heave a big sigh. "I'm sorry for what happened to you. Not every cop is a wife beater, Jamie. Really."

So he said, but she'd heard enough stories in the news, seen it happen often enough to other women who loved the men in blue. Cops got wound too tight, and then put in a pressure cooker where they were expected not to blow. Of course they blew. And whoever was nearby when it happened became collateral damage.

"I wish I could believe you," she countered. "I'm sorry, Josh. Anyway, there's a reason I'm on my own. I like it that way."

He stood there silently, probably trying to figure out what to say next.

"I'm sure your kids are wondering where you are," she added, since he didn't seem to be getting the message.

"Yeah," he said gruffly. "You're right. Good luck."

She heard him walk across the floor, felt the cold rush in as he opened the door. Then the door shut and it was just her alone in her candlelit house.

A lucky escape, she told herself, and blinked back the tears.

The snow was gone in two days and life returned to normal. Normal wasn't as satisfying as it used to be, Jamie realized as she finished up a batch of caliente fudge for the gift basket she was contributing as a door prize for the Christmas festival. Emma had contributed a quilt, which was going to be raffled off, with the proceeds going to the food bank. Heart Lake Holidays was always a big celebration, and she and Emma had been planning to go together for weeks. But now Jamie wasn't sure she wanted to go. She was bound to run into Josh and his kids there, which would be awkward. It would also remind her of what was missing in her "normal" life. That was the last thing she wanted, but she couldn't bail on her friend. Emma needed to get out and have some fun, take her mind off her troubles.

At nine, the shop phone rang. It was Emma, wanting to bail on going to the festival.

"What? Why on earth do you want to do that?"

"I'm just not in the mood. Anyway, I don't have any money to spend."

Emma needed this, and she was going to go to that festival and have fun even if Jamie had to drag her there and pin her lips up in a smile. "Well, I've got money. And I want to go," Jamie insisted. Actually, she did, she realized. No matter what she told herself, no matter how much she kept trying to protect her heart, she wanted to go and at least get a glimpse of Josh and the girls, torture herself over what she didn't dare take. "Come on. If you're really good, I'll get you one of those giant candy canes."

Emma sighed. "Okay. I guess."

"It'll be fun," Jamie insisted. "Take your mind off your troubles."

"I don't think anything can do that, but I'll come."

So, they closed up shop early on Saturday—nobody really hit the shops when the festival was going, anyway—and went to the center of town, where the main drag had been transformed into a fairground humming with booths and tents hung with cedar swags, tinsel garlands, and twinkle lights. After a lunch of vegetarian chili and cornbread from the Family Inn booth, they browsed their way down the street, checking out the jewelry, hand-knit scarves, and paintings. Jamie insisted on buying a pair of silver heart-shaped earrings for Emma as an early Christmas present. Then they drifted to the parade route to wait for the Christmas parade at two, which heralded Santa's arrival (always in the back of a pickup truck stuffed with volunteer elves who threw candy to the crowd). This year Tony DeSoto had the honor, and he'd been bragging about his upcoming Santa debut to everyone who came into his wine shop.

"I wonder if it's going to snow again," said Jamie as she rubbed her mittened hands together for warmth. "It sure looks like it."

The old Emma would have immediately expounded on the joys of a Winter Wonderland. The new, depressed Emma simply said, "The weatherman only predicted a thirty percent chance of snow."

Jamie studied her friend. Emma's mouth looked like it had forgotten how to smile and she had dark circles under her eyes. Worst of all was the darkness in her eyes. "Don't give up, Em," Jamie begged. "Things are going to work out."

Emma shoved her hands into her coat pockets. "I know."

The words were right, but her tone of voice was wrong, and Jamie knew Emma was only agreeing to shut her up. She wished there were such a thing as Santa. She'd ask him to bring Emma a fabulous new life for Christmas.

"Jamie!" called a little voice.

"Jamie!" another echoed.

"Here comes your fan club," said Emma, managing a wistful twist of the lips.

Jamie turned to see Lissa and Mandy swimming through the crowd toward her. They were wearing winter coats and mittens and their curls stuck out from under floppy stocking caps. They both sported big smiles and their cheeks were kissed red from the cold, their eyes shining. She felt a painful tug on her heart. Why hadn't these girls come with an accountant or a minister? Behind them she saw Josh, pushing politely through the crowd. He didn't have to push hard. His size alone encouraged people to part before him.

The girls were in front of her now. "Santa Claus is coming," Mandy informed her breathlessly.

"That's what I hear," she said, smiling. "Have you guys been totally good this year so he can bring you what you really want?"

They both nodded.

"What do you want for Christmas?" Emma asked.

"A new mommy," said Mandy.

Lissa frowned at her little sister. "Mandy, Santa can't bring us a new mommy. Daddy has to find her." To Emma and Jamie she explained, "She's just a baby. She doesn't know how it works."

"I am not!" cried Mandy.

Josh was with them now and frowning. "Are you two behaving like we talked about?"

"Sorry, Daddy," they both muttered.

Then, back on track, they started chattering about what they'd done and seen so far. "We got to ride the merry-go-round," said Mandy. "And Daddy got us hot choc'late."

"Sweet," said Jamie. She tried to keep her gaze focused on the girls, to not look up, but she couldn't help herself. He was looking at her, desire plain on his face. She quickly refocused her attention on the girls. *Well, that helped a lot.*

"After the parade we get to buy something," said Lissa. "I have ten dollars to spend."

"Me, too," said Mandy. She slipped her hand into Jamie's. "Will you come with us?"

"Oh, we're almost done," Jamie said. Looking at Josh, she could feel her cheeks heating.

"Don't bug the ladies," he said sternly.

"They're not bugging us," put in Emma. "And we still have to check out the arts and crafts booths."

They had just done that. Had Emma been having an out-of-body experience? Jamie turned her face so only Emma could see and scowled at her.

Emma ignored it. Suddenly she was really smiling and her eyes were starting to light up. Great. So now Emma was figuring to live vicariously through her friend's love life. Except this was not a love life. This was a no-love life. "We did the booths. Remember?"

"Yeah, but I saw something I want to look at again."

Emma pointed up the street. "Look, guys. The parade is starting!"

Sure enough, there came the Heart Lake High marching band, and behind it the convertible with the mayor perched in it, all dolled up in a red coat and a Santa hat.

"I can't see," Mandy protested. Josh lifted her up onto his shoulders and in the process wound up standing closer to Jamie. She tried hard to swallow a hiccup.

And then another. This was ridiculous. She stood and fumed as the guys from Fire Station Number Nine drove past in their fire truck, siren blaring.

"There's Sam," said Emma, elbowing her. "Sam," she called, and waved. Not that he could hear her with all the noise.

Right behind the fire truck came Heart Lake's finest, bringing more noise and flashing the lights on their patrol cars. Why wasn't Josh in one of those cars instead of here, next to her, giving her the hiccups?

The swing-dance club paused for a quick performance, shaking their hips to Kellie Pickler's version of "Santa Baby." "I thought we were going home after this," Jamie said to Emma out of the corner of her mouth.

"I want to stay longer," Emma said. "You're supposed to be trying to cheer me up. Humor me."

"This is not a movie moment," Jamie informed her.

"Not yet, but it could be."

No it couldn't. They should have left before the parade. It was a lame parade anyway.

"Santa Claus!" cried Mandy, pointing.

Even though she was frustrated and totally irritated with her friend, Jamie couldn't help smiling at the sight of Tony DeSoto perched on the back of a flatbed truck and surrounded by candy-throwing elves, waving, and holding his padded belly, faking a Santa laugh. Speakers blared "Santa Claus Is Coming to Town."

"This is just like *A Christmas Story,*" Emma gushed. "Well, the parade part anyway."

"I'm glad you're enjoying it," Jamie said. "Next maybe you'll get a miracle on Thirty-fourth Street."

"I'd take a miracle on Lake Way," Emma replied.

Her smile suddenly vanished, and Jamie wanted to kick herself. *Way to go, bigmouth.*

As penance, after the parade she stayed and wandered the booths with the girls and Emma, Josh keeping a respectful distance between them. Like that helped. With every step, every turn, she was aware of him like a giant guardian angel in a blue parka and jeans.

Lissa drifted into the tent where Jamie had bought Emma's earrings. The girl had expensive taste.

Emma followed her right on in, saying, "Oh, Jamie bought me some earrings here."

Of course, they all had to troop in.

"Look, Daddy," said Lissa, dragging him over to the table. "Can we get these?"

Jamie positioned herself by the door and pretended to watch the people drifting past, in and out, trying to keep some distance between herself and Josh.

Even though Lissa had lowered her voice, Jamie couldn't help hearing her tell her dad, "I want to get these for Jamie."

Not only was the dad falling for her, so were the kids. This was so not good. She stepped outside the tent, but she could still hear.

"I don't think that would be a good idea," said Josh.

"Why not?" There was an element of whine in Lissa's voice now.

"It would embarrass her. We don't know her that well."

"Yes we do," insisted Lissa.

Now Mandy chimed in. "Jamie's our friend."

"I want to get her these," Lissa insisted. "I have money."

"Those are more money than you have."

"I have money," piped Mandy.

Jamie wanted to burst in and say, "Don't, girls. I'm a bad investment."

"They're still too much," Josh said firmly.

"Daddy, can't you give us a little more?" begged Lissa. "I'll do extra chores."

This was awful. She moved away, burying herself in the crowd of people.

A moment later Emma, Josh, and company joined her. Lissa was pouting and Josh had lost his easy smile. Emma looked thoroughly confused, as though she'd just seen a movie with an ending that didn't make sense.

Jamie knew she wasn't really responsible for this, but she couldn't help feeling as if she, somehow, had to rescue the afternoon. She fell in step alongside Lissa. "That was really nice of you to want to buy me earrings."

"You heard?" Lissa looked at her, chagrined.

"I did. But your dad is right. It's important to learn not to spend money you don't have. And besides, heart earrings are more of a boyfriend-girlfriend thing, aren't they?" She was painfully aware of Josh walking behind them, probably pretending not to listen.

"But you bought some for Emma," Lissa pointed out, shooting down that argument.

"Well, they're for BFFs, too."

"I wanted to give you something," Lissa muttered.

"You've given me smiles," Jamie said, hugging her.

"I want to give you a present," Lissa said simply.

As if Jamie would always be in her life. She almost wanted to cry. "Sometimes the most special gifts are things you make, like drawings."

"That's for little kids," Lissa said in disgust.

"Or cards. I know lots of grown-up ladies who like to make cards."

"I guess," said Lissa, sounding unconvinced.

"The best gifts aren't always things we buy, they're gifts from the heart that help us remember special times together. Honest."

Lissa nodded, digesting Jamie's words of wisdom.

"Look, Daddy, hats!" cried Mandy, running ahead to a booth sporting all kinds of goofy hats, and Emma took off after her and Lissa, leaving Josh and Jamie to follow along behind. Subtle as always.

"Thanks," he said.

"No problem," she said, keeping her gaze straight ahead.

"It's not that I didn't want her to give you those," he added.

"I know." She kept her gaze straight ahead.

"I just don't want to make you feel like we're pressuring you somehow. Although if I thought it would work, I would," he added, and she could hear the smile in his voice.

Now she couldn't help but turn to look at him. "I'm sorry, Josh. You seem like a great guy."

"Actually, I am."

"It's just too scary for me."

"I wish you could bring yourself to trust me. What if we turned out to be perfect for each other? What if, instead of scaring you, I made you feel safe?"

She shook her head. "I always thought I'd feel safe with Grant. The year I was married to him was the scariest year of my life."

Josh nodded. He shoved his hands in his coat pockets as they walked. "I hope you find somebody who makes you feel safe. You deserve it. Until you do, maybe we can be friends."

"Do you really think that's a good idea?" asked Jamie.

"No, but it beats not seeing you at all."

Jamie nodded to where Emma stood, modeling a Cat in the Hat stovepipe hat for the girls. "There's your perfect woman."

"She's great. Too bad she's not you."

They joined the others and Lissa held out a cap for Jamie to try on. It was orange with a coxcomb and designed to make her look like a giant chicken. She struck a pose. "It's me, dontcha think?" The girls giggled and Jamie plopped it on Lissa's head. "Oh, no. It's you." She held one of the hand mirrors so Lissa could check it out.

The child smiled at her reflection. "Can we get it, Daddy?"

"It's your money," he said.

"No, it's my treat," Jamie insisted. "Mandy, you pick one out, too." That was bright. Here she was trying to distance herself from this family and now she was buying funny hats for the girls. And right after giving Lissa a lecture about not buying gifts. She needed a shrink.

By four the temperature was dropping and the sky was turning gray and the air was smelling like snow. "Well, girls," said Josh, "what do you say we go home and let Grandpa cook up that pizza?"

"Pizza!" cried Mandy, jumping up and down.

"Can Jamie and Emma come?" asked Lissa.

Josh gave Jamie a you-can't-stop-a-train shrug, and before she could come up with an excuse Emma was saying, "Sure. We can come."

"Okay, we'll see you there," Josh said. He pulled Jamie aside and whispered, "Just friends. I promise."

Just friends was so not going to work, not when every time she was with him she felt like a female Dr. Jekyll and Mr. Hyde, with Jekyll fretting that this experiment was a bad idea and Hyde wanting to grab Josh and swing from the chandelier together.

"Nice of you to commit us," Jamie growled at Emma

after they'd gotten directions and were walking to Jamie's beater.

"If you don't go after this guy you need to be committed," Emma informed her. "Anyway, I want to go. I have no life."

"I'll take you home and you can drive yourself."

"You've got new, all-weather tires and I don't," Emma argued. "I need your car."

"I'll loan it to you."

"I can't drive a stick. You're stuck. This will cheer me up," she added. "I want one of us to live happily ever after."

Jamie grabbed her arm and shook it. "Don't talk like that. We're both going to live happily ever after. You'll see."

It almost felt like happily ever after at Josh's house as they sat at the kitchen table, eating George's slightly burned pizza and playing Sorry! The house was a simple tract home with rooms done in neutral colors. Jamie had seen a painting of the girls hanging in the living room as they passed through on their way to the kitchen. It looked like the work of an amateur, short on skill, long on love, and she couldn't help wondering if it had been painted by the girls' mother. Other than a well-worn crocheted afghan on the big, brown leather sofa, motherly touches were sadly lacking. Still, there in the kitchen, warm from the heat of the oven and filled with the sound of little-girl giggles, it felt like home.

"I won!" Lissa finally crowed as she moved her piece to the finish. "I'm good, I'm good," she chanted.

"And modest, too," observed Josh, who had actually done his share of crowing when he won the first game.

"Daddy, stop making fun," Lissa said, and gave him a shove.

He pretended to fall off his chair, making the little girls

giggle and the big girls smile. He resurfaced with a come-back. "You have to be humble if you're going to be the Virgin Mary."

"Daddy, that's not for real. That's pretend." But still obviously important. Lissa turned to Jamie and Emma. "Can you come to our Sunday school program next week and see me? Mandy's going to be an angel," she added to sweeten the pot.

"Oh, gosh, we can't miss that," Emma answered for both of them.

"I'll have to check my calendar," Jamie said evasively. Lissa looked instantly worried. "But I'm sure I'm free," she added, and the child beamed at her. *Great. Is this how you distance yourself? You're only making things worse for everyone. WHAT ARE YOU DOING?*

"Okay," George said as he finished wolfing down the last piece of pizza. "Who wants root beer floats?"

"I do," chimed the girls.

Jamie looked out the window and saw fat flakes of snow falling. Even though she'd probably be fine with her new tires, she wasn't looking forward to driving home in the snow.

Josh followed her gaze to the window. "I hate to tell you this, but it's been coming down for the last twenty minutes."

"Oh." That meant the roads would already be bad.

"How about letting me drive you both home after our floats?" Josh suggested.

"Good idea," George seconded.

"But my car," Jamie protested.

"Dad and I can bring it to you as soon as this latest mess melts away. Or I can drive your car."

"Then how would you get home?"

"It's not that far to walk from your place."

Two miles in the snow? That was crazy. "We'll be fine,"

Jamie decided. "But we'd better leave now." She stood and Emma followed her lead.

"Okay," Josh said, and went to the coat closet. But when he was done fishing around for their coats he'd gotten his parka out, too.

"Oh, no," Jamie protested.

"Oh, yes." He grinned. "It's easier than pulling you out of a ditch anyway."

She sighed and resigned herself.

"Grandpa, can we make a snowman?" asked Mandy, root beer floats now completely forgotten.

"It's cold out there," George protested. "Why don't you see if our guests will help you and your dad make one before they leave. Since you don't have to worry about driving in the snow now," he explained to Jamie.

George and Sarah were in cahoots, Jamie was sure of it.

"Great idea," said Emma, and a moment later she was rushing out the door after the girls.

George and Sarah and Emma were all in cahoots.

Reluctantly, Jamie followed them outside.

Josh was already busy, helping Mandy roll a snowball into something bigger.

"This is getting out of hand," Jamie whispered to Emma.

"No," Emma corrected her. "This is getting good. Remember that scene in *The Family Man . . .*" she began.

That was it. She'd had enough of Emma and her movies and her matchmaking. She grabbed a handful of snow and deposited it down her friend's back. "What movie is that from?"

Emma let out a yelp and squirmed away. She bent and picked up a handful of snow, but Jamie was already darting across the lawn.

In another minute they were all hurling snowballs at each other. Finally the focus shifted to Josh, with all the girls pelting him. He held up a hand. "Okay, okay, I give."

"I want to finish the snowman," said Mandy, who was starting to shiver.

"You're getting cold, little girl," Josh observed.

"But I want to finish . . ."

"I know, I know. We'll work fast. Everybody help."

A few more minutes and they had a snowman standing in the front yard with branches for arms, two tennis balls for big, googly eyes, and a carrot nose, and the chicken hat Jamie had bought for Lissa sitting on its head. And two little girls were laughing hysterically.

"Okay, now. Inside and take a hot bath," Josh commanded. "And I expect you two to be in bed in your pajamas with your prayers all said by the time I get home."

"Yes, Daddy," they chorused. Then, before they went in the house, Mandy turned and hugged Jamie fiercely. Not to be outdone, Lissa hugged her from the other side.

"That was a real movie moment." Emma sighed as she and Jamie started for the car while Josh nudged his daughters back into the house.

"This is not the movies," Jamie reminded her. "And after the Sunday school program I'm cooling it with these guys."

"Those kids need a mom."

"Go for it," Jamie told her. "You've got my blessing."

"I would if I thought there was a chance. I saw how he looked at you. He's hooked."

"I'm into catch and release," Jamie retorted.

Josh trotted up to them, ending the conversation. He opened the doors for them, and then took over the driver's seat, squeezing his massive frame behind Jamie's steering wheel. Moving the seat back helped some, but he still looked too big for the car.

He shouldn't even have been in the car at all. What was she thinking? "You so don't have to do this," she reminded him.

"I know. I want to." He smiled at her. "Makes me feel noble."

"Okay, fine," Jamie said irritably. "If you get hypothermia, don't blame me."

"I'm too tough for that," he said, and edged the car out onto the snowy road.

They had a couple of slippery moments, but Josh easily kept the car on the road. By now, most people in their right minds were tucked safely indoors so the town lay quiet as they sledded around the frosted lake, which lay under a blanket of white, fringed by fir and alder trees with snowy coats.

"It's like Narnia," Emma said softly.

"It does feel magical," Jamie had to admit. If this were some other man, some other time, she'd have sworn she was falling in love.

They got to Emma's safely. Josh waited until she was through her front door before sliding the car away. It was a small, chivalrous gesture, and Jamie was beginning to suspect that it was typical of this man.

"While we're out is there anything you need from the store?" he asked.

"I'm fine," she said.

"I know," he said with a smile, "but do you need anything?"

"I'll be okay."

He nodded and fell silent, and they drove the rest of the way with only the soft hum of her radio going. Sheryl Crowe and Sting began to sing "Always on Your Side." She suddenly wanted to cry.

She dammed the tears back and quickly got out of the car the minute it came to a stop in her driveway. It was still snowing, gently though, with little flakes drifting down like the last remnants in a snow globe.

Josh unfolded himself from the car and walked around

to where she stood by the passenger door. He lifted her hand and put her car keys in it. "Back safe and sound."

"I'm sorry you have to walk home in the cold."

"Me, too." He closed her hand around the keys. "Call me if you need anything," he added.

"I'll be fine," she insisted. "I'm sorry . . ." About a lot of things.

"It's okay." He gave her hand a squeeze, then pulled a flashlight out of his coat pocket and set off down the driveway.

She watched him walk away under an arch of bowing trees, snow drifting around him, and was possessed by a sudden, crazy urge to chase after him, to grab him and kiss him and tell him to come in the house and get warm. Instead, she ran inside the house and shut the door and locked it.

Josh had gone to college in Idaho, so snow didn't bother him. He was at home skiing on it, driving in it, and walking in it. He also liked to end a day in the snow in front of a roaring fire.

Lissa had been conceived in front of a fire on a snowy night. That one last ski run had chilled Crystal to the bone and he'd been more than happy to warm her up. And boy, had she gotten warm in a hurry. It made him hot just remembering.

But the memory quickly cooled, leaving him feeling empty.

He could have done a good job of warming up Jamie Moore if she'd have let him in.

If he wasn't a cop.

Josh couldn't help what he was. His life path had been set from grade school when he was on the Safety Patrol, holding out that flag at the crosswalk, helping students get safely from one side of the street to the other. Boy Scouts,

Ski Patrol—if it involved helping other people and keeping them safe, he'd done it. It was probably in his DNA. How did a man change his DNA?

He didn't. He trudged on. Jamie had been right about one thing. It was a long way from her house to his.

TWENTY-THREE

*H*eart Lake was still a winter wonderland on Sunday morning, but that didn't stop Josh from making sure the girls got to Sunday school. Crystal would haunt him if he didn't. He also made sure Lissa made it to her new friend Damaris's house. They had all kinds of special girl plans for the afternoon, and Liss hopped out of the truck with a plastic bag filled with mysterious essentials for a good time and a two-liter bottle of pop because Crystal had been big on never going to someone's house without bringing something and he suspected that she'd want her daughters to do the same.

On his way home he drove past Jamie's driveway. He couldn't help wondering what she was doing to pass the time. She had plenty of wood for her stove; he knew that. Maybe she'd thought of something she needed from the store. Remembering how cute she'd looked the night before in that black sweater and those butt-hugging jeans, he could think of something he needed.

Damn it all, there had to be a way to convince this

woman that he wasn't like that piece of shit she'd been married to. He wanted to help her heal her broken heart, but going over to her place when she'd made it clear she didn't want him around would be dumb.

Almost as dumb as wanting her in the first place. He forced himself to drive on by.

He resisted the same temptation on Monday when he was on patrol and saw that her shop was closed. If she needed anything she had his number. She had his number. Period.

He frowned. Women sure complicated a man's life.

He finally finished dealing with the fallout of morning traffic accidents due to icy roads and decided to swing by and check on Mrs. Kravitz and see if she needed anything. There was one woman who would be happy to have his help.

"How nice of you!" she declared. "I was just wondering how I was going to get to Vern's to pick up my blood pressure medicine."

"I'll get it for you on my lunch hour," Josh promised. "Anything you need from the store?"

"Oh, I couldn't."

"Sure you could. What would you like me to get?"

Ten minutes later he left with the ten-dollar bill she'd insisted on giving him and a list of groceries that would probably total closer to twenty. But he wouldn't tell her that. Instead, he'd mysteriously lose the receipt. How many other folks were in Mrs. Kravitz's shoes right now? he wondered. He stopped by the station to see who else was around and found Martinez at his desk, writing a report. "Hey, when you're done with that, I've got an idea."

They had finished making calls and were dividing up their list of known needy subjects when Chief Romeo walked in. "This is a chance for some good PR," said the chief after Martinez told him what they were up to. "You two stay put a minute."

"Gawd," muttered Martinez. "How much you want to make a bet this ends up involving Quinn?"

Sure enough. The chief returned wearing a big grin. "Okay, guys. You both got a ride-along."

The two cops exchanged looks.

"Martinez, you're taking Mayor Quinn. Armstrong, you've got Lezlie Hurst from the paper."

Josh let out a heavy sigh. "You know, Chief, we weren't out for publicity."

"I know. But it's good for the force. People need to see us as the good guys. So here's the deal. You said one of you was picking up stuff for the food bank?"

"Yeah, me," said Martinez.

"Well, now I want both of you to go. We'll get a shot of you guys and the mayor getting stuff at Safeway, then you can do a photo op at the food bank. After that, you can just get on with it."

Josh frowned.

"Get all this done and get the ladies back by four. Temperatures will be dropping and we'll probably be up to our asses in bent fenders by five. And, Armstrong."

"Yes?"

"Make sure you smile for the camera," added the chief.

No need, thought Josh, the mayor will smile enough for all of us.

He was right about that. The mayor not only smiled. She talked, starting the minute Lezlie showed up. Josh tuned most of it out.

"This is such a great idea," said Lezlie when the mayor finally came up for air.

"We think it's a wonderful way to serve our community," the mayor said, beaming. "This is why we're all here."

This is why some of us are here, thought Josh. He looked at his watch. Almost two. Their allotted good-deed time was shrinking. "If you're ready, Mayor, I think we'll get rolling," he said. He walked out of the station, Martinez falling in step with him, and leaving the mayor no choice but to put her money where her big mouth was and follow.

"I'm still a little unclear," said Lezlie as they pulled out of the police headquarters parking lot. "Was this the mayor's idea?"

It was now. "I think she said that, didn't she?" Probably.

"Not exactly. She just led me in that direction, hoping I'd think it."

Lezlie Hurst was a smart cookie. "Well," said Josh, "you know how it is with things like this. One person gets a glimmer and then others jump in and it becomes a great idea. Sort of like in a think tank."

"Who got the glimmer?"

"Does it matter? The important thing is what we're doing, not who thought of it."

Lezlie nodded and wrote in the tablet she had balanced on her lap.

Of course, that was the right thing to say, but part of him wished he'd gone ahead and taken credit for the idea. Surely a certain woman would be impressed if she knew he was a Good Samaritan.

Then again, he'd been a Good Samaritan and driven her home and walked all the way back to his house in the snow and all he'd gotten was cold feet. But not nearly as cold as Jamie Moore's. Hers were frozen as solid as her heart.

"I knew it," Emma said, when she saw the Wednesday edition of the *Heart Lake Herald*. She stuffed the article about Josh into her purse to take with her to the

Chocolate Bar. This was bound to convince Jamie that Josh was the perfect man. Then it would only be a matter of time. At least someone would get a happy ending for the holidays.

Her ending wasn't going to be so happy, not after her meeting with Mr. Pressman at the bank. Of course, she'd known it for months, but now she *knew*. There was no way she could keep her doors open. Come January there would be new retail space for rent on downtown Lake Way, and Emma would be looking for a job. Obviously, she was no business wonder babe like her avatar, Tess L'amour. She could probably get a job somewhere as a sales clerk, though. She knew how to ring up sales. Just not how to make them happen.

The snow was mostly melted now and the streets were clear. No longer snowbound, half of Heart Lake seemed to be out, either walking or driving down Lake Way, finishing errands or heading home. If only a few more of those people had found their way into her shop she wouldn't be facing such a bleak new year.

No tears, she told herself sternly. *This is not the end of the world*. It only felt that way.

If she didn't have the article about Josh to give Jamie she'd have bagged their weekly chocolate binge. A million mochas couldn't make her feel better today.

Sarah had beaten her to the chocolateria and was settled in at one of the bistro tables. She smiled a greeting at Emma, and pulled her purse off the chair next to her to make room. Jamie was at the counter, finishing up with one last customer.

Shirley Schultz.

Emma's despondency began to morph into something with a little more fire. What was Shirley doing in here, buying truffles, when she still owed Emma money for that last bit of fabric robbery she committed at Emma's big sale? She ignored the open chair and moved up to hover in back of Shirley.

Jamie had just rung up the sale. "That will be six thirty-two."

Shirley opened her purse and began the money hunt that was so familiar to Emma. But instead of coming up empty she pulled out a ten-dollar bill.

"Hi, Mrs. Schultz," Emma said. "Needing a chocolate fix?"

Shirley gave a start, then turned around and smiled at Emma. "Emma. How are you, dear?"

"I'm just fine, except for the fact that I'm about to lose my business. How are you? Oh, I see you found some money. Got any extra in there?"

"Oh, dear, I'm afraid that's all I have."

"Well, you can give me that change and I'll subtract it from the bill you owe me. It's only the size of the national debt, but don't let that worry you." Before Shirley could pick up the bag with her purchase and escape, Emma grabbed it. "Wow, thanks. I could use some chocolate. That's really sweet of you." She pulled out a truffle and popped it in her mouth. "Mmm, good." She felt like Jim Carrey in drag, doing something wildly psychotic. It felt good. Everyone should get in touch with her inner Jim Carrey.

"My chocolate!" protested Shirley.

"Oh, I thought maybe you bought it for me since you felt so bad that you owe me money. Gosh. I'd buy a truffle for you, but I seem to have forgotten my checkbook!"

For a moment, silence reigned. Jamie, who was never at a loss for words, gawked at Emma. Then she felt an arm around her shoulder. "Emma," Sarah said gently.

"Well, I never," huffed Shirley.

"You're right you never," Emma said, her voice

hysterical. "You and everyone else in this town. Nobody thinks about how someone like me is supposed to stay in business or pay her rent or eat." Her Jim Carrey moment ended as quickly as it began. Emma dropped the bag on the counter and burst into tears.

"It'll be okay," Sarah said, and tried to hug her.

But, of course it wouldn't. She knew it, they knew it—everybody knew it. And now she'd just eaten Shirley Schultz's chocolate. And she couldn't stop crying. She pulled away, saying, "Give her another. I'll pay for it. I'm sorry, Mrs. Schultz. I'm . . ." *A failure, a loser, all alone, unemployed. Take your pick.* She couldn't stay here a minute longer. She turned and fled from the Chocolate Bar.

Shirley Schultz finally spoke into the stunned silence. "That young woman has a serious problem."

It was all Sarah could do not to grab her skinny neck and wring it.

Jamie spoke up before she could say anything. "Yes, she does. She's too nice. It's no wonder she can't stay in business when people take advantage of her," Jamie added, looking pointedly at Shirley.

"Well, I'm sure I don't," Shirley said stiffly. She snatched the bag with the one remaining candy and marched out of the shop.

"That old leech," Jamie muttered.

"She is," Sarah agreed. "But she's the symptom, not the problem." Jamie was right. Emma was too soft. "Come on," she said. "Let's go find her."

They tracked Emma down at home. Her eyes were red and her makeup was streaked.

"Fix your makeup," Jamie commanded. "We're going out."

"I don't want to go out," Emma snapped in a very un-Emma-like voice.

"It's free food. Don't turn it down."

They took her to Brewsters Brews where Samantha Brewster took one look at her and sent over a margarita on the house. Sarah watched in horror as Emma tipped the glass and chugalugged.

Finally Jamie pulled her arm, forcing her to set down the drink. "Take it easy, will you? Now, talk. What's going on?"

Emma stared at the scarred wood table. "I talked with Mr. Pressman at the bank today. We crunched the numbers and we agreed that it would be best if I . . ." She paused to take a shaky breath. "Turned the key on my business."

It was every business owner's worst nightmare, of course. Sarah laid a comforting hand on her arm. "I'm so sorry."

"Me, too," said Jamie, taking the other arm. "That so totally sucks."

"I'm a failure," Emma sobbed.

"No you're not," Sarah said fiercely. "Failures don't even try. You try harder than anyone I know."

"I had such high hopes. You know, I actually had some people sign up for my next quilting class. If I could have just stayed open a little longer." Emma unwrapped the table setting in front of her and used the napkin for a handkerchief.

She would have simply postponed the inevitable, Sarah thought sadly.

"I'll get a job," Emma said. "I'll go work at Fabricland or Macy's. Maybe I'll get a job at Savemart in the fabric department. I'll probably see half of Heart Lake there," she added bitterly.

"Maybe you could teach quilting classes on the side," Sarah suggested gently. "You know, through the park department. That's what you love the most, isn't it? That would be the best of both worlds. You'd have a paying job and still get to do what you love."

Emma nodded, forcing a wan smile. "I'll have my business loan paid off by the time I'm . . . fifty," she finished on a sob.

Sarah resisted the temptation to tell her that fifty wasn't old. "This will work out somehow. You'll see."

"I'll have to move home with my parents. Lucky them."

"You can move in with me," Jamie offered.

"You don't want me. Nobody wants me, not even my cat." Emma picked up her glass and finished her drink. "Can we get another?"

So far the only "we" drinking was Emma, but Sarah said, "Sure," and signaled the waiter. "Three margaritas."

Jamie produced a small Chocolate Bar bag and held it in front of Emma. "Here. I brought medicine."

Sniffing, Emma pulled out a white chocolate truffle. "Everyone in town's going to think I'm crazy."

Neither Sarah nor Jamie had to ask what she was talking about. "Shirley had it coming," said Jamie.

"I think I'll move," Emma decided. "All those good deeds—why did we bother? This town has no heart and it doesn't deserve any angels. I'm never donating a quilt to anything again. I'm never making a quilt again!"

"You don't really mean that," said Sarah as the waiter arrived with their drinks. "It looks bad now, but think of all your favorite movies. It always looks bad for the heroine at first. But somehow she finds a happy ending."

"Unless she dies in the end," Emma said, and took a deep drink.

"You're not going to die," Sarah said firmly. "Now, a toast. Here's to new beginnings."

"To new beginnings," echoed Jamie.

Emma didn't say anything. She was too busy drinking. They ordered dinner, but she ate little and drank more.

By the time they left the restaurant she was singing "The Bitch Is Back" at the top of her lungs. As they passed a table of gawking middle-aged women who had stopped talking to stare, Emma announced that there would be a big fire sale on Saturday at Emma's Quilt Corner. "Tell everybody," she finished, waving an arm.

"I'm sure they will," Jamie said, guiding her out.

"I'll put the ad in first thing tomorrow. Seventy-five percent off. What the heck! Eighty percent. Do I hear ninety?"

They took her home and helped her into bed, then locked the door and closed her in to sleep off the booze. If only she could sleep off the misery as easily.

"She's going to have a killer headache," Jamie predicted.

"That's the least of her problems," said Sarah. Poor Emma. She tried so hard, dreamed so big. She and Jamie both. Sarah wished she were a fairy godmother. She'd give both girls a pile of money and a handsome prince.

Except she'd tried to give Jamie the handsome prince and Jamie had slammed her heart's door on him. What, by the way, had she done with the *Herald*? She'd meant to show Jamie that article about Josh. It would have been good for Emma to see, too. Maybe it would have encouraged her to read that someone in Heart Lake was still doing good deeds.

But Emma needed more than encouragement right now. She needed money.

Sarah went home feeling suddenly pooped. She put on her slippers and settled on the couch in front of the TV.

She began flipping through the channels toward the Food Network, past the latest search for America's top model, a stupid sitcom, and a rerun from the seventies on the oldies station. And there on AMC was *It's a Wonderful Life,* which would, of course, play all month long on one channel or other. She hadn't watched it in years. She set down the remote and got sucked into watching George Bailey and Mary Hatch fall in love.

By the end of the movie, she was smiling. She called Sam at the station.

"I'm behind you a hundred percent, babe," he said when she'd finished explaining her idea to him. "We've got that money for an emergency and this sounds like one to me."

TWENTY-FOUR

Emma woke up with a screaming headache on Thursday morning. She took two aspirin and went back to bed. To heck with the shop. It wasn't like she had customers banging on the door to get in anyway. She pulled the covers over her head and played dead. It wasn't hard. Her life was over.

By afternoon the headache was gone and she had no excuse to avoid dealing with the details of death. She had to put an ad in the paper for her going-out-of-business sale, make signs for the windows, and cancel the fabric order she'd placed earlier with the Timeless Treasure rep.

She dragged her heavy heart to work where she called the paper and put in the ad. It cost her twice as much as usual because she was a day past the deadline. But at least the ad would come out on Saturday, just in time for the sale. The woman taking the information was polite and businesslike. And uncaring. Not a single, "Gosh, I'm sorry."

Big surprise. No one cared. The campaign to put the

heart back in Heart Lake had been a bust. You couldn't replace something that had never been there.

On Friday she sat all alone in her shop, feeling like a prisoner on death row and thinking about her stupid, rude behavior to Shirley. Boy, that had been the worst kind of movie moment. She hoped Mom and Grandma didn't find out.

Mom and Grandma. Just thinking about them made Emma want to cry. They had both given her money so she wouldn't have to take out such a big business loan. She had sure let them down. Mom had sacrificed her kitchen re-model. She should have redone the kitchen.

If ever there was a time when a girl could have used a comforting talk with her mother this was it, but Emma couldn't work up the nerve to call and deliver the depressing news yet. She wished she could talk to someone. Sarah probably was finishing up at the bakery, up to her elbows in flour, and Jamie was busy running her growing business. Pretty soon she'd be hiring help. She probably wouldn't call Emma, though, not after the way Emma had run Shirley Schultz off.

The memory of her dream came back to mock her. She had so envisioned the people of Heart Lake coming together to make something beautiful—what a bunch of hoo-ha.

A grand total of four women came in and bought fabric and that was the extent of her business. When she shut up shop at five she was ready to cry but willing to admit that deciding to pull the plug had been the right thing to do. She hadn't heard from Jamie to see if she wanted to hang out and she was too embarrassed over her bad behavior to call her friend, so a lonely Friday night loomed ahead of her. *Ugh*.

That margarita she'd had on Wednesday had tasted pretty good. Maybe she'd swing by Brewsters and get another. She got as far as going into the pub, but all those tables packed with laughing friends worked like an invisible force field, keeping her out. She turned and fled, settling for running by Safeway and picking up a bottle of peach-flavored wine and a movie. She'd have her own party.

By ten o'clock the movie was over, the bottle was nearly empty, and Emma was facedown on her bed, fully dressed and drifting toward oblivion. No one in her family drank. She was charting new territory. *Hometown girl makes good.*

Saturday her ringing phone about split her head open. She grabbed the receiver with one hand and the spinning bed with the other and managed a weak hello.

"Where are you?" demanded Jamie.

The words charged in through her ears and banged around in her head. "Don't yell," she protested.

"It's noon and your shop is closed and you have customers."

"Tell them I'm closed for the day. I'm sick," Emma said, and hung up. She squeezed her eyes shut and begged the evil genie whipping the bed around to please stop.

Ten minutes later someone was banging on her front door. She couldn't get up. She couldn't move. She was never going to move again. She was also never going to drink again, either. What had she been thinking, anyway? "Go away," she moaned.

The banging stopped. A moment later it started again at her bedroom window. "Get up and open the door." The voice came through the window muffled, but it still wasn't hard to recognize. Jamie again.

"I'm sick," Emma called, then winced at the pain she'd caused herself.

"Let me in or I'm going to break this window."

Emma staggered to the front door. Her head was going

to explode. Oooh, she would so never do this again. Ever. She opened the door and Jamie marched in. Blinding sunlight followed her. Emma held up a hand to protect her sensitive eyes and moaned. "Shut that."

"Geez, you're a mess." Of course, Jamie wasn't. She was wearing her favorite red leather jacket that she'd found in an upscale thrift store, her perfectly fitted jeans, and red cowgirl boots, and was carrying her favorite red leather purse. "You're hungover," she accused. "What would your mother say?" she added as she led Emma into the kitchen. She got a glass of water, then steered Emma to the bathroom, where she pulled Advil out of the medicine cabinet and shook out two pills. "Here. Swallow this," she instructed. While Emma swallowed, she started the shower running. "Strip and get in," she commanded. "I'll be right back with clothes."

Emma got out of her clothes and into the shower and got the shock of her life. *Cold. Freezing cold!* With a screech she fumbled for the shower knob. Was Jamie trying to kill her?

"Don't you dare turn the temperature up," came a voice behind the shower curtain. "You need to wake up. Wash up and get out. I'm making coffee."

Emma washed up in record time and stumbled into her clothes. She blew her hair almost dry and stuffed it into a scrunchie, then went to the kitchen.

Jamie had shed her jacket and was now busy making toast. She looked Emma over. "Let's put some makeup on you."

"I don't need makeup," Emma said grumpily.

"Trust me," Jamie said as she poured coffee. "You do." She plopped the toast on a paper towel, placed the mug in Emma's hand, and then marched her back to the bathroom. "Okay. You drink. I'll work."

Emma's reflection was completely depressing. Next to

her hot friend she always looked plain and boring. But today she looked plain, boring, and half dead. And she felt completely dead. All she wanted to do was go back to bed. "Why are you here?" she moaned as Jamie began smearing foundation on her cheeks.

"Because it's Saturday and you are supposed to be open for business."

Saturday. Open for business. Going out of business! "Oh, my gosh. My sale!" Emma set the mug on the bathroom counter and turned to dash out the door.

Jamie grabbed her by the arm. "You're already pathetically late. Five more minutes isn't going to make any difference." She returned the mug to Emma's hand. "I called Sarah and told her we were going to be another twenty minutes late."

"Called Sarah. Why?"

Jamie's eyes widened. She blinked, looking like a crook who had just made a misstep under interrogation. "Because she's waiting for the sale to start."

The sale, the sale. "I'm late for my own sale," Emma fretted.

"People will wait," said Jamie. "Eat your toast. Now, look up."

"Don't poke my eye out."

"I won't if you stand still. Quit fidgeting." She finished with Emma's eyes and surveyed her handiwork. "There. That's better. Now, lipstick. Where's your lipstick?"

"I don't know. I lost it. It doesn't matter anyway. Let's go."

Jamie growled and disappeared. A moment later she was back, her own lipstick in hand. "We are so taking you to Macy's for a makeover for Christmas."

Lipstick and a spritz of perfume and Jamie was finally done. "Okay, let's go. Bring the coffee."

And then they were off, Jamie driving as if she were at the Indianapolis 500. "Slow down. You're making me sick," Emma protested. Actually, the thought of having to preside over her going-out-of-business sale was making her a lot sicker than Jamie's driving.

Jamie took her foot off the accelerator and looked over at her. "It's going to be okay. Trust me."

Emma pressed her lips tightly together and nodded. Her friends had obviously committed themselves to getting her through this day. She'd make them proud and be brave. And gracious, even to Shirley.

"By the way, it's probably safe to tell you now that your sale ad didn't make it into the paper," Jamie said as they came down Alder to the four-way stop.

Emma's heart dropped clear down to her toes. "It had to. The woman I talked to promised."

"I know," said Jamie. "We canceled it."

"What?" What kind of friends did she have?

"Trust me," said Jamie as she squealed through the four-way stop and turned left onto downtown Lake Way.

Down the street Emma could see a crowd of people. Behind them . . . what? It looked like a marching band. She let down the car window and strains of "We Wish You a Merry Christmas" floated in to her. "What on earth?"

"It's the welcoming committee," Jamie said, and started honking her horn.

"What are you doing? What's going on?" Was she still really in bed, having some kind of weird dream?

Now she noticed that every parking place on downtown Lake Way was taken, and the crowd extended all the way down the sidewalk and clear onto the little cobblestone street she usually drove down to park her car. Only one space remained, right in front of her shop, and in the middle of it stood . . . "Santa Claus?"

He waved at them and stepped aside and Jamie pulled into the spot. The crowd cheered. Some people were holding up quilts like banners at a football game.

Jamie turned to Emma with a smile and said, "It's a wonderful life, Emma Swanson."

"What?" Okay, she was dreaming.

Santa opened the car door. "Ho, ho, ho. Merry Christmas, Emma," he said in Sam Goodwin's voice.

"Sam?" she squeaked.

"No. Santa." Behind him stood Lezlie Hurst from the paper, snapping pictures.

She began to take in familiar faces. There was Mom and Grandma and Ruth Weisman and Emma's friend Kerrie, and Hope from Changing Seasons Floral, and Kizzy who owned the kitchen shop. And there was . . . Shirley Schultz? Beaming at Emma as if Emma were her long-lost friend.

"I don't understand," said Emma.

"You will in a minute," a familiar voice said in her ear.

She turned to see Sarah standing in back of her, dressed like Mrs. Santa and holding a huge silver holiday ice bucket.

"I hear you've been a very good girl, doing nice things for the people of Heart Lake all year," said Santa Sam. "And now they want to do something good for you." He crooked an elbow for her to take. "What do you say we open for business?"

Still gaping, she took his arm and let him lead her to the front door of her store while everyone cheered and the band played "Santa Claus Is Coming to Town."

"Give me your key," he said. She fumbled out her key and handed it over and he ushered her into the shop, with people squeezing in after her.

In a matter of moments the shop was full. Sarah set the ice bucket on the counter. "Okay, people, it's time to

celebrate Christmas early and show that we've got heart."
Everyone cheered as she ceremoniously dropped in a
check. Then, while the band stood outside and played
"The Twelve Days of Christmas" people crowded forward to put checks and cash into the bucket. Shirley
Schultz squeezed toward the front with her contribution,
saying, "I think this squares us. Merry Christmas, dear."

Emma stared in wonder, tears streaming down her
cheeks. Now Mr. Pressman from the bank was actually
contributing to the bucket. "No one wants to see you go
out of business, Emma," he said. "I hope this helps."

Was this really happening?

From nowhere, several little girls dressed up like elves
appeared, bearing plates of Christmas cookies. Two of
them Emma recognized as Lissa and Mandy Armstrong.
And there was Josh and his dad.

"Merry Christmas, Emma," said Josh, and dropped a
check in the bucket.

Her mom pulled her aside and hugged her. "Sweetheart,
you should have told us you were struggling."

"So you could dip into your savings again?"

"It's all going to be yours someday anyway," Mom reminded her. "We'd rather help you now, when we're alive
to enjoy watching you use it."

Emma hung her head. "I just couldn't waste any more
of your money."

"Since when is opening a lovely shop where you teach
women how to make works of art a waste of money?" her
mother said, and hugged her again.

Jamie had been circulating with plastic glasses and
Santa and Sarah were filling them with, thank God, no
champagne, just sparkling cider. It would be a long time
before Emma could even look at a bottle of alcohol.

Jamie climbed up on the counter and raised her glass.

"A toast," she cried. She looked down at Emma. "To my friend Emma Swanson, the richest woman in Heart Lake."

She got down and hugged Emma while the band struck up "Auld Lang Syne" and everyone started singing.

"Oh, my gosh," said Emma, "it's just like in—"

Jamie held up a hand. "Don't. Say it." And then she smiled and hugged Emma. "You're still in business. This should help you turn the corner. Merry Christmas."

It was such a movie moment. Emma burst into tears.

TWENTY-FIVE

On Sunday at seven P.M., Jamie sat almost front and center at Lakeside Congregational Church, with Josh and his dad on one side of her and Emma on the other. Emma sat smiling and watching with rapt attention as the angel choir with Mandy perched toward the top sang "Hark! The Herald Angels Sing."

Coming in to church with Emma had felt a little like being part of a celebrity entourage. It seemed like half the congregation wanted to greet her, congratulate her on bringing the town together, or slip her a check. No wonder she was beaming. Heart Lake had given her a miracle and she'd be able to keep the shop open another six months; hopefully, enough time to plant her business roots deep in the community.

Now that they were seated the focus was off Emma and on the kids, and Mandy, with her earnest smile and big, brown eyes was cute enough to steal the show. But not enough to make Jamie unaware of the fact that she and Josh were sitting shoulder to shoulder. She'd promised herself that after tonight she wouldn't see him again, but maybe that was one of those promises that were meant to be broken. Maybe she should get to know this man better. Maybe he really was as easygoing as he seemed. What if he was? What if her theories about cops had been all wrong? What if this man represented healing rather than hurt?

A little girl in a red velvet dress walked to the microphone and began reading the Christmas story. "'. . . and she wrapped him in swaddling cloth and laid him in a manger.'"

On cue, Lissa laid a baby doll in a straw-stuffed wooden cradle as a redheaded, freckle-faced Joseph stood watch. Jamie could have had daughters like Lissa and Mandy if she'd only made the right choice the first time around. A deep yearning tugged at her heart, saying, "You could have these girls if you made the right choice now. Come on, what are you waiting for?"

A heart-back guarantee, maybe. A chance to see the future and know she would never get hurt again. Who ever got something like that, though?

The shepherds came and the three wise men made their way down the aisle, the youngest tripping over his bathrobe and almost taking out the two in front of him. More little ones recited poems while Lissa solemnly watched over the baby Jesus. The angel chorus sang one more number, and then the program closed with everyone singing "Joy to the World." After that it was off to the fellowship hall to drink punch and eat cookies.

Mandy and Lissa found their dad and grandpa immediately. Mandy reached for her daddy, who hoisted her into his arms, but Lissa ran to hug Jamie. "You came."

"Of course I came. I couldn't miss your stage debut," Jame said, hugging her back.

"Did I do good?" she asked, her eyes bright.

"Absolutely," said Jamie.

Lissa moved close to her dad for a hug.

"You did great," he told her. "I was proud of you."

Just what every little girl wanted to hear. Had someone told him that or did he know it instinctively?

"What about me, Daddy?" asked Mandy.

"You were the best angel of them all," he said, and tweaked her nose, making her giggle.

"Can we get cookies?" she asked.

"Go for it," he said, lowering her.

The minute her feet touched the ground she was darting through the throng after her sister.

"How about you ladies?" Josh asked. "Want some punch?"

"Sounds great," said Emma.

"I'll help him," George said, and disappeared after his son.

"That man is perfect," Emma said. "Did you see the article about him in the *Herald*? I meant to give it to you."

"No."

Before Emma could go into detail a woman came up to her to remind Emma that she had been at the quilt shop the day before. And given five dollars.

Now Josh was back with punch. "Lissa has a present she's dying to give you. Can you come by the house?"

"A present. But I thought—"

"It's nothing she bought at the festival. I don't have any idea what it is," he said. "Look, I know you're not interested, but if you could just humor me in this one thing."

Now was the time to tell him she was rethinking that, but George had joined them and was handing Emma a punch cup, and then the pastor's wife was introducing herself. She'd tell him later. She'd drop off Emma, and then go to the house and find a moment alone to tell him. Just the thought of taking such a big chance made her heart speed up. She took a sip of her drink, then hiccupped.

Josh raised an eyebrow.

"Must be something in the punch," she muttered.

Emma talked most of the way home, about the people she'd seen in church from the day before, about how cute the girls were, how nice the program was, how it all reminded her of her own childhood. Jamie let her talk on, pretending to listen while fear and hope argued the case for starting a romance with Josh Armstrong.

They were almost to Emma's place when Jamie realized her friend had fallen silent. "You're quiet all of a sudden."

"Just out of steam, I guess," Emma said.

"No," Jamie said slowly. "That's not it. What's wrong?"

Emma sighed. "Oh, I was just—" She bit off the sentence and looked out the window.

"Just what?" Jamie prompted.

"I know it's ungrateful, but I was just wishing I had the whole happy ending. Maybe if Pye came back . . ." She shrugged. "There's something kind of depressing about going to something fun and then coming home to an empty house."

There were worse things to come home to. Jamie knew. "So, move in with me already."

"No offense, but you don't have the right plumbing." Emma traced a heart on the car window. "I wonder if I'll always be . . ."

Jamie had stopped in front of the duplex now. "You won't. You'll find someone."

Emma nodded, but didn't look her in the eye.

Maybe that was just as well, because Jamie wasn't sure if she'd find doubt there or reassurance. With her own track record Jamie was hardly in a position to be forecasting romantic success for her friend.

"See you Wednesday," Jamie said. "We'll have lots to celebrate."

That brought back the old Emma smile. "Yes, we will. Life is good," she added with a determined smile.

She shut the car door and ran to her front porch. Jamie watched as she surreptitiously looked under the nearby bushes for a certain ingrate cat. Stupid animal. Oh, well. Come Christmas Emma would have someone special in her life again. It wouldn't be the two-legged variety, but it would have to do.

If only a girl could go to a man control shelter and pick out a mate. Ha! Man control. Too bad there was no such thing.

And so here she was, speeding off to take a chance on another man. She should hold out for a cat.

Lissa and Mandy greeted her at the door when she got to Josh's. Both girls were in their pajamas. "Daddy said we could stay up extra if we hurried and got ready for bed," Mandy explained.

"Come on in the living room," Josh said to Jamie, and led the way.

A fire was crackling in the fireplace and rumpled sleeping bags decorated with Disney princesses lay on the floor in front of it like abandoned cocoons. Mandy climbed back inside hers, but Lissa picked a carefully wrapped shoe box off the coffee table and gave it to Jamie. "This is for you."

"Aw, that was nice of you," said Jamie.

"Open it," Lissa urged, jumping up and down on her tiptoes.

It was almost more tape than wrapping paper, but Jamie got it undone and open as quickly as possible.

There, tucked inside a ton of tissue paper, lay a little white milk-glass hen on the nest. Just like Sarah's—the one that had gone missing. But it couldn't be the same one. Jamie could feel her smile faltering.

Lissa didn't notice at first. She was too busy explaining. "You said the best gifts were gifts that helped us remember special times together. This will help you remember when we got chicken hats."

Jamie ran her fingers over the chicken. Sarah's had a chip in its tail, so this couldn't be . . . there was the chip in the tail. "It will." What should she do? "Thank you," she managed. She was very aware of Josh studying her. She felt her cheeks warming. And then. *Hic. Oh, geez, not now.*

"Jamie, could I see you alone a minute?" His voice was carefully neutral. "Come on out in the kitchen."

"Daddy," Lissa protested.

"We'll be right back," he said. He turned and walked to the kitchen, expecting Jamie to follow.

She looked at her watch. "Actually, I should get going."

"This'll just take a minute," he said.

She followed him out with a wildly beating heart and a determination to lie.

He flipped on the light and turned to face her. In a low voice, he asked, "What's wrong?"

"Wrong? Nothing. I was just, it was such a surprise."

"Not a good one. Tell me what's going on."

She forced herself to look at him. "I . . ."

"Come on, Jamie. You've tried your best to lie to both of us about how you feel about me and I get that. You're scared. But right now, for some reason, you're lying to me about that stupid chicken my daughter gave you and I'm scared. Tell me what's going on here."

She bit her lip. How did she tell a cop that she suspected his daughter was giving her stolen goods? *Oh, God.*

"Please."

"It's just that, well, it looks like a little chicken Sarah had in her kitchen. She told me it . . . disappeared."

"After one of the baking classes?"

"She wasn't sure."

"Is this the chicken?" He wasn't yelling. He was calm. But determined.

"I'm pretty sure."

"And is there a reason you're pretty sure?"

"Sarah's had a little chip on the tail. So does this one." She shrugged. "Circumstantial evidence. Probably lots of these chickens have chips on their tails."

He took a deep breath and nodded, then walked out of the kitchen. Jamie followed him. She thought her heart had been going fast before. That was nothing. Now it was at the races, roaring around the track.

Mandy had fallen asleep in her sleeping bag. Lissa sat on the couch, next to her grandpa. Both looked puzzled.

Josh knelt in front of her. He pulled the trinket out of the box and held it up as if he were about to do a one-on-one show-and-tell. "Liss, I need you to tell me where you got this chicken."

He was trying to stay calm, but Jamie could detect anger in his voice.

So could Lissa. She looked at him, her brows suddenly heavy with suspicion. She clamped her lips shut in a pout.

"Did you buy it somewhere?"

"No."

"Mrs. Goodwin had a chicken just like this one. It's gone missing. Did you take her chicken?"

Panic flitted across Lissa's face. "No, Daddy."

"Tell me the truth," Josh said, his voice getting firmer.

"I didn't take it," she insisted, her voice defensive.

This was how things escalated to ugly. "Josh," Jamie pleaded.

He waved her to silence. "Liss, this is serious. You need to tell me."

"I didn't take Mrs. Goodwin's chicken," Lissa said, her own little voice angry. She tried to take the knickknack out of his hand and he closed his palm over it. "Give it to me!" Now she was off the couch, red-faced and teary.

"Liss, how did you get this chicken?" His voice was getting louder.

Did he realize how much bigger he was than this child, how completely scary he must look? Jamie's heart was thudding against her chest now. If he struck that child, if he dared to strike that child . . .

"It's mine. You can't take it!" Lissa cried. "I want to give it to Jamie. It's mine!"

Now Mandy was awake, struggling out of her sleeping bag. "Come on, baby," George said. "Let's get you into bed before the fireworks really start." He picked her up and carried her off down the hall.

Meanwhile, Lissa's tantrum was ramping up. "You can't take it," she cried, pulling at her father's hand.

Josh moved the coveted chicken out of reach. "Lissa."

She stamped her foot. "It's mine! It's mine!"

His big hand came down on the coffee table with a thud that sounded like thunder and made Jamie jump. The table shuddered under the impact. He leaned over his daughter, looking like some kind of ogre. "Lissa Rae, you are not telling me the truth!"

Suddenly Jamie wasn't seeing the frustrated father in front of her. She was seeing a husband in a rage, sweeping all the candles she'd just made from the kitchen table onto the floor. Then he turned and came toward her, his hand raised. "Don't! Stop it, stop it!"

Both Josh and Lissa turned to stare at her in shock.

She was on her feet, ready for either fight or flight. When had she jumped off her chair? The room was warm, but she was suddenly freezing. She rubbed her arms and said, "I need to go."

"No," Lissa cried. "Don't go." She scrambled over the coffee table and ran to Jamie, throwing her arms around her. "I didn't steal the chicken. I didn't. I traded for it fair and square."

"Traded," Josh repeated, mystified.

Lissa was sobbing now. Jamie knelt and the child threw her arms around Jamie's neck. "I don't want Damaris to go to jail."

"Damaris?" Josh's voice overflowed with shock and confusion. In one step he was to Jamie and Lissa.

If he laid a hand on this child . . .

He knelt and touched Lissa's shoulder and she whirled and threw herself into his arms. "Don't send her to jail, Daddy."

He picked his daughter up and settled on the couch with her on his lap. "No one is going to send Damaris to jail, but you need to tell me what you know."

"She'll get in trouble," Lissa wailed.

Josh stroked his daughter's hair. "Yes, she probably will. But you know what?"

Lissa shook her head, but kept crying.

"She'll also learn that it's wrong to steal. She did take the chicken, didn't she?" Lissa nodded and he wiped the tears from her cheeks. "And if she learns now that she can't take things that aren't hers then maybe she won't do it when she's bigger, when she could get in lots and lots of trouble and go to jail. Isn't it better to help your friend now so that won't happen?"

Lissa's sobs were dying down. "But she won't be my friend anymore."

"Maybe not," said Josh. "But you'll be a good friend to her if you help her be honest. Sometimes being a friend is about more than being liked. Do you understand?"

She sniffed. "I think so."

"Good. Now, tell me what happened."

And so the whole story came out. Lissa had seen Damaris snitch the chicken, but, not wanting to get her new friend in trouble, she'd kept quiet. "And when I was at her house, we were trading and she asked if I'd trade my hair beader, and I wanted to give Jamie something special. So I did," she finished, and started crying again.

Josh heaved a big sigh. "Baby girl, you knew it wasn't really her chicken to trade. That made what you did wrong. Do you understand?"

Lissa wrapped her arms around her father's neck, burying her face in his shoulder. "I know, Daddy."

It took a few more minutes to settle her down. Learning that she wasn't going to be punished finally did the trick. "I think you've already learned your lesson. Don't you?" he asked. She nodded and he kissed her. "You were a brave girl to tell me. I'm proud of you for doing that. Now, go get Grandpa to tuck you in bed."

Too embarrassed to look at Jamie, Lissa nodded, slipped off his lap, and ran down the hall.

Josh and Jamie sat on opposite sides of the living room, neither speaking. The fire in the fireplace continued to crackle.

"I'm sorry about all that," he said at last.

She nodded. Just as Lissa had found it hard to look at her, now Jamie found it difficult to make eye contact with Josh. "What are you going to do about the other girl?"

"I'm going to talk to her parents, see if I can convince them to take her to Sarah, return this, and apologize."

Suddenly, there was nothing more to say, so Jamie nodded and stood. She was surprised her legs could hold her, shaky as they felt.

"I'm sorry you had to get pulled into this," he said.

"Me, too," she said. "I should go." And stay gone. There

could be no future for the two of them. Maybe there could be no future with her and any man. The image of Josh pounding his fist on the coffee table replayed itself in her mind. Men were too unpredictable. Too big. Too dangerous.

He followed her to the door. "Jamie," he began as she opened it.

She didn't stop, didn't look at him. She just ran down the walk and got into her car. Then she drove off as fast as she could.

TWENTY-SIX

$\mathcal{M}$onday night found Jamie over at Sarah's for dinner. "It's not as free as you think," Sarah had said after Jamie made a crack about never turning down a free meal. "I've got a ton of Christmas presents to wrap and I'm hoping you'll help me."

It sounded like a great way to earn a meal to Jamie. Now she pushed away her plate. "I'm stuffed."

"One piece of my lasagna and you're stuffed?" Sarah made a face. "I've had birds that eat more than you."

"Do you know how many calories are in lasagna?" Jamie countered. "Anyway, I had two helpings of salad."

Sarah shook her head. "You hardly ate anything. I feel guilty putting you to work."

"Like playing with ribbon and paper and all those cool trimmings you always get is work?" Jamie said, rolling her eyes. "Bring it on."

"You asked for it," said Sarah. "I hope you have enough strength for this. It's going to be a long evening. But don't worry. I'll make sure we quit in time for us both to get a good night's sleep."

"There is no such thing," Jamie said, following her into the living room.

"Still getting up before the crack of dawn?" asked Sarah.

"Oh, yeah. You can't believe how many holiday orders I'm getting."

"I think I can. Your chocolates really are to die for."

"That's about what I'm doing these days. I'm not used to working as hard as you. It's killing me."

Sarah already had a collection of gift boxes in varying shapes piled on the couch and paper and ribbon on the floor and coffee table. "Let's see, I still need to get scissors and tape. I'll be right back." She picked a folded newspaper off the corner of the coffee table. "Did you ever see this?" she asked, handing it to Jamie.

"Oh, the article about Emma's shop?"

"No, something else," Sarah said, and vamoosed.

Jamie looked at it and frowned. There, in front of the food bank, stood Josh Armstrong and another cop, their arms full of boxes of bread. Mayor Quinn had positioned herself between them and was displaying a Jackie Kennedy smile. Boy, Sarah didn't miss a beat. Jamie set the paper aside. She wasn't even going to read this. What was the point?

The caption under the picture read: *Heart Lake Police Force Does Its Part to Keep the Heart in Heart Lake.* Very catchy. She wasn't going to read any more.

She picked it up. *Today Heart Lake's finest went above and beyond the call of duty, helping residents cope with the complications that come from snow and icy streets. Police helped deliver food to the food bank and assisted senior citizens with transportation to doctor appointments. Although Josh Armstrong, the mastermind behind the idea, refuses to take credit . . .*

"Isn't that cool?" said Sarah.

Jamie gave a start and dropped the newspaper. "Yeah. It's great to see that people have really gotten in the spirit of this."

"He's a good man, kiddo," Sarah said as she put the scissors and tape on the coffee table.

"With a temper." There, that should settle it. Jamie grabbed a box with a shirt in it. "Who's this for?"

"Okay, I get the message. But just remember, everyone has a temper, male and female. There's a world of difference between temper and abuse."

"I know that," Jamie snapped.

Sarah wagged a finger at her. "Hey, don't lose your temper."

Jamie pointed a finger right back at her. "You know, Santa does not bring chocolate to women who give their nieces a bad time." The doorbell rang. "Is somebody else coming over?"

Sarah shook her head, looking mystified.

"Maybe it's your buddy from across the street," Jamie teased.

"He's history, thank God," Sarah called over her shoulder.

A moment later Jamie could hear the rumble of a male voice and Sarah saying, "Come on in." And then she was back in the living room with Josh right behind her.

Okay, this was a setup. Except Josh looked as surprised to see Jamie as she was to see him.

"Sit down," said Sarah. "I'll make us some coffee."

"I'll help," Jamie offered, and started to get up.

"Stay where you are," Sarah told her. "It doesn't take two people to make coffee."

She sat back against the couch cushions with a hiccup.

He shook his head at her. "No need to be nervous. I'm

not going to hit you. That's not me. Oh, I did hit somebody once."

Ha! She knew it.

"I popped Lloyd Schmeckel in the nose in fifth grade when I found out he'd caught my sister on the playground and looked down her shirt. Does that count against me?"

If it weren't such a serious subject, she would have smiled.

"When I was a senior my dad caught me drinking with my buddies and grounded me. It was right before the big homecoming game. I was a wide receiver and I was good. Let me tell you, I was mad as hell that I wasn't going to get to show my stuff at homecoming, so mad I punched a hole in my bedroom wall. I worked for my dad every Saturday for the next six months to pay off that temper tantrum."

"So, you're telling me you don't have a temper?" Right. She'd seen for herself.

"No, I'm telling you I would never raise a hand to anyone, especially a woman."

"You are three times as big as your daughter. You scared her when you hit that table."

"You mean I scared you."

"She was upset."

"Of course she was. And yes, she was scared—scared she was going to lose her friend, scared I'd be mad at her and disappointed in her, scared she'd get in trouble. But she wasn't scared I would hurt her. Think about it. Did she run from me? Cringe? Would my dad have let me hurt her?"

Jamie chewed her lip, reliving the scene. Lissa had been upset and crying, but she hadn't been even remotely afraid to throw a tantrum or throw herself into her daddy's arms.

"I wish I could convince you to trust me, to take a chance," Josh said softly.

Deep down, desperately, she wanted to. She wanted a family of her own to wrap presents for at Christmas, to bake with, to hang out with. She wanted to sit in a church pew, not as somebody's friend, but as a proud mom. But, "I can't." The words barely came out.

"Are you sure? Look, I get that you're scared. I'm scared, too."

She stared at him, surprised.

"I'm scared that if I finally convince you to go out with me things still won't work out and my girls'll be crushed. I'm scared that if things do work out you'll . . ." He stopped and cleared his throat. "I've already lost one woman I loved. I don't want to lose another. Hell, I'm scared most of the time that I'll screw up with the girls. We're all scared of stuff, Jamie," he added softly, "but what are you gonna do, curl up in your closet?"

"I have a life," she informed him. "I have a business."

"You have a heart, too. What are you going to do with that?"

She didn't know. So she said nothing.

He nodded, his lips pressed together. "Yeah, so I guess there's no room for me in your life or your heart." He turned his back on her and called, "Hey, Sarah, how about that coffee."

Awkward silence enveloped the room while they waited for Sarah to reappear. She returned bearing a tray of steaming mugs and a sugar bowl. "You don't take cream in your coffee, right?" she said to Josh.

"Just black is fine. Thanks," he said, and helped himself to a mug.

Sarah sat down and handed Jamie a mug. Then, careful not to look at her niece, she started stirring sugar into her coffee. Jamie was sure she'd been eavesdropping from the kitchen. "What brings you here, Josh?"

"Actually, I'm meeting someone here in . . ." He checked his watch. "About five minutes."

"Anyone I know?" asked Sarah.

"One of your baking students. She has something of yours to return to you."

Sarah looked at him, understanding dawning. "My milk-glass hen."

"That would be it."

Sarah sat back and took a deep drink from her mug. "How did you end up involved in this?"

"My daughter had it. She'd traded something for it."

Sarah's eyebrows shot up. "But she didn't know."

"She knew. Dad is bringing her to the bakery tomorrow to apologize."

"Oh, but she didn't take it," Sarah protested.

"She knew who did and she didn't do anything. I understand that she was worried about losing her friend, but I want her to get in the habit of doing what's right, no matter what."

"Very wise," Sarah approved.

The doorbell rang. Josh motioned for Sarah to stay seated and went to let in Damaris. Sarah turned to her niece. "If you let this man get away I am going to have you committed."

And then Damaris was in the room, her mother standing behind her with her hands resting protectively on the girl's shoulders. So this was the demon child who had driven Sarah nuts. Right now she just looked like a frightened little girl. Her mother wore a coat over a nurse's uniform. Jamie wondered if this was the poor woman's lunch break. Some way to spend your lunch break.

Damaris looked up at her mom as if for assurance and the woman nodded.

"I'm sorry I stole your chicken, Mrs. Goodwin,"

Damaris said, holding out the knickknack. "It was wrong." She began blinking furiously. In spite of her efforts, tears leaked from her eyes.

"Thank you for returning it," Sarah said. "I appreciate that."

"Do you hate me?" Damaris asked in a small voice.

Sarah gave her a pitying smile. "I'm sad about what you did, but I don't hate you."

Damaris burst into tears and covered her face. "I'm so sorry."

Sarah went to the child and hugged her. "I know. We'll put this behind us, shall we?"

Damaris nodded, still clinging to her. "Can I ever come over again? I promise I won't take anything."

"Of course you can," Sarah said, and stroked her hair.

"Thank you," said her mother, who now had tears in her eyes. "Come on, sweetie, let's go."

Damaris nodded and followed her mother out of the room, keeping her gaze focused on her feet. Josh saw them out the door.

Jamie expelled a breath and fell back against the couch cushions. "I feel like I'm in a soap opera."

Now Josh was back. "Thanks, Sarah," he said. "You probably helped that kid more just now than you'll ever know."

"Time will tell," Sarah said.

Then nobody said anything. Sarah was probably busy mulling over this latest encounter with Damaris. What was Josh thinking? Jamie knew what she was thinking: yes, she probably should be committed. She had to be completely insane not to give this man a chance.

"I'd better be going," Josh said at last, and started for the door.

Sarah stood and walked with him. "Thanks for coming. And for sorting this all out. You're a good man, Josh."

"I try," he said.

He did. Jamie wasn't sure she'd ever met a man who seemed to try so hard on so many fronts. Still, she sat rooted to the couch, assessing her sanity, and let him walk out the door.

TWENTY-SEVEN

Christmas came with just enough white to dust the lawns, leaving Heart Lake residents free to roam back and forth and enjoy the holidays. With the kids and grandkids, Sam's folks, her sister and brother-in-law, and Jamie and Sarah's other niece, Krysten, Sarah's house was full. So was her heart. She basked in the joy of Christmas morning while her granddaughters ripped into presents with excited squeals.

"It's so good to be home," said her daughter, Stephanie, hugging her.

"Amen to that," said her son the starving actor, helping himself to another piece of Sarah's Danish puff pastry.

If only she could keep them all here. Forever. There was nothing like family.

But later, after the Armstrongs had arrived, and Lissa and Mandy had presented her with Martha Stewart's latest Christmas book, she had a sudden epiphany. Family was important, but family was an ever-growing, always changing animal. The more you opened your heart, the bigger it got.

"Who's the hunk?" Krysten asked Jamie after dinner as the sisters loaded the dishwasher.

"Just a friend of the family," said Jamie.

"Hmm. I wouldn't mind getting friendly with him," said Krysten. "Is he taken?"

It shouldn't have bothered her that her little sister was interested in Josh. "He's a cop."

"So I guess that means you don't want him. He's not like Grant, is he?"

A montage of Josh scenes flashed through Jamie's mind. She saw him with his daughters, hoisting them onto his shoulders, laughing when he lost at Sorry! She saw him kneeling in the snow, changing that woman's tire, saw the picture of him in the newspaper, his arms full of food for the food bank. "No, he's not at all like Grant." He wasn't! *Well, duh.* "I think he's got someone."

Emma hurried home from her parents' house anxious to check on the new baby. It had been so sweet of Sarah and Jamie to give her a cat for Christmas, and the kitten, which she'd christened Angel, had quickly captured her heart. Most of it, anyway.

"Mommy's home," she called as she set her grocery bag of presents on the hall floor. A fat little ball of orange and white fur skittered down the hallway, anxious to welcome her. "Have you missed me, sweetie?"

She picked up the kitten and it immediately started purring.

She cuddled it to her and walked into the kitchen. "Are you ready for your Christmas dinner?" Silly question. The new baby was always ready to eat.

She mixed some Kitten Chow with a big spoonful of canned cat food and set the bowl on the floor. "There you go. Eat up."

Angel crouched in front of the bowl and dug in. "You are such a pretty baby," Emma informed the kitten as it ate. "Maybe after you're finished we should put on some Christmas music and do some quilting. What do you think of that idea?" It sounded pretty okay to Emma.

Except it was Christmas and she was finishing out the day on a note of okay? Christmas wasn't a time to be alone in an apartment. Maybe she'd go over to Sarah's for a while. They'd be happy to fold her into the crowd.

But no matter how long she stayed, she'd still have to come home alone. "You know what," she told the kitten. "I think while you're eating, I'll just go check in with Tess." Now that she had a few pennies to spare, she'd been allowing Tess to spend a little money. Tess had bought a new condo and even hosted a Christmas party. "I should have had a Christmas party this year," she told the cat. "I have some great friends."

Fortunately, Angel was just a baby and Emma didn't have to explain about her less than stellar love life.

The doorbell rang. Maybe Jamie was done with Christmas at Sarah's and had decided to stop by. Emma hurried to the door and opened it.

There stood a man in jeans and a red parka. He wasn't drop-dead gorgeous like Josh Armstrong. In fact, he had all the makings of a geek: glasses, a cheap haircut, skinny legs, which meant that an equally skinny torso lurked beneath that bulky coat. But he had a cute face and a nice smile, and in his gloved hands he was holding . . . "Pye!"

The black cat launched himself from the man's arms, landed on the floor, and ran off down the hall, probably anxious to find something to shred while she stood in the doorway, ready to cry with joy. "Where did you find him?"

"My mom actually found him hiding under the bushes out by the back porch," said the man. "She volunteers at the animal shelter and she saves every lost cat poster she finds. And every cat," he added.

"Gosh, I looked for him everywhere. Where did you say you live?"

"Oregon."

"Oregon?" she stammered.

"But my parents live three blocks over," he added with a smile. "I'm up visiting for the holidays."

And probably busy with his family. Oh, well.

He nodded in the general direction of the prodigal. "Your cat's got an interesting name. What's Pye stand for?"

"Pyewacket. I named him after the cat in *Bell, Book, and Candle*."

"Great name," he said with an approving nod.

She could have kept him standing there talking for the rest of the day. But the door was open, and Pye could run away again. And Angel could follow him right out. "I shouldn't keep you there, standing in the cold."

"Then ask me in," he suggested.

Tess could wait.

Once inside, her visitor pulled off a glove and held out a hand. "My name's James Stuart."

As in Jimmy? It had to be a sign.

She shook his hand. It was warm, just like his smile. "I'm Emma Swanson."

His eyes got big. "Are you the woman with the quilt shop?"

She nodded.

"My mom has bought stuff from you. She's new here. In fact, she was at that fund-raiser at your shop." He shook his head and smiled. "I'm sorry I missed that. It sounded like something right out of a movie."

Emma stared at him. "What did you say?"

"Uh, like something out of a movie?"

"That's what I thought you said." She didn't have to get hit over the head with a cosmic hammer to know what to do next. "How about some eggnog?"

The sugar buzz finally wore off and the girls fell asleep in the car on the way home from the Goodwins'. Josh and George carried them into the house and laid them out in their beds, shoes and all. Crystal would probably have insisted they wake up and brush their teeth. Josh just let them sleep.

He got a beer for his dad and himself and they slouched companionably on the couch. "Man, that was pandemonium," George said. "All those people, kids running everywhere."

"Aw, you loved it," said Josh.

"You need to find a woman."

Where the hell had that come from? Josh stared at his dad.

"I mean a new woman. I don't think Jamie's ever gonna come around, son. She's damaged goods."

Josh gave a snort. "Well, Merry Christmas to you, too," he said, and took a long drink of his beer.

"I'm just saying I think you might need to know when the game is lost. That's all."

"I know." Josh walked to the living room window. "It's starting to snow again."

"I thought this place didn't get a lot of snow," Dad said in disgust.

"Me, too. Oh, well. The girls will love it."

"Yeah, they'll love dragging their poor, old gramps out in the cold is what they'll love," Dad said grumpily. He picked up his half-finished thriller, ending the conversation.

Josh continued to stand by the window, watching the flakes fall. If Crystal was here she'd have dragged him outside for a walk. If Crystal was still alive . . . But she wasn't. He downed the last of his beer and dropped the bottle in the recycle. He felt restless. Maybe he'd take a walk in the snow by himself. A walk down Memory Lane, he thought bitterly. It looked like memories were all he was going to have.

"I'm going out," he announced.

"Go ahead," said his dad from behind his book. "Freeze your balls off."

Not a bad idea. Maybe life would be easier if he could forget he was a guy. He put his coat back on, shoved his feet into his boots, and slipped out the door. The snow was already coating everything white, including the street. He was glad he had the week off. Tomorrow would be a fun day, filled with fender benders and grumpy commuters.

He was halfway down the block when a familiar Toyota came sliding down the street. It skidded to a crooked stop at the curb. The passenger window slipped down. "It's snowing," Jamie informed him.

"Yeah, I noticed."

"I'm afraid I'm going to get stuck. Would you mind driving me home?"

Actually, he would. Dad was right, the game was lost. What was the point in staying on the field?

But he couldn't let her drive off alone. She'd wind up in a ditch for sure. He walked around to the driver's side. "Move over."

She obliged and he climbed in behind the steering wheel and moved the seat back. "This car is a tin can," he grumbled.

"I'm thinking of getting a new car. Something a little bigger."

"Why bother? This works for you, and you probably get pretty good gas mileage."

She frowned slightly, like he'd said something wrong.

"How did you like my family?" she asked.

"They're great. The girls had a good time."

"I'm glad. My sister liked you."

"Yeah?" What, now she was setting him up with her sister? Well, why not? It was time to move on. He should do that. What kind of perfume was Jamie wearing, anyway? It smelled good.

She didn't say anything more. Instead, she hiccupped.

Josh frowned at her. "Okay, why are you nervous now?"

"I'm not," she insisted.

She really was the world's worst liar, but he let it go.

They were almost to her driveway when Jamie suddenly blurted, "I told her you were taken."

He almost slid off the road. "What?"

She hiccupped again.

Now what was going on in her head? He nudged the car through the snow up to her house. They both got out and he walked around to the passenger side and held out her keys. "Here you are, home safe and sound." He remembered the last time he'd brought her home in the snow. He'd wanted so badly to come in.

This woman was both his best dream and his worst nightmare. Things had never been this complicated with Crystal. Was she up in heaven, laughing at him?

"Would you mind coming in and building a fire?" Jamie asked in a small voice.

Did she have any idea how she was torturing him? "Yeah, actually, I would. I'm sorry, Jamie. I don't know what is going on in your head, but I can't do this."

"I'm not sure I can, either, so I'd really appreciate it if you'd give me some help." She grabbed him by the coat and pulled him toward her.

Surprised, he let her.

Now they were standing body to body, heart to heart. She reached up and took his face in her mittened hands. "I hope you bend," she murmured.

He did. And then his lips touched hers and that was all it took to start a bonfire. He wrapped his arms around her and kissed her long and thoroughly. She finally pulled back, looking slightly dazed. He hoped Crystal was smiling. He was.

He took Jamie by the hand. "Come on. Let's go inside and build a fire."

A NEW SEASON

A newcomer to Heart Lake on this Saturday afternoon might have thought that there was a big January sale going on somewhere down by Emma's Quilt Corner. In spite of the dusting of snow on the ground, every parking space on downtown Lake Way was taken and a good-sized crowd of people milled along both sides of the little no-name cobblestone street in their coats, hats, and mittens.

Emma, Sarah, and Jamie stood up toward the front of the crowd with their nearest and dearest, taking it all in.

"I can't believe this turnout," said Jamie.

"A lot more than at our kickoff meeting," Emma agreed. "I think maybe we did make a difference."

Sarah gave her a one-armed hug. "You bet we did."

"I think everybody's here now. It would be nice if we could get on with this before our tails freeze," said Jamie.

"Don't worry," said Josh, hugging her from behind. "I'll keep your tail warm."

Emma's new boyfriend, James, had driven up from

Oregon to help her celebrate the success of their good-deed campaign. He smiled at that and took her gloved hand.

"Oh, good. Finally," Jamie said as the excited crowd parted to let Mayor Quinn through.

"Always making an entrance," Sarah said in disgust.

"Let's hope she doesn't take too long to make an exit," said Jamie, hunching her shoulders against the tiny snowflakes that were starting to fall.

Now the mayor was in front of the new street pole at the corner. Its top was covered with a big sheet of canvas held on by a giant red ribbon bow. She raised her hands for silence. "As you all know, we are honoring three special women today. It's easy to take the place where you live and the people you live with for granted. Thank you, ladies, for saving us from that." The crowd exploded into applause and hoots as she awarded each woman with a commemorative plaque and shook her hand.

"Thank you," Sarah said, speaking for all of them. "A town can't come together unless everyone cooperates. Many of you were at the grange earlier this week and shared some of the good things you've been doing for each other, and that just proves my point. The honor belongs to all of you."

Her speech earned even more applause than Mayor Quinn's. Madame Mayor almost managed to look genuine when she smiled and hugged Sarah as everyone clapped.

The mayor reached up and pulled off the bow and the canvas with a flourish to reveal the new street sign. "I now declare this street Angel Lane in honor of our three good angels, Sarah Goodwin, Emma Swanson, and Jamie Moore."

"Wow," breathed Emma as everyone clapped and hooted.

"Just like in a movie," said James, putting an arm around her shoulder.

The little no-name alley now had a name, and Heart Lake was, hopefully, a more closely knit town. Mission accomplished.

There was nothing left to do but celebrate, so the three friends and their biggest fans went to the Family Inn for pie and coffee.

"I feel like I'm married to Mother Teresa," said Sam, as the waitress freshened his coffee cup. "You could probably run for mayor right now and win by a landslide."

"Don't tempt her," said Jamie with a grin. "There's probably nothing she'd like better."

"Good point," said Sam. "And if you became mayor I'd really never see you."

"Don't worry," Sarah assured him, and gave him a kiss on the cheek. "I've got my hands full keeping you in line. The last thing I need is to have to worry about a whole town. But it felt good to know that I've made a difference right here where I live."

"I agree," said Emma. She smiled at James. "And tonight I feel like the luckiest woman alive."

"Second luckiest," Jamie corrected, taking Josh's hand.

"Well, then, here's to three lucky women," said Sarah, raising her coffee cup. "And to giving season. May it last all year long."

FAVORITE RECIPES

Sarah and Jamie thought you might enjoy making some of their favorite recipes.

Happy eating!

From Sarah

HERBED BISCUITS

2 cups flour
4 teaspoons baking powder
$1/2$ teaspoon salt
1 tablespoon fresh rosemary
$1/2$ cup butter, room temperature
$2/3$ cup milk
1 egg

Sift dry ingredients into a mixing bowl. Cut in butter as for pie crust, then add the milk and egg. Mix until you have dough, but don't overmix. Roll out dough into a $1\frac{1}{4}$-inch-thick round and cut with a biscuit cutter (or cut into squares with a knife). Bake on ungreased cookie sheet for 20 minutes at 350°.

Makes 6 to 9 biscuits, depending on what size you cut the biscuits.

RAISIN PIE COOKIES

FILLING
1 cup raisins
1/2 cup sugar
1/2 cup water
2 1/4 teaspoons flour
1/8 teaspoon cinnamon and nutmeg

COOKIE
3 1/2 cups flour
2 teaspoons baking powder
1 teaspoon baking soda
1/2 teaspoon salt
1 teaspoon vanilla
1 cup sugar
1 cup shortening
1 egg
1/2 cup milk

Mix all of the filling ingredients in a small saucepan and cook over medium heat, stirring constantly, until thick. Remove from heat.

Cream together shortening and sugar in mixing bowl, then add egg and milk. Sift dry ingredients and add to sugar, shortening, egg, and milk. In manageable batches, roll out the dough to about 1/4-inch thickness (as for sugar cookies). Cut out with round 6-inch cookie cutter (or, if you don't have one, a drinking glass), and lay out rounds on ungreased cookie sheets. Reserve enough rounds to top each bottom round.

Put 1 heaping teaspoon of filling on top of each cookie round. Top with remaining rounds and then crimp the edges together as if making a little tart. Bake for 15 minutes at 350°.

Note: This recipe makes approximately 28 cookies, depending on whether you use a biscuit cutter or make your cutouts the old-fashioned way, using a drinking glass. You might be able to squeeze out another cookie or two from the dab of dough left in the bowl, but Sarah prefers to either toss it or let her granddaughters play with it as this kind of dough can get tough after too many encounters with the rolling pin. Anyway, making creations out of leftover cookie dough is a great way to introduce little girls to the fun of playing in the kitchen.

PUMPKIN COOKIES

COOKIE
1/2 cup butter
1/2 cup shortening
1 cup sugar
2 cups flour
1 teaspoon baking soda
1/2 teaspoon salt
1 teaspoon cinnamon
1 cup canned pumpkin
1 egg
1 cup raisins
1/2 cup chopped walnuts or pecans

FROSTING
3 tablespoons butter
1 tablespoon cream cheese, room temperature
4 teaspoons milk
1/2 cup brown sugar, packed
1 cup powdered sugar
3/4 teaspoon vanilla

Cream shortening, butter, and pumpkin in mixing bowl; blend in egg. Sift together dry ingredients and blend into pumpkin mixture. Fold in raisins and nuts. Drop by spoonfuls (Sarah uses a regular dinner spoon) onto an ungreased cookie sheet. Bake at 350° for 15 minutes.

Combine butter, milk, and brown sugar in a saucepan. Cook over low heat, stirring constantly, until dissolved.

Remove from burner and add cream cheese. Stir until smooth. Add powdered sugar and vanilla. Spread over warm cookies. Let dry completely before storing.

Makes about 3 dozen.

OATMEAL COOKIES

$1/2$ cup margarine
$1/2$ cup sugar
$1/2$ cup brown sugar, packed
1 egg
$1^1/2$ cups flour
$1^1/2$ cups rolled oats (Sarah uses the old-fashioned kind)
3 teaspoons baking powder
$1/2$ teaspoon salt
2 teaspoons orange extract
$1/2$ cup white chocolate chips
$1/2$ cup dried cranberries

Cream together margarine, sugars, and egg. Add extract. Sift together dry ingredients and add to creamed mixture. Finally, mix in white chocolate chips and dried cranberries. Drop by rounded tablespoons onto ungreased cookie sheets and bake at 350° for 15 minutes.

Makes about 28 cookies, depending on how much of the dough disappears before getting to the baking sheet. These cookies go fast, so Sarah recommends doubling the recipe.

GINGER COOKIES

¾ cup shortening
1 cup sugar
¼ cup molasses
1 egg
2 cups flour
2 teaspoons soda
½ teaspoon salt
½ teaspoon cloves
½ teaspoon ginger
1 teaspoon cinnamon

Cream shortening and sugar until smooth. Add molasses and egg and cream until thoroughly mixed. Sift dry ingredients. Add to creamed mixture. Sarah doesn't do this, but you can chill for an hour if you want a dough that is easier to work with. Form dough into 1-inch balls and bake at 350° for 12 minutes or until browned and flattened.

Makes about 3 dozen.

SARAH'S HUCKLEBERRY COFFEE CAKE
(Adapted from a recipe by Rana French)

CAKE
3 cups flour
1 cup sugar
1 tablespoon baking powder
1 teaspoon salt
1 teaspoon cinnamon
1 teaspoon vanilla
1 cup butter or margarine, softened
2 eggs, slightly beaten
1 cup milk

FILLING
2/3 cup sugar
1/4 cup cornstarch
2 cups fresh or frozen huckleberries
3/4 cup water or huckleberry juice

TOPPING
1/4 cup butter
1/2 cup sugar
1/2 cup flour
1/4 cup slivered almonds

For filling, combine sugar, cornstarch, water (or juice), and berries in a medium-sized saucepan. Cook over medium heat until thickened and clear. Set aside to cool.

To make cake, sift flour, baking powder, salt, and cinnamon into a mixing bowl, then add sugar. Cut in butter to form fine crumbs. Add eggs, milk, and vanilla. Stir until blended. Spread half the batter in 2 greased round 8-inch pans. Divide filling between the 2 pans, spreading evenly over each batch of batter. Drop remaining batter by spoonfuls over filling.

Prepare topping by cutting butter into previously blended flour and sugar; then stir in nuts. Spread topping on top of cakes.

Bake at 350° for 40 to 45 minutes. (If desired, one coffee cake can be baked in a 13 × 9 × 2-inch pan.)

Makes 16 pieces.

Note: Sarah uses wild huckleberries, but frozen raspberries or blueberries also work great.

DANISH PUFF

PASTRY BASE
1 cup sifted flour
$^1/_2$ cup margarine
2 tablespoons water

TOP
$^1/_2$ cup margarine
1 cup water
1 teaspoon vanilla
1 cup flour
3 eggs

ICING
1 cup powdered sugar
$^1/_2$ teaspoon almond extract
2 tablespoons milk
1 cup slivered almonds

For pastry base, measure flour into a medium-sized mixing bowl and cut in margarine as for pie crust. Sprinkle with water and mix with a fork. Divide into 2 balls. Put on a large, ungreased cookie sheet and pat into two long strips 12 inches by 3 inches.

To prepare top, put margarine and water into a small pan and bring to a rolling boil. Add vanilla and remove from heat. Stir in flour quickly. When smooth, thick, and slightly cooled, add eggs one at a time, beating till smooth. Divide in half and spread evenly over each strip of pastry. Bake at 350° for 1 hour (or until brown and puffy—Sarah always checks it at 40 minutes). Let cool.

For icing, mix powdered sugar with extract until smooth. Spread over both pastries and top with slivered almonds.

Serves 8 to 10.

CALIENTE FUDGE
(Courtesy of Maria Parra-Boxley, Dulce Passion Bakery)

1 can sweetened condensed milk (14 oz.) (La Lechera)
3 cups semisweet chocolate chips
1 tablet Nestlé Abuelita authentic Mexican chocolate drink mix
2 tablespoons cinnamon spice blend

CINNAMON SPICE BLEND (POUR INTO A SMALL PLASTIC ZIP SANDWICH BAG AND COMBINE):
1 tablespoon Saigon cinnamon
1 tablespoon ground ancho chile pepper
1 tablespoon ground red cayenne pepper
1 tablespoon Cinnamon Plus spice blend (The Pampered Chef)

Line an 8- or 9-inch square pan with waxed paper. In a heavy saucepan over low heat melt tablet of Nestlé Abuelita authentic Mexican chocolate drink mix on one side. When you see it begin to melt on one side turn it over to melt the other side (tablet will not fully melt until combined with sweetened condensed milk). Add 3 cups semisweet chocolate chips and stir in 2 tablespoons cinnamon spice blend (cinnamon spice blend can be decreased or increased according to your heat taste buds). Continue to stir slowly so your chocolate doesn't stick and burn. The chocolate and spice mix will start to get heavy and clumpy. At this point add the sweetened condensed milk and keep stirring until well combined. Turn off heat and pour the fudge into prepared pan. Let cool and chill for 2 hours or until firm. Turn fudge onto cutting board; peel off paper and cut into squares. Store loosely covered or at room temperature.

Makes about 2 pounds of fudge.

PRUNE TRUFFLES WITH ARMAGNAC
(Courtesy of Kathy Nordlie)

¾ cup (4 ounces) pitted prunes, each prune cut into eighths
¼ cup Armagnac
⅓ cup heavy cream
6 ounces bittersweet chocolate, such as Lindt or Tobler, broken into small pieces
1 tablespoon unsalted butter at room temperature
½ cup toasted pecans, finely chopped
½ cup cocoa powder for coating

In a small bowl, combine the prunes and the Armagnac. Cover tightly and let sit at room temperature for at least an hour to soften.

In a small saucepan, bring the cream to a boil over moderately high heat. Add the chocolate and remove from the heat. Whisk until the chocolate is melted and the mixture is smooth. Beat in the butter.

Drain the prunes, reserving 1 tablespoon of the Armagnac. Add the prunes, the reserved Armagnac, and the pecans to the chocolate mixture, mixing until well combined. Transfer the mixture to a shallow bowl and refrigerate, uncovered, until firm, at least 3 hours.

Coat your palms with the cocoa. For each truffle, form about 1 teaspoon of the cold truffle mixture into a ball, rolling it between your palms. Place the truffles on waxed paper. After the truffles are shaped, dredge them lightly in the cocoa, then toss gently from palm to palm to remove any excess. Place each truffle in a paper petit four cup and refrigerate for at least 1 day to let the flavors mellow.

Makes about 30 truffles.

WHITE CHOCOLATE LEMON FUDGE

1 cup cream
3 teaspoons butter
2 teaspoons shortening
4 teaspoons lemon extract
24 ounces (3 boxes) Baker's white baking chocolate
1 cup shredded coconut
1 cup powdered sugar

Break the chocolate into small pieces and put in a large bowl, along with the shortening. In a small saucepan, bring cream slowly to a light boil. Pour the boiling cream over the chocolate and keep stirring until the chocolate is melted. Beat well, as if for ganache. Add powdered sugar, lemon extract, and coconut, and pour into a 9-by-9-inch glass baking pan. Let sit for 2 hours or until firm.

Makes 9 to 12 pieces, depending on how you cut it.

Note: This is truly the best fudge on the planet. Jamie stumbled onto it quite by accident, early in her truffle-making career. When the ganache didn't set up (it probably would have if she'd been a little more patient!) she tried to roll it into balls and dip it in melted white chocolate anyway, hoping against hope the truffle fairies would fix the mess. All she got was a tray full of blobs that looked like they had candy leprosy. Disgusted, she scooped up the mess, combined it with the leftover white chocolate for coating, then mixed in some powdered sugar and dumped the whole thing in a 9-by-9-inch glass pan. And shockingly, she wound up with incredible fudge. It just goes to show, nothing is ever wasted in the kitchen if a girl is clever!

PRETZEL TURTLES
(QUICK AND EASY)
(Courtesy of Carol Isaacson)

One bag Rollo candies
One small (16-ounce) bag small, knotted pretzels
One medium-sized bag (6 ounces) of pecans

Lay out pretzels on an ungreased cookie sheet. Put a Rollo candy on each pretzel. Put in oven at 250° for 4 minutes. Take out and top each with a pecan. (Press pecan in lightly.) Put in refrigerator to harden for 3 minutes. (Don't leave in the fridge. Jamie's not sure why you shouldn't leave them in the fridge, but Carol told her not to, so she doesn't!)

You can make up to 57 of these if you use a whole bag of Rollos. You'll probably have extra pretzels left. Eat the evidence.

CHOCOLATE MINT PIE

Single baked pie crust (you can use a prepared crust or
    make from scratch) or prepared chocolate crumb crust
1 cup butter
2 cups powdered sugar
4 ounces (squares) unsweetened chocolate, melted
4 eggs
¾ teaspoon peppermint extract
2 teaspoons vanilla extract

Using mixer, cream butter and sugar together. Add melted
chocolate and blend well. Mix in eggs, one at a time, then
flavorings. Pour mixture into shell and freeze until solid.
Can be served with whipped cream, chocolate shavings,
peppermint candy, or coconut.

Serves 8.

Note: You can actually serve more since this pie is so rich
that a very small serving goes a very long way.